Crimson Gauntlet An Apocalyptic Lit RPG Adventure

Crimson Gauntlet An Apocalyptic Lit RPG Adventure

❦

I.O. Adler

Lucas Ross Publishing

Contents

Level Zero	1
Level One	15
Level Two	49
Level Three	66
Level Four	100
Level Five	157
Level Six	193
Epilogue	212
Developer's Note	220
	221
About The Author	222

Level Zero

1

Eddie Rush's First Rule of Winning? Never be late for a game.

Guild law, and something I enforced as a guild officer.

Here I was, running behind schedule by hours and gunning my scooter out of the Golden State Care Home parking lot onto the boulevard.

Forty patients in need of a paratransit shuttle driver, and my evening replacement was a no-show. Mr. Montgomery, my daily regular, had been late following his periodontal appointment and was in a chatty mood, making my last pick up and drop off go long.

On Wednesday raid night.

Of course, every night but Tuesday was raid night, but you get the picture.

A hundred players were waiting, with twenty more looking to fill the slot of anyone not equipped, buffed, prepped on strategy, and on their toon in front of the instance gate ready to rock the house.

In this case, Night World's third expansion pack, Grave Warden's Curse, and the Twilight Crypt's third boss, Covadine the Mad. Our guild, Grace Over Pressure, was hitting its head on what should have been a straightforward spank-and-tank fight, but the wraith stage and the swarming insect damage were taxing our healing group's ability to keep up.

I was the top damage-dealing archer and guild officer by the grace of having been with the group since its last game. Long of tooth, and currently short on time.

Traffic was mercifully light, thanks to the evacuation orders.

My scooter maxed out at thirty-five. I adjusted my glasses to better see my dashboard clock. Quarter to eight, and it would take me twenty minutes to get home. My game rig needed a restart and had just finished downloading an operating system update, along with Tuesday's game patch.

Screwed. So screwed.

Laura, aka Rosette, the mass-buffing and disease-curing level-eighty Druid, was a guild leader who tolerated zero crap and demanded punctuality.

Was that her texting me now?

I was heading for a yellow light. No way to make it, and while the Bell Park PD was noticeably absent from the roads for the past week, I knew if I pressed my luck, I'd catch the red and get pulled over and have to deal with a traffic stop and a last fatal hit to my commercial driver's license. I braked hard.

Text to voice over my helmet speaker. "Message from: Laura."

She was going to be chewing me out for not being logged into the game thirty minutes ago to herd the cats. Even a guild of dedicated players determined to graduate from cutting edge to bleeding edge with new content required a firm hand.

Anything less, and our main competition guild-wise on our server, Bellum Cultura, would leave us in the dust. They beat Covadine the Mad last Saturday and took down the Platinum Abomination on their first try.

"Server's down," my phone said in its ever-pleasant husky woman's voice. "Meetup at Tasty's. Did you get your package?"

What package? But that was it from Laura.

"Email," I said and my phone obliged.

Seventeen messages, mostly junk, but one from Janus Brand International.

Did You Receive Your Package? The email header was a long confidentiality clause followed by a yes/no toggle waiting for my response.

The second email of note was from the parcel service. *Package delivered two hours ago.*

The light turned green. I sped forward at a measured clip. The thought I had received my package from Janus made me giddy. The sensation was instantly offset by the realization my roommate had signed for the most important delivery of my entire life.

2

Lawrence-Not-Larry lay sprawled on our couch, the TV blasting a screeching K-pop ballad as an anime show's credit roll scrolled by. He wore his headphones on as he tapped on his tablet, smashing fruit with a virtual sledgehammer.

"Larry?"

He muttered something unintelligible. The place reeked of...well, Larry. I kept to my room, mostly. It's where my gaming rig was set up, wedged between my futon and the small closet holding the rest of my worldly belongings.

Hot and stuffy. Typical for a midsummer evening. No AC, and the fans we owned barely made the air breathable.

I checked my room. No package on the futon amongst the rumpled sheets or on my desk. My ceiling fan whirled above my head, shuddering as if it were a mad machine waiting to drop down and chop heads.

My eyes were almost watering as I leaned in close enough so Larry couldn't ignore me. "My package?"

He grunted. Made a vague gesture to his left.

The clutter on the small table was mostly ignored mail neither of us could bother to gather and take down to the recycling container. On top of it was a battered box large enough to fit a pair of shoes. Taped, with labels declaring Fragile and Handle with Care!

Guaranteed to earn an extra punting by the delivery anthropoids.

My heart was in my throat as I grabbed the package, turning it end-over-end and discovering gaps in the cardboard along the corners.

This was the piece of hardware I'd need to make it into Janus Brand International's alpha test, and it had been stomped upon.

It was with no small amount of trepidation I used a grimy butter knife to pry apart the tape along the box's end.

A second box waited inside. Pristine white, unblemished, intact. I pulled it out like it was Hanukkah and this was the last gift I would ever receive.

The sealed tape had a reflective hologram. A laminated tracking chip popped away as I pried the box apart. A mummified bundle the size of a grapefruit waited inside. More tape, more labels.

This product is proprietary hardware for authorized users only. If you have received this, you are responsible for the hardware's use as mandated by your confidentiality agreement. Violating your agreement or sharing details, photos, or design specification of the enclosed prototype will result in

Blah-blah-blah. I had skimmed the NDAs as thoroughly as I would any end-user license. JBI had invited me to its new game, Crimson Gauntlet, a virtual sim, and I would have sold my soul to be a part of it.

Speaking of End User License Agreements:

Use of this product constitutes an agreement to the terms of use. Some users may experience dizziness, seizure, and light sensitivity. Other side effects may be possible. We encourage you to consult a physician before playing.

I owned a VR set already. I skipped the rest.

A third silver label sounded less threatening.

Game release day TBD but soon! Be ready!

"Find it?" Larry called from the couch.

I ignored him. With the care of a surgeon, I stripped the last layer away.

A wire headset, but closer to a pair of reading glasses. Smaller than the bulky eye coverings of the VR gaming rigs available on retail. Skimpy, actually. Hooks around both ears, a copper-colored frame, impossibly-thin lenses, and the tiniest rectangular housing behind the right lens.

That's it?

The small block was solid, perhaps holding a battery, a receiver, or both.

They fit perfectly over my glasses. But what was the point?

I went through the package again. Where were the earpieces, the video display, the rest of it? The email didn't mention a second package. No paperwork besides the stickers.

It was all wrong. The next iteration of gaming was supposed to be full sensory. I was expecting a haptic ensemble, like a SCUBA suit. Crimson Gauntlet was supposed to be less an online experience and more a drop-in-and-forget-your-old-life sim, with monsters and loot and quests galore, if the early hype was to be believed.

The third label's last line? *You won't believe the life you're about to live.*

I took the flimsy headset off and gave them a last look before stuffing them back into the box. "Yeah, right."

"Huh?" my roommate murmured from the couch.

"Nothing, Larry."

I slammed the door on the way out.

3

Tasty's Diner popped on my map app, but I didn't need directions.

I pulled into the lot twenty-five minutes later. Enough cars and light. A lot of vehicle break-ins lately, according to the other employees at the retirement home.

The diner was the place you'd go to soak up a late-night drinking session, or take a cheap date who deserved better than the usual fast-food selections every town north, south, and east of here had two of along the highway.

For an online guild, having six of us living so close was a two-edged sword. We'd become friends of sorts, even though we rarely met up. Too busy online. Chewy and Bennett both had families. How their wives dealt with a nightly raid schedule was a mystery. Kermit and Shadow had moved closer recently. Both worked tech, and both had found apartments close enough to the San Francisco Bay Area so they could drive in, but far enough away so they could afford rent.

And Laura?

She lived on an old farm just north of Bell Park and hadn't shared enough about what she did when not playing.

We had a seventh guild member not too far away who had made a few of our meetups. Kip. Somewhere up in the hills east of Sacramento on Highway 50, heading towards Tahoe. Kip had been our top healer until his death in a car crash a year ago.

The door to the diner stuck as I opened it. The air smelled heavy of bacon, fried food, and powdered sugar. Syrup in five flavors waited on each table, and a display case of pies and donuts stood prominently next to the Please Wait to be Seated sign.

There they were.

My guildmates sat with coffee and pie, huddled in a corner booth.

A handful of diners occupied a few tables and the counter, but it was a light crowd for a place once so popular with slackers and retirees. And then there were the evacuations. While not mandatory, the Army and the Sheriff Department posted blinking road signs and ran sound cars encouraging everyone to leave.

The radio message mentioned spiking radiation levels in Redding. Sacramento was next, the doomsayers said, and inevitably Davis, Bell Park, and a dozen other communities. But if Redding and the northern third of California were contaminated from whatever happened in Seattle and Portland, where were the refugees?

Fake news.

My mom in Colma kept texting me to come down. My replies were always the same.

Maybe next weekend.

Besides, my boss needed me. So did my guild. Staying with my mom and her new husband was out of the question and I doubted I'd find a crisis center where I could set up my rig. None of my fellow diehards were leaving, either.

At the table, Laura was holding court. Not in a bad way, just the queen bee doing her thing, with an infectious confidence and passion.

"...I posted the video on our forum. Bellum Cultura used the DoT bug after the server reset to bring down the Platinum Abomination. Let's see them try that Saturday after their instance resets. We stay heavy on bleeds, spam-heal the melee, and have all the ranged stick close to Hagar."

Hagar, my toon's name.

Shadow glanced up from his phone. "Nice of you to show up."

Dark eye liner, shiny raven-black long hair, and a gray trench coat. Heavily creamed coffee and apple pie waited before him. He had a walnut brown Messenger bag tucked against his lap. A fresh bandage high on one cheek.

"Cut yourself shaving?"

"Something like that." He scooched over so I could sit. He was back on his phone, pinging away at a game with a zombie head eating babies.

Laura glanced at me with her green eyes. "You're late."

"Sorry. So…the Platinum Abomination?"

"Yeah. No one's tried to stack up for cover behind the mining cart. You keep heals-over-time on the ranged, pop your Major Succors early to get past the cooldown for stage two, and we grind him down below half by the time the guard rush begins."

Kermit and Chewy both were mostly done with their pie. Sweet potato and blueberry, respectively.

Bennett, the big married guy who always sat next to Laura, dabbed crumbs from his wispy beard. "What about the lava surge? It hits the edge of the map by the cart every three minutes."

Laura nodded patiently. "Yeah. Timer's in the UI. Formation collapses in before running back out for cover."

"Means we get hit by bone shards."

"That's what potions are for."

Shadow didn't look up from his device. "And invulnerability glyphs." The trace of a smile dimpled his face.

"Not everyone has that," Bennett said.

"I do."

Kermit snort-laughed. The oldest member of our guild, around forever, and spoke with a British accent I always thought sounded fake. "Grinded two months for a trinket."

"I like to win."

"We all do. Premature to worry about the Platinum Abomination if we can't take down Covadine."

Laura turned her coffee cup in her hands. "We'll get him. We all just need to focus. Maybe a night off is what we need to get our heads on straight."

The server came by and I ordered coffee. My hands were jittery enough, but what the hell. I cleaned the lenses of my glasses and considered the specials board behind the counter. I wasn't really hungry. When she brought the thick mug of java, I added my sugars.

Laura tilted her cup in Kermit's direction, and then toward Bennett. We all clinked.

"To lost players, and the toons we knew and loved."

"To Kip," Chewy said.

"Manabanana," Shadow corrected, remembering Kip's character name.

I was late for the toast. After an attempted sip, I set my surprisingly scalding cup of coffee down.

The topic changed. Chewie complained about his wife and Bennett commiserated. Neither woman played Night World. Laura was posting a group photo to our forum, while Kermit polished off his sweet potato pie. Shadow played his game. The zombie made a yum-yum sound after every fifth baby head.

I took out the glasses. The wave of disappointment couldn't be overstated. What knucklehead packed these things into my box instead of the VR hardware that was supposed to drop me into gaming nirvana?

No On switch, no label, no ports, and no instructions.

They looked like an art piece designed by a high schooler taking first-year metal shop and discovering the wonders of solder. Too industrial for steampunk. Solid enough. Light as a feather.

I slipped them on over my own glasses. Something pinched the skin on the side of my head. I tore them off and felt the housing behind the right lens. Had the hard edge cut me? A dot of red from the side of my face.

Shadow lowered his phone. "What have you got there?"

"It arrived from JBI. Supposed to get the Crimson Gauntlet VR goggles but all they sent was this."

Chewie was wiping his pie plate with his finger. "I got those too. That's the hardware. It's the first part of whatever they're sending."

"There was no other package. It's some kind of mistake. These aren't anything."

Voice low, Shadow pointed at the glasses. "Did you miss the confidentiality terms? Those aren't meant to be seen in public. You're not supposed to take pictures of it, show it off, leave it at a bar, or talk about them. With anyone."

"We're all part of the alpha."

"Your funeral. JBI lawyers are no joke."

"I got mine too," Bennett said. "I locked them in my office."

"See? Even Bennett is smart enough to follow basic instructions. Maybe he won't be the first to die in tomorrow's raid. Unlike last night."

Bennett smirked before flipping Shadow off.

After rubbing the glasses in a failed search for whatever had pricked my head, I slipped them on again. "It's not like these things are the next big phone. No one here cares. And I think they sent us the wrong device. There's no power, no interface to bridge with my gaming rig, no—"

Motion outside.

The diner window reflected too much interior light to see clearly, but an orange glowing shape darted past in the parking lot. Glasses off again, I squinted. The shape was gone. A dog or something, perhaps with a glowstick attached to its collar. Whatever it was, it had vanished beyond the first row of parked cars.

Laura scowled. "Shadow's right. You don't want to show off those things and have someone post a picture. It won't be good for you and it won't be good for us."

"No one's going to share anything," I said sheepishly.

"Maybe not one of us, but you never know."

Kermit chuckled. "'Cutting Edge Tech Marvel Unveiled at Bell Park Dive.' But Eddie's right. There's more hardware coming. Janus, in all their wisdom, decided two boxes would be better than one. Best to tamp down your dreams, my friends. I've been through a few alpha tests and I'm not holding my breath it won't be anything more than a pixel walk through a grassy field. Let's brush up for tomorrow, shall we? Less sucking, as the kids say."

We talked about strategy.

Could Bennett respec his arcane talents to improve his to-hit rating? We had three other light mages, none present, who underperformed and needed better gear. Or they needed to be swapped out with our hungry second-tier raiders who were less experienced with the bosses in the Twilight Crypt.

Chewie and Kermit went back and forth on reorganizing the melee DPS into two squads and sticking close to the Platinum Abomination during the third stage or falling back to the mining cart for a big heal during the last phase of the fight.

As he tapped his clean plate, Chewie kept repeating the same thing. "We slack on bleeds or he regenerates."

"Bosh. We die, we wipe," Kermit countered. "We have to retreat to get in healing range."

"This assumes we even make it to the third stage," Bennett said.

Laura watched them bicker. Serene, intent, and gripping her mug tight. She wore a camo tank top and her arms showed her inks. The text of the Second Amendment in scrollwork along her right forearm. Below it, "Liberal and I vote." But "vote" was struck through, and the word "shoot" scrawled in next to it. Her left arm had a diagram of a woman's reproductive system wrapped in barbwire.

"No changes to the plan," she said. The table fell silent. "Strategy's up on the forum. Melee stays in range in a single group. Forget the mining cart. We mess with the strategy now, we'll be back at the first boss wondering why we can't progress. We're going to make it to the third stage, and the Abomination's going down."

She had everyone's attention except me and Shadow. Still on his phone, his zombie head kept eating babies. I had the glasses near my face and was staring through the lenses.

The two of us knew the fight. We weren't the ones who had been caught in the open and died. I had posted the notes while Shadow had edited the instruction video with big arrows and labels so everyone would know what to do.

Motion again, this time near my scooter. I had pulled it up into the gloom behind the electric vehicle charging station. Was someone sitting on it?

I edged out of the booth. "Excuse me. Someone is messing with my ride."

4

Bennett followed me out the door. He had his cigarettes and lighter in hand. "I needed to get up. My ass is killing me."

As the door swung shut behind us, I noticed the streetlights beyond the parking lot were out. The freeway was dark too. Cars still raced along, their headlights bright.

Tasty's Diner was up on the frontage road off I-80. The Chevron and Jack-in-the-box at the crossroads should have been beacons but it was as if the night had swallowed them.

I headed across the lot towards the charging stations.

Bennett was right behind me. "Hey, Eddie? I know this is out of the blue. I was thinking about asking Laura out."

"You're married."

"Not really. I mean, Sheila and I have separate bedrooms. She sees other men. We stay together for the kids, you know? If I asked Laura to coffee, would it...would it make it weird?"

Too dark to see clearly. I turned on my phone's flashlight and directed the beam around. Nothing. Imagining things. Then I noticed my scooter's dashboard console was smashed and the battery wires in front of the motor severed.

A pool of coolant poured from beneath a hatchback parked beside the closest charging station. The front body panel above the tire had been peeled away and the hood was bent. I got closer and confirmed it too had loose wires. Something had wrecked its engine.

Bennett followed behind me and rambled as he sucked on a menthol cigarette. "I mean, you and her and Kip would sometimes do those early breakfasts before I came to town. That's something I need in my life, and she's, well, you know, Laura. I wouldn't be the first guildie to date her."

"Bennett, be quiet."

Something metal snapped on the far side of a nearby pickup. I directed my light and hurried to get a look. Kids with tools stealing batteries and catalytic converters?

"It's just I really feel connected to her. It's not like there's anyone else in my life right now. I—what is that?"

The pickup truck sat on a raised suspension. Its hood had been pried open like the hatchback's.

Something clinked at the front bumper. A round steel cage about the size of a basketball stood next to the raised curb of the nearest planter bed lining the lot. It had metal barbs, hooks, and other parts bolted or wired to it, as if it were a sculpture project of found metal junk someone had abandoned.

No sign of the vandals. No sign of what had made the noise. Something about the metal wire ball reminded me of the glasses. Pieces of shattered computer peripherals lay scattered on the ground, like someone had smashed a CPU motherboard. Had they come from the vehicles?

Bennett approached with his own phone light directed at the round ball. His beam quivered. "Isn't that the weirdest thing?"

"I wouldn't get close to it."

He reached for it. When it moved, it was fast. A quick snap, a blur of motion, and Bennett was stumbling back.

"Aaah! Aaah! It cut me!"

He clutched his hand as his phone, cigarettes, and lighter tumbled. Blood dribbled to the asphalt. A piece of meat had landed on the ground nearby. A digit of his forefinger.

I pulled him along with me towards the diner entrance.

The wire basket had moved. It now stood in the glow thrown from the windows of the diner. Not so much a ball anymore, but an upright thing standing on two back legs. Its arms were blades on hinges. It leaped, landing on the roof of a sedan in one of the blue accessible parking spaces. It sprang down to the hood. With both arms upraised like a praying mantis, it plunged the blades into the car and began tearing metal and plastic.

The car's alarm blared.

An old man with two canes brushed past them as he hurried towards the vehicle. The metal creature ignored him as he approached, but once he got close, it froze.

I pushed Bennett away as I moved to grab the man. "Sir? Sir! Get away from it!"

He stood at the front bumper of the sedan with a cane raised. He poked at the creature.

It vibrated like an over-wound toy. Clicked. Pounced. It struck the man, who fell backward against me. We all went down. The man screamed as something *thunk-thunk-thunked* into him. Warm sticky liquid spattered as I pushed him off and scrambled backward.

The machine perched on top of him, its knife forearms a blur.

My head smacked a concrete planter. Nowhere to crawl. The thing would leap onto me next. My Crimson Gauntlet headset had slipped from my collar where I had tucked them.

I almost cast them aside when a red flashing in the lenses caught my eye. Something had switched on.

Instead of getting up and running, for some reason I put them on.

Words, too many words. A disco ball display of red data.

The machine was finished with the man. It flashed its knives and trembled like a coiled spring.

In the lenses, a target square appeared on top of the thing.

Two words stood out among the barrage of text: Punch and Shoot. Punch was grayed out. "Not in Range" in smaller case letters. But Shoot displayed brightly beneath the target.

The metal machine jumped.

I raised my hand defensively to ward it off. Flinched and blinked on the word Shoot. A flash of light leaped from my hand. The killer contraption blew to pieces. The parts braced my face and scattered around me. When I looked about, all that remained was fragments.

Bennet was trying to help me up. "Did you see that? What happened to it?" He had his wounded hand tucked under an armpit.

The game glasses. The Shoot and Punch options were gone, as was the target reticule. But the surrounding night was lit up with indications floating in midair.

Welcome to Crimson Gauntlet!

Enemy: Rat (Level One) Defeated!

Achievement: Baby Steps. Defeat your first opponent.

Achievement: Greenhorn. Use a skill.

Experience gained. You are now...

Level One

1

"What's going on out here?" Laura shoved past the customers clustered around the door to Tasty's Diner. "Oh my god, your hand!"

She hurried to Bennett. He showed her his bloody arm before drooping. I caught him and eased him to the sidewalk. He wasn't out, but his eyes were rolling. Sweat covered his face.

"Stay awake, Ben," she said.

I tapped his cheek with my fingers. "Bennett? Don't pass out. Someone get a first aid kit."

"I have one in my truck."

I grabbed her hand. "Wait. Don't go into the parking lot."

"Why not?"

Her puzzled expression vanished as she looked at the fallen form of the old man. The dark pool of blood was a glistening shadow.

"Something attacked us."

"What do you mean, something?"

"It was metal and fast. It's gone now."

"Then I'm getting my gun."

The diner's lights went dark. From the power lines, a champagne cork *pop* and a spray of sparks from a transformer. The only lights came from a dozen phones in the diners' hands and the vehicles along the freeway.

A pinch in my skull. I put my hands to my glasses but didn't want to take them off. More words appeared, but they were distracting.

Bennett needed an ambulance. We needed the police. I unlocked my phone. No signal.

"None for me either," Laura said.

Bright fog lamps blazed as a truck drove our way along the frontage road. Had someone called the cops? Or was it an ambulance?

I patted Bennett's shoulder. "You're going to be okay."

It was a hundred yards off, maybe two. Then I saw orange dots swarm up around the vehicle. The lights went out. From the darkness came a terrific crash, a boom, followed by rending metal and shattering glass.

Then, silence.

Laura turned her phone light on. Blinded me. I pushed it away from my face. Tried to focus on what was going on down the road.

My cluttered UI made room for the twelve orange dots near the crash site.

"I'm going to my truck," Laura said.

Bennett groaned and tried to sit up. I helped him. Kermit hurried over from the diner. He had a hand on Bennett to steady him. From a jacket pocket, he produced a cloth handkerchief and was wrapping the stump of a finger while getting Bennett to keep pressure on the wound.

Laura had made it to her vehicle. The dome light came on. She cursed as she climbed inside and unlocked the glove box.

An orange glow winked to life near the charging station. My scooter? I stepped around the nearest car for a better look.

A second ball of metal sat on the asphalt. It hadn't been there before. A swarm of tiny cockroaches ran in neat lines between it and my scooter, with a second stream running into a hole in the back of one of the charging stations. Each roach trucked along with a piece of wire, silicon, or steel in its mandibles.

My UI gave the ball a label.

Rat (Inactive).

I wanted to punt the thing, but then noticed three more balls under similar construction along the back line of parked cars. Each had a similar label in soft orange. The army of roaches were assembling more of the little murder machines.

From down the road, the horde of orange dots around the crash hadn't come any closer.

Each popped up with an orange label. All were level-one rats. How long before the ones in the cocoons became active?

Laura had a revolver in hand. She checked the load before snapping closed the cylinder. "What are those things?"

"I don't know. One of them sliced Bennett's finger. It chased us before attacking the man. And then I…"

"Where is it now?"

"I destroyed it."

"Was it a dog? A coyote? What are we talking about?"

I realized she either wasn't listening or guessed I was panicked and hadn't seen it clearly. "It wasn't an animal. It was made of metal and looked like a ball, just like the ones there. But then it jumped up and came after us. It had knives for hands. We need to leave."

She directed her light around and scanned the darkness beyond the parking lot. Then she climbed into the cab of her truck. Tried to start the engine. Nothing happened as she kept turning the key. A stream of curses followed.

At the front of her vehicle, I found another line of roaches climbing the front passenger tire and dropping to the ground with fragments from the engine compartment.

"Laura, come see this. It's not going to work."

Shadow and Chewie had come outside and gathered with Kermit and Bennett. A few other patrons were filtering into the parking lot. A woman screamed at the sight of the murder scene and ran back inside. Chewie crouched next to Bennett while Shadow inspected the dead man.

Laura gave up trying to start the truck.

I brought her around the front and directed my light onto the roaches. "It wasn't a coyote or dog or mountain lion. It was a machine. And somehow, I blasted it. These bugs appear to be making more."

"What do you mean?"

"It's the game, Laura. Crimson Gauntlet. The headset they sent. The screen told me the game was live. This is all part of it."

She shook her head as she hurried back to Bennett and the others.

I stomped on a roach. It wriggled beneath my foot. I grounded down on it. When I lifted my foot, I saw a smear of wires and plastic. But there were too many of them.

I hurried after Laura. Every time I made a fist, a prompt appeared.

Punch (Default) and **Shoot (Default)**.

No Target.

As I glanced at my guildmates, each had a gray, almost invisible reticule. Not targetable with either of my game skills. Except for Shadow. A red label hung over him.

Shadow (Level 0/Allied Player).

He wore a pair of game glasses. He was looking at me while holding up his hand with the palm out before making a fist. Swung it in the air. Right hook, left upper cut. He chuckled, as if getting a joke no one else had heard.

"You brought your glasses," I said.

He adjusted them before looking out across the lot. "I wasn't going to leave them at home."

"You and me both."

We had witnessed a murder, Bennett was hurt, and our vehicles were being systematically destroyed by metal roaches. We needed to find a phone or a car that worked. But all I could think about was calling out Shadow about his rant about confidentiality. I was about to say something when I noticed movement out on the frontage road.

The horde of orange dots from the crash down the road was heading our direction.

2

I helped Bennet sit up straight on the curb. "Can you get up?"

He was bathed in sweat and stiff, but at least he wasn't a wet noodle anymore.

Kermit directed his phone light at me. "He shouldn't be moved."

"We don't have a choice. Help me get him on his feet. Does anyone's car work?"

Chewie had his key fob in hand. Clicked it. Nothing from his hatchback. "There are bugs all over the ground."

"Yeah. That's not the only thing we have to worry about."

Two of the diner patrons hurried to their cars. The key fobs didn't work. No dome lights lit up, and no engines started. Every vehicle in the lot was out.

The approaching orange game markers had halved the distance towards us. At this rate, they'd be here in less than a minute.

More faint labels appeared. When I paid attention to them, they brightened, the letters a hazy blue.

A virtual tag hung over a phantom box next to the vehicle recharge station.

Asset: Transportation.

Another inside the diner near a window: **Asset: Food.**

And next to the dead man: **Loot: Coin x 1.**

But then the menu presented tabs that obstructed my view.

Game introduction. Boost Stat Selection. Chaos Levels. Experience Tracker. Combat Log.

Too much. I dismissed it all. But taking the glasses off felt like a mistake. I left them in place.

Shadow waved his hand at the red glow next to the dead man. "You going to pick that up?"

The loot. I tilted my head down. My eyes didn't see anything; the glasses did. A red coin. When I reached for it, it vanished as my fingers brushed it.

Picked up: Coin x 1.

Achievement: Save it for a Rainy Day. Loot your first coin.

I now had an inventory to the left of the other tabs awaiting my attention.

"They're getting closer," Shadow said.

Kermit and Chewie had Bennett standing.

Revolver at her side, Laura continued to study the night. Nodded. "I don't understand what's happening, but I hear something. Everyone inside now."

The other patrons retreated past her.

Shadow lingered outside the door. "This is a mistake."

"Bennett won't make it far."

"He hurt his hand, not his leg."

I found a slide lock at the base of the doors and backed away as the orange marks approached us. The glasses could zoom in, at least a little.

From the darkness, tiny mechanical animals hopped towards the diner. All of them were labeled **Rat (Level One)**. They bounded on top of the first cars before spreading out.

Laura squinted. "What's happening out there?"

"Over twelve of them. They'll have the place surrounded."

"I count fourteen," Shadow said.

Two of them jumped towards the entrance. We backed up. One slammed the door with a shuddering smack against the glass. The second one struck it even harder. They took turns, backing up a few feet before rocketing forward.

"What's going on?" one patron cried. "What are those things?"

Phone lights cut everywhere, alternately blinding me and illuminating the interior of the diner. Finally, one patron directed his light at the door. He was a man in his thirties who had been seated at the counter eating a burger. Leather jacket, buzz cut, blue coveralls.

Laura aimed her pistol. "Hold the light steady."

A fracture ran the length of the glass door from top to bottom. When the next rat sprang and whacked the glass, fresh cracks spider-webbed around the point of impact.

Laura's pistol thundered. I flinched and shielded my ear as a second shot exploded. Two neat holes punched in the glass door. One rat had skittered back and began running in circles. Its hind legs had been blown off.

The second rat stood dead still, with a small hole in its breastplate. It twitched before resuming the assault on the door.

Laura cocked the hammer of the revolver.

Shadow stepped in front of her. "Wait."

"Get back, you idiot," she growled.

He ignored her. Raised his hand and put it to the glass. This time, when the rat jumped, it flashed both blades and was about to shatter the door and double-skewer Shadow.

His hand flashed. The rat exploded into a million pieces.

Player: Shadow is now Level 1.

He stepped back, his eyes darting. He was reading.

Laura sidestepped him. "Where's the other one? You're blocking the light!"

"You don't need your gun."

He stepped out through the door.

"Wait!"

I hurried to follow him. Shadow approached the wounded rat. Raised his hand and blasted it. Like the others, it blew apart.

From inside the diner, someone screamed. Glass shattered. But before I could move to see what was happening, rats came for us. I put my back to Shadow's. Raised my hands. My every instinct was to run. I wasn't holding a weapon. The only thing that told me my hand was anything more than flesh and bone was the glasses.

Coming too fast. I swatted at one as it jumped at me. It was like slapping a bowling ball as I deflected the rat. It raked my arm as I ducked and shielded my face.

Shadow blasted one out of the air. "Use your skills!"

Punch (Default) and **Shoot (Default)** both lit up.

I sighted on the rat. It had landed at my feet and spun, its blades ready to blender me.

I'd made it through life never having thrown a real punch at anyone. But if this was a game, I had to know what everything did.

My interface must have known what I had in mind when I clenched my fist. The rat moved for me at the same instance I thrust my hand in its direction. I also activated my Punch skill. I connected. The machine blasted into pieces even as I felt something pop in my knuckles. Pain shot up my hand and through my wrist.

Three more came for us. These circled for a moment before rushing forward simultaneously.

I realized I didn't need to strike the things. My interface told me I had a second skill. I raised my hand, palm out, and chose Shoot.

The rat died.

Shadow killed his too, but the third feinted even as I tried to squeeze off a second shot. Shoot was grayed out, with a stopwatch animation circling the skill. Something in my UI protested. It was too fast for my brain to register the words, but my Shoot and Punch skills needed a full second before I could use either again.

"Raaargh!" Laura charged and smashed the Please Wait to be Seated sign into the thing.

Shoot lit up. I blasted it. Once again, the attack option turned gray. A cooldown. Had to be.

Chewie, Kermit, and Bennett followed Laura out the door. The screaming inside grew louder. My target screen filled up. Fourteen, fifteen, twenty. Rats swarmed the diner's interior.

Laura had her weaponized sign ready to swing.

I looked at the exit to the parking lot. The coast was clear.

"This way. Run."

3

Shadow played rear guard as I led our procession forward. Only two ways to go along the road. One would take us towards the truck I had seen crash and the gas stations and fast-food joints at the nearest intersection. The other way led out towards the farms on the west side of town.

A strip mall a few miles to the south had a 24-hour urgent care.

Bennett trotted along under his own power. "Wh-what about the other people?"

Laura had one of his elbows. "I hit two of them with my .357. They didn't die. How did you kill them, Eddie?"

"Like I told you: it's the game."

"Crimson Gauntlet? The sim?"

"Yeah. A message flashed on my lenses. The game is underway."

"What does that have to do with any of this? It doesn't make sense."

I took the game lenses off. Instant pain lance through my skull. But I offered them to her. She declined.

"It's what happened," I said. "The game's dropped AR labels on everything. You, me, all of us. The diner and everyone there, too. Only me and Shadow are listed as players. The machines that attacked us—rats—are level-one monsters."

"Bullshit."

"I have a Punch and a Shoot skill. That's what made them explode."

"It's true," Shadow said. "I leveled up. Eddie and I are level one. The rest of you are like NPCs."

Non-player characters. People controlled by the computer inside a game.

Chewie laughed nervously. "I'm not an NPC."

"You're not a player, either."

"Only Shadow and I are for now," I said. "At least until the rest of you get your glasses on."

Kermit appeared eager to take the lead. "Let's stop talking about a game. We get to the service station and call the cops. Land lines can't all be down. We need an ambulance. The police. Whoever sent those battle bots after us has to be around here somewhere, controlling them."

I wasn't so sure. The darkness around us felt like it had texture. Blinking away the headache wasn't working. Once the lenses were back on, instant relief.

No more traffic on the highway. Only a few emergency lights burned up ahead, no doubt battery powered. In the distance, a few faint points of soft illumination glowed. Facilities on generators?

We passed the wrecked truck. It was a large Ford F-350. Raised suspension, rollbar, cab larger than my bathroom, and a front rack for ramming kangaroos and smaller vehicles. It lay sideways in a ditch.

Our phone lights revealed the damage to its windshield and grill. The hood was bent open. Three metal balls rested in the mud in front of the truck. Lines of roaches carried their offerings of scrap parts to each of the meshy nests.

Rat (Inactive) on each ball.

"Keep going," I said.

Laura didn't budge. "You said those things come from these nests?"

"Like a cocoon. Yeah, I think so."

Shadow went to the closest ball. Punched down on it. It blew apart. He visited the other two and likewise destroyed them.

Loot: Coin x 1 from one of them and he collected it. He spent a moment staring and poking the air.

I got closer to see what he was seeing. "What?"

"I finished a quest."

"What quest? I didn't see a quest."

"Kill five rats. Good experience. You should have accepted it before they attacked."

"I was busy."

"Aren't we all?" Even in the poor light, I saw his grin. "Level two soon."

4

The window of the gas station office was already broken. Shattered glass lay everywhere. Display racks of energy drinks, soda, chips, and candy had been knocked over.

Too many shadows to see clearly.

Laura leaned in through the busted window. Her revolver stayed at her side but she held her phone high. "Hello? Anyone here?" No one answered. "Eddie? Those glasses show you anything?"

My interface wanted to tell me something but for the life of me, I couldn't pull up the notifications.

"Hey!"

"Sorry. No. I don't see anything inside. At least there's no game element in there."

"Then keep watch."

She pushed the broken door wider and stepped inside. Her light played about as she moved between the aisles towards the front desk.

"Trouble?" Shadow asked me.

"The menus and alerts all went away."

"Double blink. Clears the screen. Do it again, and it brings it back. Select a notification and give it the slightest nod to dismiss it permanently. Look at a tab to open it."

I double blinked. The Welcome to Crimson Gauntlet message appeared, along with a regurgitation of the confidentiality clause. The loot and enemy notifications were gone. Part of a combat log, no doubt, but I couldn't find it.

Selecting a tab required more than looking. I had to think about it. Whether the game understood some micro gesture of mine or it read my mind, I didn't know, but it took concentration before I could open the tab listing my character information.

An ability list had my two attacks, Punch and Shoot. No other information presented itself. I waved my hand in front of my face. There had to be a way to contact whoever was operating the game. I had to tell them something was going horribly wrong.

Our correspondence with Janus had been via email and their online forum. Crimson Gauntlet until that day was vaporware. We'd need a computer and internet and power to tell them the game was out of control. Bennett was hurt for real. I had a scratch along my arm that could have been my throat by another several inches. Nothing in my hand felt broken, but it was sore from punching the rat. And then there were the people at the diner.

I shuddered. I didn't want to think about what those rats were doing to them.

If Shadow and I were the only ones with game glasses, what could we possibly do against all those creatures?

"Phone's dead," Laura called from inside the gas station.

Kermit fetched paper towels from a dispenser attached to a trash bin between the pumps. He helped Bennett re-wrap the hand. "Will those things chase us?"

I took a break from my interface. "Rats. The game calls them rats."

"Bosh. Rats aren't made of metal with knife hands."

"They are if they're what the game considers a level-one monster."

"Does that mean there's level-two monsters?"

"I don't know."

Bennett winced as Kermit pressed a second wad of towels around the nub of his finger. "A level-one creature almost killed us. I don't want to wait around to find out if there's worse things out here."

"My house is closest," Kermit said. "A few miles' walk."

Chewie had been silent since the truck, checking his phone screen every minute. "Why your house? Mine's not much further away down in Merrydale. I need to get home to Carol."

"I want to make sure my wife's safe too," Bennett said miserably.

Shadow gazed at the night. "Those are all options. I want to head east."

I couldn't see what he was seeing. "Why? What's there?"

"An objective."

Laura emerged from the gas station office. "There's two bodies inside."

"Any rats?" I asked.

"No. And I refuse to call those monsters rats. Follow me."

She had a set of keys and unlocked the rolling door to the garage. Smog Checks and Oil Changes. No Appointment Necessary. The door stuck. I got under it and pushed. It slid halfway up before stopping. It wouldn't go further even with both of us pushing.

With her phone light, she surveyed the garage interior. "Grab tools. Anything that might serve as a weapon. And either come inside or put your phone lights away."

Chewie shut his light off and stayed with Kermit and Bennett. I didn't see where Shadow had gone, but I followed Laura as she went to a tool chest fixed to a wall. One key unlocked it. She selected a socket wrench and tested its heft before taking a larger one. She offered me the smaller wrench.

I refused. "I'm good. You saw what I did to the last thing that attacked us. Shadow can do it too. Standing up to those things with tools and whatever ammo you have left is a bad idea."

"I'm not planning on getting into another fight. We keep quiet and stay dark and get out of here."

"And go where? We don't know where this ends. Chewie and Bennett want to head home. And Ben needs a hospital. Shadow is wandering around out there doing Lord knows what."

She went through a few drawers and sifted through the contents. "I don't hear a solution."

"Tell us which way to go, and they'll follow."

"I got us away from the restaurant. We pick a direction and take it. What else do you want?"

"A plan. We've been through this before in-game. We'll waste time arguing about what to do."

"No arguments. We move. Taking care of Bennett is number one."

"I agree. But you need to acknowledge that Crimson Gauntlet is what's going on out here. Right now, only me and Shadow have our glasses. We all need them. Which means we need to do more than just run and hope nothing else finds us. Bennett's place is closer than the urgent care. If we make it and things are bad in his neighborhood, we find his wife, get his glasses, and keep going. Kermit or Chewie's place next. That way, we're ready for anything that comes up."

"You think we're prepping for a raid?"

"I don't know what we're prepping for. But Shadow and me are the only ones able to beat those things. And if they're listed as level one, it means there's higher level creatures to worry about."

"Noted."

I was about to say more when a glow caught my eye through the window. I slipped past Laura. Outside, Bennett had sat down again.

Kermit crouched next to him. "We'll be leaving soon. We'll get you home, get you fixed up, and feeling better."

Doing his best to shield his phone's glow, Chewie was once again checking it. "Find anything useful, Eddie?"

"No. We're getting out of here."

I headed around the corner. A flatbed truck with its front end up on a pair of jacks stood in the dark. The faint light came from behind it. A blue cube was tucked against a stack of old tires. If I raised my glasses, the object vanished.

Asset: Crafting.

Shadow appeared from the rear of the garage. "I found one just like it behind the dumpsters. Let me take it."

"What is it?"

"I don't know, but I'll figure it out."

When he tried to reach past me, I grabbed for the blue cube. When my fingers touched it, it burst in a flash like a soap bubble.

Asset Destroyed. Chaos Level: +1.

"You idiot! You ruined it!"

"I was trying to pick it up."

"Not like that, you don't. Read the tooltip."

He made a quick check around the truck.

I focused on my UI. There, among the notifications I had dismissed earlier, was a bland paragraph titled "Interacting with Game Assets."

To pick up or move assets and loot, extend a single digit and hold to acquire the object. Retract the finger to drop it. Only one item may be held at a time. Quick touch will automatically add items to your inventory. Extended touch allows an object to be transferred, traded, or moved within the game world.

Achievement: Butterfingers! Destroy a game asset.

Achievement: A Taste of Chaos. Earn your first Chaos Point.

My combat log wanted my attention.

I had "punched" the object for one damage, enough to destroy it. One Chaos Point for me, whatever that was. The crafting asset had disintegrated because I hadn't taken the time to read the manual.

What had I done to myself?

I looked up Chaos Points.

Chaos Points are acquired by committing acts of antisocial behavior, including the destruction of player-accessible assets and anything the game engine considers griefing. See heading Griefing.

I knew what griefing was. Training mobs, or mobile game objects such as monsters, onto other players, killing non-combat NPCs, breaking the game world, lying to newbies on how to do stuff, and otherwise doing things to affect another player's ability to enjoy the game. Like killing them in PVP as they respawned.

Some considered it a sport.

Every game company had a policy against griefing along with penalties, including game bans.

Crimson Gauntlet awarded Chaos Points.

Shadow and I joined the others at the garage entrance. Kermit was distributing a six-pack of energy drinks. I took one and popped it open. The sickeningly sweet berry jubilee-coffee concoction tasted like heaven.

Laura motioned for us to follow. "This way. Bennett's house is closest. We stick together, keep quiet, and figure out what's next after we get there. Questions?"

Shadow bumped me as he moved past. "Try not to break anything else."

A dozen lame rejoinders came to mind. None worth saying.

5

A siren wailed on the road ahead. Flashing reds and whites.

Kermit stepped off the curb and waved. "It's the cops. We're saved!"

I stopped him. "Something's not right. Look!"

But he wouldn't be able to see it. Even in the glare I could make out the orange tags of a dozen level-one rats on the car heading our way.

The police cruiser shot past us as everyone ducked behind a parked delivery van.

More were coming. A second vehicle, large, a big rig without the trailer, barreled after it. The tractor was lit in orange.

Goliath (Level Ten).

Shadow was the first to stand. For a mad second, I thought he was going to blast it. We kept low as a pair of riderless motorcycles whizzed past in the same direction. They also had tags.

Viper (Level Five).

The two vipers caught up with the goliath, and they vanished into the night.

If there was someone in that cop car, God help them.

The delivery van and the surrounding cars had their engine compartments torn open. No metal balls or roaches, though. Had the little scavengers finished their plunder?

"Your place is on Twin Oaks?" Laura asked Bennett.

He nodded. "Number 142." We continued in the dark. I kept seeing hazy blue tags around the homes in the dark, and more near an apartment building parking lot. But with everything blacked out, I didn't want to hazard going off alone, and Laura was leading us fast along the roadside while avoiding the overgrown sidewalk.

Shadow trailed behind. I lingered near a weed-infested driveway where he had slunk off. A blue tag too far away to read vanished. He reappeared a moment later.

"What did you find?"

"Crafting assets, mostly. They're everywhere."

"Maybe don't go running off on your own."

"We're heading in the wrong direction. You know that."

I didn't, but I kept quiet. I hadn't found any quest tracker or map. The time I had already spent concentrating on the menus and tabs was taking its toll. A dull ache was building behind my eyes.

A stretch of farm road led us to a trailer park. Lakeside Mobile and RV Gardens. The street leading in was Twin Oaks. One of the eponymous oak trees stood above a dry, round fountain in a roundabout near an office and clubhouse. I didn't see a second tree.

Twin Oaks was a loop, according to a sign with a map and the lots labeled by number. Bennett's place was at the far end.

Bennett walked faster as we passed the dry fountain. "You think Kirsten's okay? Everything's so dark here. You don't think those things got here, did they? What would they want with anyone here?"

Laura nudged him and pressed a finger to her lips. "Quiet down." To me, she asked, "Any signs of those things?"

I scanned the trailer park. It was blacked out like everything else. My glasses weren't picking anything up. "I don't see anything."

"It's clear," Shadow added.

"Wait. We don't know that. The glasses seem to work with line of sight. It means there could be hundreds of the things hiding. The street's narrow."

"Eddie and I will scout ahead."

Laura nodded. "We'll be here. Be careful."

I caught up with Shadow as he strolled ahead down the center of the row of single-wides. Mailboxes, planters with honeysuckle and bougainvillea, rock gardens with decorative statues of deer and gnomes, and covered parking slips next to each home. Further along the curving street were larger units, double-wides with picture windows. Some had cozy front or side porches with sitting areas.

Speed bumps every thirty feet. Some were unpainted. I tripped over one.

Shadow waited for me to catch up. "Keep up, noob."

I kept my voice down. "Why are you so eager to be here?"

"Why are you so eager to let Laura call the shots?"

"She's looking after everyone."

"She's not in the game; you are. Don't join her cult like the others. It's...boring."

Before I could respond, he went to collect a crafting asset next to a propane grill beneath an overhang. I stayed in the center of the street. I was afraid to trip and didn't want to use my phone light.

So few cars. Had most of the residents evacuated?

"Hurry," I called.

When Shadow didn't answer, I moved along the side of the mobile home, bumping into a shin-high stack of cinder blocks.

"Shadow?"

The game asset had vanished. Shadow wasn't there. I felt my way to the back corner of the house. A few dim solar powered walkway lights glowed in the back, highlighting a small vegetable garden in planter beds and a back shed. The nearby units' rear yards were mostly open, with no fences dividing them.

"Where are you?"

When I heard no answer, I returned to the street. I got my phone out and directed its light around me. The dark felt oppressive, as if it had grown in substance. If Shadow was screwing around or off collecting loot, I wasn't going to wait.

A redwood tree in the middle of the road had a curb around it, dividing the lanes. Beyond it shone a dozen soft blue lights. I moved to the nearest one tucked beneath a set of stairs leading to a single-wide's front door.

Asset: Transportation.

Not wanting to destroy it and earn more Chaos Points, I touched it with my forefinger. It vanished and my UI told me I had one transportation asset in my inventory.

Achievement: Pack Rat. Collect your first game asset.

What had I just picked up?

Transportation assets can be used to secure transportation resources.

Thanks for nothing, tool tip.

I moved to the next blue box. It was poorly hidden inside a plastic toy pedal car.

Asset: Crafting.

This too I picked up. It occurred to me that whoever was controlling the game had gone through the trouble to place these things in the game world. I didn't see any cameras or projectors. Maybe there weren't any and it was all happening through the glasses. But the device on my face had to be receiving a signal from somewhere despite the phone service outage and the blackout, didn't it?

As I went to investigate a third asset across the street, I heard something metal fall and clang in the dark. I froze. The sound had come from a double-wide with a Camaro in the parking space.

An orange glow appeared. A level-one rat. Two more joined it and they scurried towards me.

I retreated. My foot caught another speed bump. I turned in time to raise my hand and blasted the closest one with my Shoot skill. The rat dropped. The second one flew at me, faster than I could react. I caught it with my hand and flung it aside. Something—a knife claw, its hind leg, its teeth—raked my wrist. Before it could move, I shot it too.

The third one sidewinded to my right.

I was up on my haunches when its eyes flared and electricity crackled. A brilliant jolt of lightning forked into me. Burning and pain. The shock knocked me back onto my butt. My muscles convulsed, and I almost bit my tongue in half.

What had happened?

The rat had a label.

Shock Vermin (Level Two).

A meter at the bottom of my UI had dropped almost to nothing. **Health low!**

The glowing rat hopped towards me. Bigger than the other rats. It flared its claws as it sprang. The Punch skill, my only chance. It caught the thing dead center and the shock vermin disintegrated.

Either my hand was numb or using the skill before punching avoided pain.

Everything happened at once. A fresh wave of rats, seven of them, emerged from the mouth of a cul-de-sac. Four of the level-one standard murder rodents and three of the level-two shock bastards.

My low health notification vanished, crowded out by a barrage of information, including three loot nodes where the rats I had killed had been. I tried to clear my vision.

The game demanded I decide, even as I forced my uncooperative limbs to move, to run. I almost did a face plant on a curb as I staggered away from the fresh wave of mobs.

Would you like...? Choose a stat...? Quest Locator Walkthrough...? Accept Quest...?

Blinked. Blinked again to dismiss the pop-ups. What psychopath had programmed a game that would nag you while in combat?

A final undismissed prompt gave me pause even as the gang of rats hopped in my direction.

Select Class.

I didn't dare set aside what might be the most important decision I made in the game. But there was no time to read or try to understand my choices. I left the selection window open as I scrambled to keep my balance. Made it to a utility pole and a gravel pathway between units. Around the back, I came to a power box.

A dozen metal gestating spheres waited for me, like a field of alien eggs. Rats. All were labeled inactive.

As if on cue, one vibrated. Its designation changed.

Shock Vermin (Level Two).

The ball lit up as if a flashlight had been turned on in the center of a wicker basket. The shell cracked and break away as steel fingers thrust and slash at the air, the little monster looking to murder me even before it drew its first breath.

I punched the egg. It blew to pieces and I snatched up a coin. The act triggered something, as now the other eleven spheres twitched. Iron claws scratched behind me. The gang of mobs were coming down the gravel path. With my two basic attacks having a shared one-second cooldown, I wouldn't be able to shoot or throw my fists fast enough. The low health notification reminded me that with one more scratch or jolt, I'd be toast.

Time to go, but where?

I leaped over an upside-down plastic kiddie pool and pushed through a juniper hedge. A light up on the corner of a single-wide must have been battery operated as it threw enough light for me to navigate. I was running now despite a tingle racing through my legs from the shock rat.

Around a low fence, I almost collided with a lone rat. One Punch, and it blew apart.

I picked up a coin before running again. The rest were behind me. I hurried along a pathway that cut behind the units and forked out to a marked trailhead leading to open space. I didn't read the sign. But following it away from the trailer park would take me further from Laura and the others.

I headed left towards the shadows of the nearest homes. A mistake, no doubt. I would realize this choice was a mistake when the rats got me.

The path led between more rows of homes before letting out into the top of another cul-de-sac. A dog was barking from within one of the mobile homes. Whether it was at me or something else, I didn't know.

I heard an engine. Electric, but it had a distinctive whine. Amber running lights shed enough illumination that I could tell I was looking at a motorcycle.

Viper (Level Three).

It was coming from the back of the mobile home park.

A hedge provided cover.

The riderless bike coasted past the entrance to the cul-de-sac without pause. Even in the moonlight, I could make out long scythe-like blades. I didn't want to know how the machine might use them, but I held no doubts it would be deadly.

Was it on patrol or looking for me specifically? Had the rats called it?

Too many things I didn't know.

When the sound of the engine faded, I headed for the corner. The rats hadn't followed me or I had lost them. I scooped up three more nodes of crafting assets along the street. No clue what they'd do for me, but it barely took a moment. I hadn't bothered to check if I needed to manage my inventory space.

Another emergency light burned above the front door of a single-wide. I could see the street numbers. 138, 140. 142 lay just ahead. I jogged, feeling exposed.

Bennett's house was an older place with a white aluminum handrail that wobbled when I put my weight on it. I mounted the three steps to the door. We didn't have a plan except to scout ahead. With the rats and the viper on the road, I hoped Laura and the others had the sense to stay hidden.

I tapped with my finger. Tried the doorbell but it was dead. Glanced through a side window into the pitch-black interior.

The door was locked.

Did I mention Bennett was a chatty player? Every time we grouped up, he ranted about whatever was going wrong with his life. I was one of the few who put up with it. Maybe it was because of my day job.

Mr. Montgomery and the rest of my oldsters who I drove around were perpetually starved for chatter and I was a captive audience.

Bennett wasn't so bad except when he complained about his wife. It's a reason I received so many whispers after posting in guild chat I was getting a group together for a dungeon.

Is Bennett coming?

He was a decent enough player. If he wasn't, he wouldn't be in Laura's inner circle. She didn't believe in dragging along deadwood, be they under-skilled or under-geared.

But "Kirsten this" and "Kirsten that" get old.

They kept a key hidden beneath a pot of impatiens.

How did I know? I was good at listening to blather. Bennett, even during a raid, rambled about hearing his wife coming home, sometimes having forgotten her keys or having left them along with her purse while she ostensibly went out for a walk around the neighborhood on her way to her tryst with a man down the block from them. Bennett would set the deadbolt so he could have the satisfaction of making her go through the trouble to unlock the front door.

I used the key and pushed the door open slowly.

"Hello?"

After waiting a beat for an answer, I instinctively tried the light switch. No power. My phone light was getting a workout as I played the beam around the cluttered interior.

"Kirsten? You home? I'm a friend of Bennett's. He's with us near the park entrance. He was hurt. He sent me to find you."

I stepped past the gallery wall to the living room. An overstuffed sectional leather sofa occupied most of the space beneath a big-screen TV mounted on the wall. The hallway led to a kitchen and dining room.

The red spatters on the cabinets and dishwasher were nothing compared to the dark puddle on the linoleum. It was like someone had dumped a bucket of ruby-colored paint and tried to wipe it up with their hands.

My stomach lurched when the smell hit me. Piss and blood. All the things games leave out when you're slaughtering goblins, orcs, and kobolds by the thousands.

I backed away from the scene. Paused.

The dining room table was a mess of magazines, boxes, and paperwork. Mailers, credit card offers, and bills spread haphazardly, with crumpled napkins and food wrappers thrown on top of it all. Some had made it to the floor. And there, by a knocked over chair, was a box that looked familiar.

Big enough for a pair of shoes. It was covered with packing tape, a delivery tag, and stickers.

Fragile Contents. Handle with Care!

The return address was Janus Brand International.

6

The smaller white box that had held the Crimson Gauntlet game glasses had been discarded into an overfilled wastebasket, along with the bubble wrap. Next to the bin were more of the inside packaging, the paperwork from Janus, including the NDA, and the security tape with the tracking chip. A quick inspection of the table confirmed the one thing missing was the glasses.

Where had Bennett put them?

If he had opened the box, he hopefully wouldn't have been so careless as to place them down in this mess.

A back hallway led to four rooms. Tiny bathroom first, with a sink and toilet. Next was a spare bedroom with a bare double mattress covered with clothes and junk. The primary bedroom had a queen-sized bed and two nightstands loaded with prescription bottles, crumpled tissues, and books.

No glasses on the nightstand or in the drawers. The door creaked when I closed it behind me. You don't know how loud a house is until all the sounds—furnace, A/C, fridge, fans, and humming electronics—stop. I listened. All quiet. If the rats hunted by sound, I needed to be careful.

The last door in the hallway led to an office with a gaming rig.

Marvel movie figurines lined a shelf alongside a xenomorph and some dusty Warhammer 40k soldiers. The computer rig looked more expensive than the mobile home. If I wasn't strolling through the middle of a crime scene, I'd have taken a moment to ooh and ahh. Fancy keyboard with mechanical keys that lit up, a mouse with twenty plus buttons, a chair with force feedback and imbedded speakers, and a CPU in a neon case.

Bennett's boy cave, I presumed.

No glasses on the desk. I went through the drawers. Spare peripherals, cables, mice, miscellaneous stationary, a stylus, pens, a pack of Q-Tips, and a notebook with scribbled diagrams and notes of what looked like the first encounter in the Twilight Crypt.

Had Bennett placed the glasses in his car? Did he have them with him? Or had they been dropped, misplaced, or tucked under some random piece of clutter? A thorough search would take hours. I worried my phone charge would flag, and I didn't enjoy shining my light around like a burglar. And then there was the question of what had happened to Kirsten.

The CPU rattled. The clattering sound started and stopped, started and stopped. It was as if the computer had an old fan that was struggling to turn.

Yet none of the case's neon was illuminated. I crouched. Leaned in with my light. The power bar was dark. A breeze tickled my nose. There was a rough hole in the wall and floor behind the desk, with a mountain of dust on the floor. It was as if something had gnawed its way into the home.

A mechanical roach pulled a load of silicon junk through a busted panel on the side of the computer. It vanished through the hole in the wall as another pair of roaches appeared.

The creatures were making more rats.

Ice ran down my spine as I retreated to the hall. Nothing moved, yet I had the feeling I wasn't alone. I turned the phone light off and felt my way back to the front door and looked outside.

A cluster of roaches scuttled about near a recycling container. They were assembling a nest of metal wire and computer parts. No game tag yet. Was it just now forming into something? The roaches were everywhere. Between them, the blood in the kitchen, the pack of rats chasing me, and the patrolling viper, it was time to go.

I descended the steps when the motorcycle's blue halogen headlight flared. I was blinded. The machine's engine spun up and it shot towards me from the darkness. I dove to the mobile home's front porch and drew my legs up as the machine ripped past me, impossibly fast.

Where had it come from? Had it been waiting? I hadn't seen it and it didn't have its game label until it attacked. Yet here it was. A stealth ability? Questions for later as the viper made a tight turn. I ran inside, heading down the hall and through the kitchen. My feet slid and I almost face planted on the blood-slick linoleum.

Tires squealed outside. Could it navigate the tight, cluttered spaces between the homes? A second later, I had my answer. The riderless bike slammed into the front steps, barely slowed, and hurtled through the door. It was coming through the house to get me.

The rear slider past the kitchen was ajar. I tore the door open, almost taking it off its track.

The back porch was a tiny wood deck with no railing. I dropped and hit the dirt hard, feeling something in one ankle pinch. As I rose, I fumbled with a chain-link gate to a fence. A padlock held it shut.

A loud crash inside the kitchen. Glass shattered and the engine revved. The tires burned rubber. But the viper appeared to be unable to make the tight turn to make it through the kitchen.

A nervous laugh escaped my lips. But then the viper appeared at the open slider. The engine had changed its sound. The outline through my glasses looked different, and when the machine emerged onto the back deck, I understood why.

Walking. The viper was walking upright, or more accurately, was balanced on its rear wheel while using its blades like ski poles.

I threw my leg over the fence. Felt the wire at the top snag my pants but kicked my leg free. I ignored the scratches on my palms and arms as I finished the climb.

The viper crunched down on both wheels and flew off the porch, whacking into the fence. The metal barrier buckled but held. The monster's blades whirled like swords. It chopped into the thick wire, tearing into it. It would be through it in seconds.

I ran into the weeds, not able to see enough to know where I was going. The grim certainty that at any second, the viper would run me down or carve me to pieces spurred me on. Then I came to another fence. Higher, with no easy finger or footholds.

The sharp engine purr and the rush of wheels through the weeds told me it had escaped from Bennett's yard. My breath caught and my hand shook as I turned to face it. I raised a hand towards the oncoming viper. Used my Shoot.

The ball of white hit it dead on. But unlike the rats, the viper merely flinched. The blades were aimed forward like twin lances held by a charging knight. It gunned its engine and I had nowhere to run.

A bolt of green knocked the bike down. A second bolt, and the viper was spinning, its back tire throwing weeds and dirt everywhere.

Shadow strode towards me, visible in my glasses. "What are you waiting for? Hit it before it gets up."

I fired. Fired again. Shadow's third shot knocked the viper to pieces. Shrapnel pelted me. The viper's headlight went out and it took a moment for my eyes to see.

Achievement: Big Boy Pants. Defeat a higher-level monster.

Shadow didn't hesitate to stoop and loot the coins and a pair of items I couldn't identify in time.

I stared in disbelief at the remains of the motorcycle. "Where were you, Shadow?"

"Collecting assets. Bennett's wife?"

"Kirsten. I couldn't find her. But there was a lot of blood in their house."

"Yeah, I saw signs of that too around the park. I don't think anyone here is still alive."

"We were supposed to stick together."

He ignored the comment and was hurrying towards the back of the neighboring mobile home.

I caught up with him. "Did you hear me?"

"Yeah. I'm sure anything roaming nearby heard you, too. Keep it down."

"Wait. This isn't the way back."

Shadow's voice was a purr. "I'm not heading back. At least not yet."

"Why not?"

"Because I have a quest to finish."

7

A mob of rats came for us when we emerged onto the street near the top of the park. They came from all sides. First were the garden variety level-one critters. I blasted two of them even as Shadow took down four. A mix of shock vermin were in the second wave. I went for cover behind a large mailbox. One rat discharged its load before I nailed it.

It didn't go down.

Shadow joined me behind the box. "You're still using your level zero attack!"

A rat knocked him down. Slashed. He thrust his palm up and it splintered.

Two shock vermin to my left, the wounded one to my right. I took down the wounded one as the others hopped around the mailbox. They had us in their sights. Their weapons hummed and electricity crackled. Shadow lobbed something towards them that burst in midair. I flinched. Blinked the afterimage away. Both of the vermin were down. So were the remaining standard rats that had been scurrying our direction.

No more targets.

Shadow brushed himself off as he rose. "You almost got us killed."

"I used everything I had."

"You're useless."

He looted. I stood there, my cheeks hot. "Are you hurt?"

"It didn't get through my armor."

Armor? I hadn't seen him wearing anything. "What did you use on them?"

"Something I was hoping to save for later. A grenade."

It couldn't have been a real one. The explosion had been right next to us, yet we were both alive. Every corner might hold more rats, more vipers, and whatever had murdered Bennett's wife. But I wanted to know what had happened. I concentrated on reading my combat log. Almost tripped again.

Shadow used Grenade (Level One). Shock Vermin (Level Two) took 13 damage. Shock Vermin (Level Two) took 15 damage. Rat (Level One) took 14 damage.

On it went with the rest of the rats. The least he did with his grenade was twelve points of damage. And his energy bolt? I scrolled to the start of the fight.

Shadow used Corrosive Blast (Level Three). Rat (Level One) took 18 damage and suffered from damage over time.

Was he level three? Higher?

And then there was my statistics. The best I did?

Eddie Rush used Shoot (Level Zero). Shock Vermin (Level Two) took 5 damage.

My hits did less than a third of what Shadow could do.

I didn't want to fall behind, but there was so much to read. I dismissed the combat log. Still needed to figure out the leveling prompts. Too many speed bumps to navigate as I caught up with Shadow. More game assets waiting to be picked up. Transportation, Crafting, an **Asset: Weapon** that I hadn't seen before, and then tucked in the middle of a juniper bush, an **Asset: Armor**.

Shadow collected it all and reached for the armor. "That's mine."

"I need to survive this the same as you."

"Then, in the words of our illustrious guild leader, do better."

He took the armor. Paused for a moment as if reading. "I need three Armor Assets to finish."

"Every minute we stay out here means the others might get attacked. They don't have any way of defending themselves."

He pointed. About a hundred feet off was a corner where the road turned. End of the loop that would take us back towards the entrance. A hazy orange glow hung in the air ahead of us. A hedge of oleander grew along the curb. It blocked our view of whatever enemy lurked behind it.

But as we edged closer, a label popped.

Goliath (Inactive).

8

A goliath. Like the big rig that had been chasing the cop car. A level-ten mob. And we were approaching it.

It was the largest metal cocoon I had yet seen. Almost the size of a mobile home and wrapped in a net of wire. A driveway light not too far away illuminated the vehicle's vinyl paneling, windows, tires, and a side-view mirror. I could just make out the obstructed painted lettering behind the side door. Sea Breeze.

It was an RV.

The mesh encasing the machine wasn't as neat as the ones holding the rats. Uneven, as if a giant spider had given up halfway through its wrapping of an elephant-sized behemoth caught in its web.

The ground was covered with lines of roaches streaming towards it. Supplicants visiting their idol god, each with an offering.

Throughout the mobile home park, the rats had been waking up, and here we were sneaking up on a boss.

Shadow touched a finger to his lips. I nodded. Rolled my eyes, but doubt he caught it.

Something vibrated, like a phone on a countertop set to silent. The sound was moving near the rear of the RV.

A new creature slunk around the back bumper. It reminded me of a giant desert tortoise. It had a plastic shell like a snail, and vestigial front legs that looked deformed and unable to do much more for the machine than drag it along. Its rear end scraped along the asphalt. The back of the shell trembled and clicked softly like a retractable pen. It was dribbling out tiny metal poops.

And there, before our eyes, each of the little dropped shits sprouted legs and scurried off into the night. The thing was making roaches.

Grub Layer (Level Four).

I was about to blast it when Shadow raised a hand for me to wait. The creature was creeping our way, making new roaches with every shake of its ass. It didn't appear to notice us, and we had the drop on it. But Shadow's attention was on the bugs as they scurried off. The new ones weren't heading towards the inactive goliath.

I kept checking over my shoulder as I followed him. He traced the scuttling line of bugs to a courtyard with a fountain. There the bugs were dismantling what remained of a set of electric golf carts parked next to a recharge station. The station was likewise mostly dissected. Scattered around the scene were three more assets: transportation, crafting, and armor.

"How did you know to follow those things?"

Shadow looted. "The bugs make new monsters. They also leave these behind. It's how the game must balance itself. Creates enemies while giving players what we need."

The rear hatch to one cart tumbled open, revealing a car battery. The roaches methodically clambered around it as if deciding how best to carry or tear apart their prize. But then, in an act of mechanical monster harmony, they worked together to pop the clamps holding the battery and worked to budge it out.

An asset appeared next to the cart. Armor.

Too many roaches around me. I stomped one, then another, and a third and fourth.

"Stop it!"

I grabbed the armor before he could get to it. The roaches kept doing their thing, as if the slaughter of their fellows had no bearing on their scrapping ambitions.

A resounding mechanical shriek of metal against metal from nearby. It had come from the direction of the RV.

We stepped out into the street and stared.

The large orange tag had changed.

Goliath (Level Four).

Its engine sputtered. With unseen hands, it pulled the cage-like scaffolding apart as it rolled into the center of the road. The grub layer was nowhere to be seen, no doubt having moved aside.

The goliath was awake, and I had been the one who roused it from its slumber.

9

Shadow ran past me as I took cover behind the nearest mobile home.

I chased after him. "Maybe it didn't see us."

"It saw us. The roaches are everywhere here. It can't miss us and aluminum walls won't stop it."

Its powerful engine rumbled. The goliath shuddered as it threw off the last of its metal wrappings. Its headlights flickered to life and it was rolling.

We came to an intersection. Shadow took us to the left and along a walkway, cutting behind several homes. A clatter and crash as the goliath charged around the corner, demolishing part of a single-wide, along with a decorative fence and a family of plastic gnomes.

The path let out into another cul-de-sac with a cluster of redwood trees. We cut beneath an arbor and along the side of a house. We were once again on Twin Oaks and the main loop.

The goliath screeched to a stop. Mercifully, the trees had forced it to backtrack. All too soon, it sounded like it was once again catching up. Each speed bump forced a series of tortured creaks from the giant thing as it sped to catch up with us.

Another intersection. The goliath would overtake us in seconds. Its high beams were spotlights banishing the night in front of it.

A yellow dumpster stood in front of a double-wide to our right. I pointed. Shadow followed, muttering a string of curses. The dumpster was full of refuse drywall, scrap wood, and plumbing. No roaches, no rats. We pressed ourselves against the metal as we hid behind the big box. I fought to control my breathing, as if the rattling monstrosity hunting us could hear us above the clatter.

A high fence ran along the edge of the home next to us. If the goliath found us, we had nowhere to run.

The engine throttled and sputtered as the goliath drove by. The contents of the dumpster vibrated. But the monster kept rolling. The taillights vanished around the bend as it headed towards the neighborhood's entrance. When it was out of sight, it blasted its horn. The first seven notes to every Mario Brothers game.

Had the RV owners been Nintendo fans, or did Crimson Gauntlet have a weird sense of humor?

Its lights continued to recede. A second blast of its horn confirmed it was still moving away from us.

Shadow shoved me against the dumpster.

"What are you doing?"

"Sort yourself out."

"What are you talking about?"

"Your level. Your skills. Your class. If you're only going to use your base abilities, then you're a waste of time."

I didn't want to argue. If Crimson Gauntlet was trying to kill us, the only weapon we had was our game resources.

Shadow let go but was waiting for me.

I opened the interface. Ignored the vice pressing my eyes and head as I navigated the waiting tabs.

The level-up notification flashed for my attention. When I selected it, a screen filled my vision.

Level Two Pending.

A prompt asked me to select a class. Four options. The last thing I wanted to do was read. My brain was tired. I was thirsty and needed rest.

I considered my stats. STR, WIS, DEX, HEALTH, MOVE, CHA. Everything had a value of a five except for STR. STR, or strength, was ten. A review of my combat log explained why.

To my shock, I had accidentally spent five attribute points when dismissing the level-one prompt. No option of an undo. So what did strength do for me?

Your strength affects your ability to do physical damage with hand-to-hand strikes and melee weapons. It also governs how much you can carry.

And here I had been shooting things.

But five more points waited to be spent. A second box prompted me to choose a class. My class would no doubt dictate which attributes I'd want.

The options? Hacker, Blaster, Brute, Hellion.

My lifelong gamer brain kicked in. Blaster? DPS class. Brute? Tank. But Hacker and Hellion? No clue. A game only had so many ways to divvy up its player roles. Buffing, debuffing, healer, melee, ranged, front line, support, multi- or single-target damage.

None of the four class options sounded like a healer, not that healing was something Shadow and I needed in our current situation.

Each class description felt overly terse and begged questions.

Hacker. *Learn to control Crimson Gauntlet lifeforms! Use your Corrosive Blast to take down hordes of enemies while weakening the strongest foes. Become the scourge your enemy fears!*

Blaster. *Be death from afar. Electricity, fire, and ice bend to your will as you lay waste to your enemies with the elements.*

Brute. *Go toe-to-toe with the strongest adversaries, using weapons and fists to destroy any who would stand against you. Learn to become impervious to the most powerful attacks while tearing your enemies to pieces!*

Hellion. *Guile and stealth are your tools. Luck is your friend. Deliver an unstoppable ambush from the shadows. Your adversaries will never see you until it's too late!*

It didn't sound like any of them healed. The Hacker was basically a pet class DPS, and the Hellion a rogue. Brute had damage resistance, but it meant trusting the game to keep the machine monsters from hurting you while you fought at close range. And Blaster sounded like it might be a squishy class, thus the first to go down.

Which would be the best?

"Time's ticking," Shadow prompted.

I had to pick. The goliath could return. It could also be searching for our friends. Which of these would help us escape this nightmare?

I made my choice.

You are now...

Level Two

1

Class: Hellion.

Achievement: Promoted from the Dregs. Make level two and choose a class. The game's about to get interesting...

New Skill: Stealth.

New Skill: Stab.

Stab? I hadn't found any weapons. Besides assets and coins, there hadn't been loot, at least for me. Shadow had yet to share what he had found or where he got his grenade.

The Boost One Stat prompt was next, and this time I didn't want to accidentally pick strength. While the extra damage was nice, the other attributes might prove more beneficial. Five points to distribute, and the game forced me to spend them all in one place, so no spreading them out.

Time to investigate.

Boost one stat. STR, WIS, DEX, HEALTH, MOVE, CHA.

Your dexterity (DEX) governs your chance to hit and dodge. Eye-hand coordination, ranged and hand-to-hand physical attacks, and avoiding damage are improved by this attribute. A high dexterity raises your chances of a critical hit.

Dexterity was the typical rogue attribute in so many games, yet I hesitated.

Wisdom (WIS) measures your ability to perceive the world around you. It is also half of your power pool for your abilities. A high wisdom helps resist negative game effects in combat and is the basis for any control skills.

A Hacker class stat. While it sounded good, it wouldn't benefit me.

Your health (HEALTH) is what keeps you alive. When it's gone, you're dead.

Duh.

Your move attribute (MOVE) affects your ability to navigate the game world in relation to game assets, vehicles, and enemies.

Vague. How would a stat make me run faster while evading a murder-happy motorcycle or recreational vehicle?

Charm was last.

Charm (CHA) is your ability to persuade and convince outside of combat.

Great. Charisma, essentially. Maybe the hacker with their pets? Otherwise a dump stat except for the horny bards of the world.

Less than a minute had passed, but it felt like I was reading for too long. Shadow continued to keep watch.

I chose DEX, raising it to ten. Didn't feel spryer.

The quest tracker was next, but I wasn't going to spend more time studying my interface. It tucked itself unobtrusively into the top right corner of my field of vision.

Quest available.

They hung in every direction, vying for my attention.

The crisp reports from Laura's revolver echoed through the air. I dismissed the quest notifications.

Shadow and I broke from cover and ran.

2

The goliath crouched over the clubhouse entrance. If I didn't know it was a transmogrified murder robot, I'd have guessed it had been tossed against the structure by a tornado. But the metal monstrosity had sprouted two asymmetrical arms and was using one as a bludgeon against the windows and outer wall. The second arm acted as a kickstand, keeping the thing upright.

The sound was horrendous.

Metal, wood, glass, and plaster shattered with each blow.

While the clubhouse was dark, I knew the machine was attacking it because Laura and the others were inside.

Shadow pushed locks of hair out of his face. "It's too big for us. They might be okay."

"Don't even suggest it."

He didn't reply. We had a good vantage point beneath an overhang fixed to a rusty mobile home.

The goliath's headlights tilted downward like twin suns acting as eyes. They shone around the broken wall where it was directing its blows. While the clubhouse wasn't big, the rear portion of the building remained in darkness.

I moved forward. "I'm going in there to see if I can help."

"Your funeral."

My meager skill list had three attacks and Stealth. I activated it. A squinty-eyes icon appeared top center in my HUD. Was I really going to do this?

I emerged from the shadows and walked towards the clubhouse. I had my hands out to my sides, as if afraid to lose my balance. Throat dry. Needed a glass of water.

The ear-splitting racket only got louder as the goliath tore away a window. I crossed the clubhouse's small parking lot and cut through the landscaping as I got closer to the building. Surely the machine would see me or sense me. Did level play into whether a mob could detect me? Was it based on actual vision or whatever the game considered perception?

No way to know for sure, but it was my ass on the line.

Some games, you show up in the same room as a monster, and they'd aggro even if they weren't looking at you.

Another crash from the goliath. Wood cracking and glass breaking. From inside, someone yelped. Bennet, probably. The crying grew louder as I approached the rear fire door. Why hadn't they made a run for it?

Fear of getting steamrolled, no doubt, but then I nearly stepped on the answer.

In the dark, and with me focused on my Stealth icon, I had missed three rats. They stood perfectly still near the fire door, like demonic garden statuary. But they completely ignored me.

Achievement: Wool Over Their Eyes. Sneak past a hostile monster.

The Stealth ability didn't appear to have a duration, for which I was glad. But how close could I get to the rats?

Five steps away. Four. Three.

My Stab skill lit up, as did my Punch. I was in range. So Stab didn't need a weapon. If it was stealth only, then perhaps it worked like an alpha strike ambush. Again, typical rogue/thief/assassin fare. But if I opened up on the rats, the goliath would no doubt attack me. I gave them a wide berth and rounded the back of the building.

I tip-toed through the succulents to get to a slightly ajar window. It wouldn't push open any wider. It led to a back room. A small light moved about inside.

"Hey!" I whispered. "Hello? It's Eddie!"

Chewie appeared on the opposite side of the glass with his phone light blazing. "Where were you?"

"We ran into trouble. Is everyone okay?"

"No! That thing's about to tear the roof in!"

"Anyone hurt?"

Laura was next to him. "We're fine so far. Gun's dry, not that it did much good. You and Shadow?"

"Alive. Figured some stuff out, but it's complicated. Bennett's wife…I'm not sure what happened, but she's not home."

A boom from the front of the clubhouse. The window vibrated.

"Bennett's in the storeroom with Kermit," Laura said. "We need to get out of here."

"There's rats out the back. I might be able to kill them."

"Where's Shadow?"

"It doesn't matter. I can do it. It probably means the big one will see me. I'll draw it off you. Make it to the road and I'll try to circle back and catch up."

"I saw how fast that thing moved."

"Yeah. I did too. When you hear me screaming like an idiot, that's the signal. Come out the back door and run for it."

My last comment was punctuated by a thunderclap of debris falling to the asphalt. The goliath whirred, clanked, and buzzed as it continued its relentless assault.

I hit Stealth. How stupid I must have looked as I slunk back through the plants, being anything but silent. The rats waited where I had left them.

Here went nothing. I adjusted my glasses and inched closer until the Stab option lit up. With one rat down, I would have two left to fight. And then the four-ton wrecking ball two levels higher than me would do its best to grind me into paste.

I attacked. Twin virtual claws appeared around my hand and struck the creature.

The rat exploded, as did the one next to it. Stab flashed and grayed out, as did stealth. I was visible now, but I realized Stab had taken down a second target.

Achievement: Twofer! Kill two targets with one attack.

No time to peruse the combat log. The third rat's reaction was instant. It leaped at me, its blades flashing. Despite me feeling like I was in a nightmare wading knee-deep through pancake syrup, it missed.

I punched it. It fell apart like the other two and I paused for a moment as a nervous titter escaped my lips. I had done it. Killed all three with two attacks. But then fiery beams caught me in their sights as the goliath rose to its full height.

It was tall enough to see over the side of the clubhouse. It roared.

Whatever the roaches had done to the machine included adding a horn that made the goliath sound like a T-Rex and freight train screaming in unison while turned up to eleven.

My Stealth icon remained gray. On cooldown. Or inactive because I was in combat. I backpedaled, turned, and broke out in a full sprint as I shouted and whooped.

The machine's engine roared. I didn't dare turn to see what it was doing as I jumped a curb and ran across the traffic circle and out through dead weeds and hard dirt. A road led parallel to the main thoroughfare. My hometown of Bell Park had a tiny airport close to the mobile home neighborhood, and this led there.

The lights were no longer on me. I paused. The goliath had disengaged from the clubhouse, but was stopped just outside the parking lot. It was backing up, its lights directed down. Something was moving about the thing. A high-pitch engine whined.

A motorcycle? My UI filled in what I was seeing.

Viper (Level Three).

Another one? The bike whizzed about around the goliath, hitting it repeatedly and sending up sparks.

Laura and the others hadn't emerged from the clubhouse. A good thing because they'd be danger close to the fray.

The goliath swiped at the bike, but missed. I walked cautiously forward. Raised an arm for my Shoot. But that violated our guild's tenet, and one I would repeat in our forum daily. Play to your strengths. Specialize. Maximize what you're good at. Double down with buffs, gear, and enchantments. And don't suck.

Stealth was once again ready. I must have been out of combat. I triggered the ability and slinked forward.

Every strike by the viper sent a spray of plastic into the air. Every swing and miss of the goliath was a massive whoosh of its larger arm. If it hit me, it would turn my bones to jelly. Any in-game armor class be damned.

The goliath leaned hard on its short arm. Sagged. Was it hurt? Was the viper damaging it despite being a level lower? The viper darted past, ducking under the goliath's pendulum arm at the last moment. But the goliath spun in time, knocking the bike off into the side of a mobile home where it crushed a trellis and smashed into the aluminum wall. The viper's wheels spun as its blade arms worked to extricate itself.

I hesitated. If it killed the viper, it would be free to attack me next.

A green ball of sparkling energy smashed into the back of the goliath. It sizzled.

"What are you waiting for?" Shadow shouted from nearby. "Hit it!"

I then realized why the viper had been attacking. Shadow had chosen Hacker as a class and was controlling it.

Fist poised for my Stab attack, I closed the distance to the giant machine. The claws appeared again.

The goliath lumbered towards the knocked-down viper. The enormous machine's leg-like rear limbs were the easiest target, but its arms swung and it used its forelimbs to steady itself. I moved right behind it and attacked its butt.

Unlike the rats, it didn't explode. A flash of energy erupted as my claws chopped at the thing. The surge rolled up the back of the goliath and through its limbs.

It stopped, planted its shorter forearm down, and swung its larger arm. I dove beneath the flailing limb, running around it and trying not to get squished.

I didn't have my combat log up, but the beast had a health bar. Halfway down. Which meant it was alive and well and my Stealth had been blown. My Stab popped up again and I punched it in the side. Took down another fraction of its health, but nothing like my first attack.

Shadow lobbed in more green globs. Each one stuck to the goliath's skin and hissed. The acidy green wounds were all doing damage over time.

The viper popped itself up on its wheels and peeled out as it charged.

I kept punching. Laughed. I couldn't help it. We were murdering a giant Transformer with skills and abilities only visible to anyone wearing weird glasses in a game that was trying to kill us.

The goliath pushed its body to one side, blocking me in. A third of its health remained. It punched me. The hammer blow took me off my feet and sent me tumbling. Pain replaced everything. I couldn't see. Couldn't tell which way was up. Blood filled my mouth and sweat stung my eyes.

The goliath filled my vision as I fought to recover and straighten my glasses.

But then the viper appeared. It sliced deeply into the goliath's shorter forearm, doing a tight donut around the limb and severing it near the elbow joint. The goliath toppled my way. I couldn't move fast enough. Crawled. Something heavy fell across my legs, pinning me. I couldn't attack.

"Help!" I croaked.

The goliath pivoted and appeared to be having trouble moving. The viper was repeatedly ramming itself into the giant machine's RV body and hacking down with both blades. The fiberglass splintered. Smoke from the tires choked me.

Then the machine caught the motorcycle with a downward punch that crushed it. One of the goliath's headlights still burned. It turned towards me. A bright bolt of green struck its face and it paused. A second Corrosive Blast hit the thing. It cut loose with another blast of its infernal horn. Sheer rage.

"Attack it now!" Shadow called as he ran around the back of the thing.

"I can't move!"

But my Stab skill was lit up. I slapped at the hunk of metal on top of me. A feeble blow with my virtual dual claws.

The ability triggered.

The portion of machine on my legs blew apart, freeing me. I was up and on my feet. A touch was all that was necessary. The goliath reeled as Shadow sent more green bolts. The energy surges covered it and its health bar continued to sink. Yet it wasn't dead.

Facing the thing and dodging back and forth, I tried to anticipate the next swing of its long arm. While it was having trouble and couldn't prop itself up, it remained lethal as it cut through the air with a solid whoosh with every miss.

I needed to get it out of my mind that I had to hit it with a fist.

Its hand dropped like a guillotine. The metal smashed into the ground where I had been standing. Then it backhanded me. The swat sent me sailing. I rolled and struck a curb hard. My UI lit up with my health bar.

Two hit points remaining.

My head rang and the wind had been knocked from me. I was helpless as the goliath crawled closer, raised its hand, and—

Exploded.

Shards of recreational vehicle rained over me. I shielded myself. The largest pieces fell to the street, but enough chunks of the engine crashed around me to make me curl up into a ball.

Shadow looted the body.

3

Achievement: By the Skin of Your Teeth. Lose 95% or more of your hit points. Enjoy cutting things close, eh?

Another notification pinged. Experience earned. Halfway to level three. No doubt because the goliath had been level four. Even with Shadow doing most of the damage, I benefited.

Everything ached as I got up and straightened my glasses. My bottom lip felt swollen and my cheek hurt. The ringing in my head continued. My tongue kept bleeding from where I had bitten it and my ankle complained with every step.

Two hit points left.

Had the goliath hit me any harder, I'd be dead. Whether some game mechanic saved me and governed how hard the mob struck, I didn't know.

I needed armor. "How did you do that with the viper?"

The viper lay dead at Shadow's feet. He appeared to be busy with his UI. "Class skill. I can have one pet. I'll need to find another one."

"Let's not wait around."

Laura led the others our way. "That was insane."

I spat red. "Yeah. I don't want to do that again. We should go."

"Agreed. We need to find a place to shelter and wait this out. The army, the cops, someone will come."

"Hopefully somewhere with fewer giant monsters. There are a ton of rats roaming about too, and there's more of those eggs everywhere."

Chewie kicked at a piece of the goliath. "We should have gone to my house."

Bennet leaned on Kermit for support. "Wait. What about Kirsten?"

"I checked your house," I said. "She wasn't there. And about your glasses. They got delivered. I saw the package on your dining room table. Where did you put them?"

"On my desk."

"The one with the computer?"

He nodded. "My gaming room. Kirsten isn't allowed in there and she respects my space."

"Well, I looked and they weren't there."

"Never mind the glasses," Laura said. "We'll have to take Eddie at his word that your wife is gone. She probably got out last night."

I didn't want to tell any of them what I had found. "Yeah. Hopefully."

"If Eddie and Shadow can see and fight these things, that will have to do. They'll lead us out of here. We'll find Kirsten wherever they're transporting the evacuees."

Shadow blinked a few times before taking in the group, as if just realizing we were there. "Time's wasting. Let's go."

I was the last to leave. I directed my phone light onto the wreckage. Hard to believe we had destroyed a machine this big. Five more coins waited for me, along with two armor assets and one **Asset: Weapon**. Either Shadow had left them behind, or the game had set the loot aside for me.

Something pulsed on my mini-map. My quest tracker. I hadn't taken the time to examine it, and the group was leaving me behind.

Quest: Collect Five Armor. Begin Quest?

Quest: Kill Five Rats. Begin Quest?

I hit yes to both. If I was collecting the things anyway, why not gain experience?

Quest Complete: Kill Five Rats.

Crimson Gauntlet was keeping track and granting retroactive progress. Another nudge of experience.

My armor asset collection quest was at one of five. The mini-map pinged two nearby locations for more. They were spread out across the north side of the trailer park. Too far away and I wasn't going to go roaming on my own. More would come later, or we would find a way out of this mess.

It explained what Shadow had been doing. How many quests had he already finished?

At the edges of the map in several directions, I saw available quests too far away to have descriptions. Tempting. Because if I wanted to not suck and get better, I needed XP.

Before I left the scene of the fight, I examined the wrecked viper. Shadow hadn't been able to salvage it. No pet heal skill? I'd have to ask. The thing was a twisted wreck. One of its two blades was dug into the asphalt, the other sticking upright, as if a final derisive middle finger to the goliath or to us.

The black residue on the weaponized limb could have been a dozen things, but I realized to my horror it was blood. The machine had been a killer before Shadow had charmed it.

It begged a question: how many people were dead inside their mobile homes? Why hadn't I told Bennett about the scene of violence inside his place? If it had been Kirsten's blood, she couldn't have survived. And how far had this machine virus pretending to be a game spread?

I jogged to catch up to the others.

We needed to stick together to survive the night. And Laura was right. The cops would come. Or maybe the Army or the Marines. Because Shadow and I and a couple of pairs of glasses couldn't save us all.

4

I led the way along the shoulder of the road. "I'm familiar with the airport here. One of my clients likes me to take him there."

It wasn't far, the property less than a mile from the trailer park.

Chewie scoffed. "One of the old farts you truck around and can't drive is a pilot? Bosh."

"Keep your voice down. But yes. Mr. Montgomery. He rents a hangar."

"I thought you had to own an airplane to have a hangar."

"An aircraft. I'll show you. And if we're lucky, I'll be able to get us inside."

The long road leading towards the airport from the boulevard ran straight and was freshly paved. The moon was gone, so we had only starlight. By Laura's decree, we kept our phones off and walked close, with hands on shoulders as needed as we approached the gate.

There was a security booth that was never manned, and a yard arm that would rise for any hangar tenant with a remote. We ducked under the yardarm and approached the two main buildings.

"Looks clear," Shadow said.

I confirmed it. No game assets. Hopefully, that meant no monsters. Both buildings were white. An office occupied the end of one row of hangars. The black single runway was unlit.

Kermit and Bennett peered through the office window. I kept going towards a wide rolling door. A padlock held it shut, and the combination was the same as Mr. Montgomery's birth year. He had me unlock it for him after his drop-off.

I popped the padlock and rolled up the door high enough so we could step inside.

There was an alarm panel on an interior post, but Mr. Montgomery didn't use it. With the power out, it didn't matter. The airport also had cameras and a security company that patrolled every hour. Somehow, I doubted they'd be around that night.

Laura shined her phone about. The place had a few folding chairs, a beat-up recliner, an army cot, and a TV. A milk crate held a few empty bottles and at least one full Olde English 800.

"I brought Mr. Montgomery here for his 'appointments.'"

"You said he was a pilot," Chewie said.

"I said he owned an aircraft." I directed my phone light to a corner. The basket of a hot-air balloon stood next to a door to a bathroom. "That's his aircraft. Unused, I assure you. It allows him to rent."

"And the rest home lets him come here and drink?"

"Assisted living. No one there's a prisoner."

Chewie grunted as he flopped down on the recliner.

Laura checked the bathroom before going through the drawers of a rolling toolbox. She pocketed a lighter. "Water would be useful. In case we have to hide out here for a while. Food too."

With a wide grin, Chewie offered the bottle of malt liquor.

"Not the time to get drunk, people. Let's get inside and close the door. Kermit? Bennett?"

They ducked through the door. Kermit took a blanket and settled into a chair, while Bennett went into the bathroom.

Shadow was the only one still outside.

"Coming?" I asked.

"I don't want to get boxed in there."

"If we shut the door, we can avoid being seen."

"Better to see them first."

"He's right," Laura said. "One of you should keep watch. Shadow? Stay out there for an hour, then get Eddie."

He nodded. I rolled the door closed and leaned against a wall near the exit. The others settled in. Water ran from inside the bathroom. But otherwise, it was quiet.

My queasiness had turned into nausea. Was it the blood or the adrenaline? Whatever it was, I was exhausted, but keyed up. I sat. Feigned sleep. Examined the combat log.

Shadow's Corrosive Blasts had done less than ten points of damage per hit, and that was over a few seconds. A lot less than my Stab. But his viper hit almost as hard as I did and had two attacks. It also pierced some of the goliath's armor. My hits had an added strength bonus. At least my misspent attribute points had a benefit.

My inventory was a small tab accessed from the mini-map. A few assets, but nothing else there. What good were crafting items without a way to turn them into something useful? At least the **Asset: Armor** counted towards a quest. I needed four more. No sign of how much experience a completed quest would pay. Most games made quests the fastest way to level. Stacked quests were the best, where a player could work several quests at the same time.

I opened the quest tracker. To find new quests, I would have to travel.

A few were in the direction we had come from, and more lay everywhere, but all were off the map. No doubt Shadow saw this, too.

Maybe once we got on the road again, we might have a better idea of what lay ahead. I needed to wind down and rest. But I wasn't about to sleep.

I slid the door up and joined Shadow outside.

"There are quests out there," I said.

"There's an entire game out there."

"You figured it out pretty quick."

"And I'm surprised you didn't. Eddie Rush. You were the first to hit max level on vanilla Night World. Streamed the whole twenty-two-hour marathon."

"Game hit at the right time. I was between jobs."

"I think we're all between jobs now. Time everyone realized that."

"What do you mean?"

"Did you finish your armor quest?"

"I need four more."

"How about we go out and get you those?"

"We're keeping watch."

"We'll be back in an hour. They'll keep."

3:29am, according to my phone. "We need to get sleep."

"That's not what the old Eddie would say."

I got down on my haunches and put the back of my head against the wall of the hangar. The night air felt cool and good and my stomach began to settle.

Four more armor assets. And what would level three bring me? But it was a question for later, and maybe a question I wouldn't be able to answer. Dawn might bring an end to this. I took the glasses off. Rubbed my temples. Then I put them on again and studied the darkness.

5

I'd hardly call it sleep, but my eyes had shut. I came to, neck stiff, butt on the ground, and head on my knees.

The sky was that awful blue gray you never saw unless you'd stayed up all night running instances for that one drop that the random loot gods decided you didn't deserve.

Shadow stood down at the corner. The rolling door to the hangar was closed again.

The air held a chill, but it wouldn't last long. It would be a warm day. I shivered as I got up and rolled my neck and shoulders to work out before approaching Shadow.

The view past the landing strip was wetlands, with brown low hills in the distance. Too blurry. I cleaned my glasses with my shirt.

One of the cheaper parts of town stood across the scrubby marsh. San Rivera. Postage stamp-sized cottages, a school, strip mall, and access to the waterways. But the tributary of the Sacramento River had been dry for a decade. The houses with waterfront property sat over dirt and mud, with an ever-present mosquito cloud.

Shadow stared.

I looked where he was looking. "What do you see?"

"By the school."

I could barely make out the single-level buildings, but the elementary school had a large concrete art piece depicting an abstract twisted ribbon in its courtyard that peered over the scrub. A little more than a mile off. A red flash, like arcing electricity. Was a wire down? I peered over the frame of the glasses. The light show was only visible with the glasses on. Game assets were up to something.

"A monster?"

"Uh-uh. I think someone's fighting something."

Did he have enhanced eyesight as a perk? I doubted he'd tell me. I watched the flashes for another minute and then they ended. For the briefest moment, I thought I saw a figure. She was illuminated in purple, but vanished. She didn't appear again.

My stomach grumbled and I was parched. "I'm going to look around for food."

The other hangars had fancy locks and wouldn't be easy to break into. According to Mr. Montgomery, the office kept spare keys in a safe, so that was a non-starter. Breaking into a hangar would be involved and require tools and I wasn't ready to make that much noise. Next door to the office was an unassuming door that led to a crew room.

A rock used to prop the door open worked as a window knocker. A few throws, and the spider-webbed glass was weak enough to kick in.

A card table, folding chairs, a stained couch, and a bulletin board with expired local food deals and someone advertising flying lessons. Not much more than a breakroom with a microwave and mini-fridge. It had an attached patio out back, but the curtains were drawn.

The fridge had three Diet Dr. Peppers and a moldy Tupperware container with a science experiment ready to sprout legs. There was a box of ramen noodles in a cupboard. We could make noodles, except no stove and no power for the microwave.

A last check and I was ready to leave when a game asset just outside the back slider caught my eye. A quest marker.

It hadn't been there before.

I moved the curtain an inch for a better look.

The light blue quest marker didn't have a label. I unlocked the glass door and stuck my head outside.

Quest: Survive the Wave.

I reached for it to learn more and accidentally accepted the quest. When the rats appeared on the perimeter of the airport property, I realized my mistake.

It was more rats than I could count.

Had they been hiding there the whole time? My goggles hadn't seen them. No visible roaches assembling them, either. The hopping murder machines were coming, and fast.

I slammed the glass door and ran out of the break room.

Laura was outside the hangar, the door once again open.

"They're coming!" I shouted. "Close it! Close it!"

She retreated inside, shoving Chewie back before pulling the door down. But it didn't close all the way. They both worked at the door but it didn't budge. A foot up off the ground, and big enough for the rats to get easily in.

At the end of the hangars, Shadow was firing his Corrosive Blasts. I turned towards the front of the airport. A rat appeared by the office, with two more hurrying to keep up. They bounded my way. More running to join them.

I used Shoot. Hit one, but didn't kill it. I fell back towards Shadow. Shot again. Missed. The three rats were now five, with a sixth trailing behind. They were grouping up. I only had three hit points. During the time since my fight with the goliath, I had only regenerated one health.

Shadow had three charging around him, all covered with green glowing globs of energy that sizzled at their metal bodies. But he had more coming too.

"You going to do something or what?" Shadow asked.

My breath caught as I used Shoot on the injured rat. The blast took the thing out. My Stab lit up and I slashed the next one with my virtual fist blades even as it sliced with its sword arms and tried to chop my head off. The rat went to pieces, as did the one behind it.

So Stab could take out two targets. A fourth and fifth rat were scurrying towards me, one closer than the other. When Stab finished its cooldown, I used it again. Both rats went pop.

Shadow's three monsters dissolved simultaneously as his damage-over-time attacks did their thing. The next one to attack him stopped suddenly as he held a palm out like a crossing guard confidently stepping in the way of oncoming traffic. The monster's outline went from orange to red. It then turned and attacked the next rat. The two tussled, and with a Corrosive Blast, Shadow finished it off.

A final rat didn't stand a chance when I hit it. No more hostile monsters.

Quest Completed. You survived the wave.

I panted and couldn't stop smiling.

My experience slider topped out before resetting back to zero. My hit points surged back up to full.

You are now...

Level Three

1

"Don't pat yourself on the back too hard. They were all level-one rats."

I ignored Shadow as I studied my options.

New Class Skill: Fade. Enter Stealth even with enemies nearby. Level-Two Fade allows the user to hide even while in direct combat.

Direct was the key word. The rats we had just fought had been coming after me, but the game might not have considered that "direct combat." I needed the advanced version in case things got even hairier.

Increase one skill.

That was new. Stealth, Stab, Punch, and Shoot were my options. I couldn't level Fade yet.

Advanced Stealth allowed me to remain undetected, even if I touched a monster or made noise. It allowed me to avoid detection when closely sneaking around enemies more than two levels higher than me. Later levels allowed me to extend the ability to others. Useful, but passive.

Shoot increased range and damage. The description hinted that I could use Shoot and not break stealth at higher levels, but it didn't sound like it did as much damage as the melee skill.

I wasn't sure what the point of Advanced Punch was, except it favored increased damage while Stab raised the chances of a critical hit. Advanced Stab also had two sub-choices.

Stab: Flurry or **Stab: Whirlwind.**

Flurry did extra damage to a single target. Whirlwind increased my targets to three. If there were more clusters of rats, that sounded good. I chose Whirlwind.

Boost one stat.
STR, WIS, DEX, HEALTH, MOVE, CHA.

As much as I wanted to soak more damage, I didn't want to take any, if possible. Dodging sounded better, as did more crits, even if I hadn't landed one yet.

Dexterity went to fifteen.

I looted another **Asset: Armor** and an **Asset: Weapon**. When these would do me some good, I didn't know. And my health bar was once again full, even though I still felt sore and weary.

Shadow was watching me. "If you had used your Stealth, you could have hit harder with those claws of yours."

"My Stab only spills over into one additional target. How long can you keep that rat of yours charmed?"

"It's mine until I dismiss it."

The rat cozied up next to Shadow like a well-trained dog.

To the east, the sun threatened to crest the hills. The dull, distant *whup-whup-whup* of a helicopter thrummed from somewhere, but it never appeared and the sound vanished.

I knocked on the hangar door. They rolled it up.

"What happened?" Laura asked.

"A group of them snuck up on us."

Shadow scoffed. "He accepted a quest and they spawned."

"They didn't pop up out of nowhere," I said. "They were already around us. We just couldn't see them."

Laura's face hardened. "I thought the glasses let you know where they are."

My face flushed. Here we were, life on the line, and I was guilty of a noob mistake. How many countless posts had I pinned on our forum about not triggering a trap, aggroing a pack of mobs, or prematurely starting an encounter before the raid group was ready?

I brought everyone the Diet Dr. Peppers from the break room. A check of the perimeter showed no new monsters. Laura joined me for the patrol, her revolver tucked into her belt. With the weapon out of ammo, it was as useful as a paperweight.

Kermit helped Bennett with the can of soda. He sipped, coughed, and didn't want more. The towels around his injured hand were soaked through.

Shadow snagged a can and gulped it down.

"Don't suppose you came across Tylenol or some aspirin?" Kermit asked.

"I can check again."

Chewie paced in front of the hangar. "Is that what we're doing? Staying here?"

I found the bottle of malt liquor empty by the hot-air balloon basket. "You have a better plan?"

"Those things found us at the park, and we barely made a mile before hiding here. We're sitting ducks."

"Bennett's hurt. At least here we have open space so we can see them coming. I won't activate any more quests."

"Bennett hurt his finger, not his leg. We need to keep moving."

Laura watched the exchange. "That big machine at the clubhouse came for us with no quest. The motorcycle was hunting us. And at the diner, they came for the cars in the parking lot before going after the people."

I looked at the rows of hangars. She was right. Even without us here, the machines would want what was inside them. They'd want to harvest the airplanes and tools for parts so they could make more rats, more vipers, and Lord knows what else.

I tested the hangar door. It was solid and wouldn't budge up or down. "It's daylight. There's only the main road and we'll be walking."

"Beats being stuck inside a hangar with a door that won't close," Chewie said.

Laura nodded. "Chewie's right. A door like this isn't much better than a mobile home. Best to take our chances out there where we can keep moving."

"The bike path," Bennett mumbled.

"What?"

"There's a bike path close to the runway. We passed it last night just after leaving the road. We can follow it."

It didn't take Laura's okay to get everyone up and ready to leave. Kermit passed around the last soda and filled the cans and the liquor bottles at the sink in the break room.

Where was Shadow? I found him with the rat he had charmed. It was now a **Rat: Level Two.**

He sifted through the remains. "The viper was better."

"Can you get more than one pet?"

"Not yet. And I want to get something better than a rat to replace my viper."

"What's the chance of success on your skill?"

"I'm still figuring that out."

A sharp *praaap-praaap* of automatic gunfire exploded from across the marsh. Because of the range or the sunlight, I saw no glow of game assets.

Laura was crouched and waved us towards her. "Get down. Let's go."

We moved as a group to the road. Staccato pops echoed from the distance. If this had been a normal day, I would have guessed it was a nail gun or a car backfiring.

As Bennett had mentioned, a bike path led off to the south. But next to a trail sign stood a blue game object.

I approached it.

"What do you see?" Laura asked.

She didn't appear to know what I was looking at. None of them did, except maybe Shadow. He gave me a smug look.

I was careful not to accept the quest without reading it.

Quest: Be First to Level Five.

"You got this one already, didn't you?" I asked Shadow.

Laura inspected the section of road where I was crouched. "What is it? Another quest?"

I told her. "The game wants us competing. I hit level three. Shadow got a head start."

"I guess it's good you're getting experience. It also means the game knows where both of you are if it dropped something for you."

Of course, the game was watching. But at that point, what choice was there?

First to level five in our group? First in the zone? The world? How big was Crimson Gauntlet, anyway?

I accepted the quest.

2

A blue waypoint pointed towards an unknown game asset. It hung above the nearest houses, showing something to be had out of sight from a street beyond.

Our group emerged from the bike path onto a residential road near a playground. I hadn't heard a gunshot in twenty minutes and hoped whoever it was had survived.

The street to the right headed for the thoroughfare. To the left, more single-family homes. Yards, cars, mailboxes, fences. Just no people. The silence felt thick. No cars, no leaf blowers, no airplanes.

We came across our first metal cocoon with a shock vermin just past a dumpster. Shadow destroyed it and looted a coin.

"You know the area, Bennett?" Laura asked.

"We take Mount Lassen Drive. Then we head in the same direction as the parkway."

He was right. During work, it was a shortcut I'd take with my oldsters if the parkway got backed up with after-school traffic. There was a major intersection another mile up with a Safeway, a Rite-Aid, and a few gas stations. From there, you could head east to the freeway and downtown, or towards the other communities within Bell Park further south and west. There was also a high school nearby.

Bennett had to stop. He was panting and his face was beet red. Kermit helped him to the curb so he could sit.

Laura stood over them and watched the road. Her jaw clicked. It was something she did in raid chat when she was pissed.

"I'm going to scout ahead," Shadow announced.

Chewie gestured at him helplessly. "Shouldn't we stay together?"

"Five minutes," Laura said. "Be back in five. Then we keep going."

Shadow hurried across the street towards a corner. Mount Hood Lane. I caught up with him. "I'm coming with you."

"Keep up."

For a sickly looking pasty dude, he moved fast. If there was anyone watching out their kitchen windows, we must have looked comical. Darting from vehicle to vehicle, looking about like kids with a bag of firecrackers on the run from the police.

Shadow's rat kept pace with a frantic spring to its step as it followed his every move.

The game asset was down the street. A Jeep Wrangler rested on its side where it blocked the road. Cracked or busted out windows, the passenger door ajar, and gas pooling in the gutter. Vapor fumes rose from the asphalt.

A swarm of flies buzzed about as we took the sidewalk to bypass the obstacle. A pile of bodies lay on the other side. Perhaps twenty people with cuts, severed limbs, and slack expressions. All were dressed in ordinary clothes. One was a cop.

I covered my mouth and felt my stomach turn.

Shadow slowly exhaled as he took in the scene. "Didn't think they had all evacuated, did you?"

If I'd have answered, I would have hurled.

Of course, there were going to be bodies. It wasn't like a computer game where the dead eventually evaporate into nothing. No mess, no stench, no mourning, at least not really. In fantasy land, you pop up again in moments, because where's the fun in permadeath?

We kept moving.

The blue game asset appeared to be in the backyard of a rundown flat-roof house overgrown with honeysuckle hedges and peeling mustard-color paint.

Shadow's rat made too much noise as it clattered to a stop at his heels.

A half-dozen vehicles along the section of street had been dissected.

Body panels lay about, and the insides of the skinned cars were little more than steel frames. The engines were mostly gone, as were most of the interior components save the seats. Did the bugs have no use for vinyl and faux leather? But there were no roaches.

Strange.

The home's front yard looked like a tornado had struck a garage sale. Household items, litter, a trampoline, parts of at least two bicycles, and a shredded propane grill lay scattered on the dead lawn.

Shadow took cover beside a utility pole and studied the house. "Wait here. I'll go get it."

"Why do you get to take it?"

"Because I'm almost level four. I'll be more help to us if I'm stronger. You want to get out of this alive, right? Cover me if anything happens."

He wasn't waiting for me to argue, and I didn't want to shout. He crossed the yellow grass in the side yard and checked the gate. It shook but wouldn't open. A lattice fence top leaned precariously and grew heavy with vines. He looked about, probably searching for something to climb, but came up short. He then moved towards the front door.

That was when the mobs appeared.

They sprang up from the scattered junk in the front yard. Four thin humanoid figures stood on shaky legs. At least seven feet tall. Their hands featured long hooked fingers that almost touched the ground.

Skeleton (Level Four).

Shadow backed up, throwing a Corrosive Blast at the closest monster. It barely scratched its health bar as it strode towards him.

He sent in his rat next, the animal launching itself at the monster and chopping at its head and neck with its blades. A section of metal tore away from the skeleton's shoulder and it lost a quarter of its hit points. It stumbled to one side, almost keeling over, before skewering the rat with two fingers. It held the twitching pet aloft before slamming it to the sidewalk, where the rat exploded.

"A little help!"

My Stealth skill wouldn't activate. Too close. I hit Fade. Every instinct was to retreat. Instead, I moved past Shadow towards the four metal figures. The injured one was in range. Stab lit up. But what would happen once I appeared, even if I took it out? The other three spread out in a line and marched forward.

I sidestepped the wounded one and slipped between the others.

"Hagar!"

I tried not to be distracted by him calling me by my Night World character's name. The skeletons had enormous feet. I guessed my Stealth would break if I touched any part of them. I made the entryway even as more Corrosive Blasts flew and the first skeleton died. Shadow was falling back.

The door stood ajar. I pushed it open and stepped into the front hallway of a house packed floor-to-ceiling with plastic containers, boxes, papers, books, and appliances. A hoarder? The narrow path between it all led down a hallway and to a kitchen. I went through the kitchen and tried not to breathe when the first whiff of spoiled trash punished my nostrils.

A sodden pyramid of crumpled and grease-stained bags of McDonalds and empty buckets of the colonel's chicken dominated a table, with Taco Bell wrappers on the floor. The three chairs were rusted vinyl and metal, and these had a lifetime's worth of mail. Bills, junk adverts, print catalogs (they still put those out?), charity mailers, and flyers with the faces of missing children.

I almost took a header down a single step that led to a family room. Still obscenely cluttered, but there was enough space around a TV and a recliner with a standing tray next to it. Mandarin Palace takeout boxes here, with plastic fork and soy sauce packet collection. And there, by the door to the garage, was a computer desk and a gaming rig.

The roaches had been there, judging by the breadcrumb trail of silicone and the popped side panel to the case. But the fancy illuminated keyboard and twin monitors told me the householder, or at least someone here, played. And beneath the desk was a familiar white box.

Same as the one both Bennett and I had received.

Shadow screamed from outside. It wasn't pain, but exultation. I hated to have left him. It violated my gamer code. But I wanted the asset or whatever Crimson Gauntlet was dangling in front of us to get us there.

The rear slider wouldn't budge. It took a moment of fiddling to figure out the two locks and the bar, keeping the door shut.

Once unlocked, it took all my strength to shove it open so I could wedge myself outside.

The backyard was dried weeds and a dead plum tree. There, at the base of the tree, was the game asset. A pair of Janus Brand International glasses like the ones I was wearing.

I didn't get it. What good would a second pair of glasses do for me?

As I stepped out onto the concrete slab patio, a skeleton rose from the dirt. I Faded. The skeleton marched towards me. My Stealth icon remained dark. Did it see me? It hadn't been closer than the ones out front. Then I realized I was standing on some roaches. Had crushed two of them.

I was in combat.

The skeleton tilted its head, its mouth leering. It scraped its finger blades along the concrete as it closed in.

3

Too fast.

It was coming too fast, and I didn't want to let it catch me as I squeezed back inside the house.

When it ducked and was about to enter, I thrust with my claws and hit it with my Whirlwind. I wished I had chosen Flurry as my new skill. The skeleton reeled as it lost a third of its health. A roach died too, the second victim of my multi-target assault.

My Stab lit up again instantly, the cooldown somehow not needing a full second.

The skeleton punched me before I could move. Too fast to dodge. The blow caught me in the midsection and put me on my backside. Most of my health vanished. I inched away into the family room as the monster ripped the glass door off its track. It threw the door aside, where it exploded into shards against the concrete.

When it gripped the doorframe, I attacked.

My strike shattered the skeleton's arm. Another roach died. The skeleton stumbled back onto the patio. Stab reset again. I pressed my luck and jumped outside after it. I lunged and took out the thing's spine. It fell to pieces.

Achievement: Dem Bones. Kill a skeleton.

A quick review of my combat log confirmed what I suspected. If my whirlwind skill killed something, I could use it again without pause. While the damage was still split between targets, in this case it let me drop three attacks without waiting a beat for the cooldown.

Thanks, roaches.

The roaches still alive at my feet continued their business of dismantling an air conditioning unit bolted to a bedroom window.

My hands shook as I collected the loot. The skeleton dropped two red coins and an **Asset: Armor** and an **Asset: Weapon**. One more armor and I'd finish the quest.

I picked up the glasses waiting for me beneath the tree. They didn't vanish like the coins and other items. But I received a notification.

Player Asset collected.

Same size and makeup as the ones on my face. I didn't want to remove mine. Like the other objects, I wasn't sure what I was supposed to do with them, so I tucked them into my back pocket.

The scrape of metal behind me. Another skeleton ducked outside. It stooped to pick up the skull of the first skeleton. Shadow stepped around it and caressed its arm. He took the skull, examined it for a moment, and tossed it aside. His tangled hair was all over his face and one of his trench coat sleeves had been shredded. Blood oozed from a cut running from his ear down to his chin.

"Well played, Hagar. Well played."

4

Shadow checked the base of the tree. "You left me hanging out there."

I backed away as his skeleton tagged along obediently. Its head was stooped and it kept its arms with its wicked hooked fingers tucked against its ribcage like a praying mantis.

"You should have run," I said. "I didn't think we'd make it after you lost your rat."

"I made a new friend."

"I see that. But there were three to deal with after the first one died."

"Bones here took on one of them. I whittled down the other. It almost got me."

His health bar was full.

"You leveled," I said.

"Lucky thing, too. Since I was fighting alone, the XP was mine. Don't suppose you'd give me the game glasses?"

The skeleton loomed. A mental command from Shadow, and it would disembowel me.

I patted my back pocket. "Crimson Gauntlet called them a player asset. What are they good for?"

"I'm still learning, just like you. We agreed I would take what we found. That'll best help the others get out of here."

"I think I'll hang onto them for now."

For a long second, I thought he was going to try something. Would any of my skills work on him? He wasn't a game monster. He'd see me if I Faded.

His sneer stretched the bottom corner of the cut along his face. "Your choice. Let's get out of here."

We exited through the house, Shadow and his skeleton going first. With his pet monster in front of me, the thought crossed my mind this would be the time to take it out. Stab wouldn't light up. A friendly target. Hopefully, it meant the thing couldn't touch me either.

I still didn't feel easy walking within striking distance of a seven-foot-tall skeleton with Freddy Krueger fingernails. This very machine might have been one of the creatures that had murdered those people.

We had to pass the crime scene on our way back to the group.

"Shadow, wait up. Think twice about dragging your new friend over to the others. I mean, what if it breaks control? What if it attacks them?"

"It can't break control."

"How do you know?"

"Because the game told me it couldn't. Besides, you weren't worried about Ratty. Bones promises he won't hurt anyone."

"Bones, huh? Naming your pets? You're enjoying this too much."

"And now that you have those extra glasses, what are you planning on doing with them?"

"What do you think? If we have three people who can fight, we stand a better chance of making it out of here."

He made a noncommittal grunt before flamboyantly waving Bones along, as if his pet skeleton needed to be encouraged.

5

Laura and the others were gone.

Mount Lassen Drive ran two ways, and I didn't see the group in the street or along the sidewalk.

Shadow looked in either direction before staring off into the distance above the rooftops. "I guess we took longer than five minutes."

"Then we need to find them. Leaving them here was a bad idea. There's no hiding place and they were undefended."

I hurried along the cars parked around us, scanning the homes for signs the others might have taken cover inside. If they weren't hiding, they must have continued along the street. Or had something come after them, forcing a retreat back the way we came?

A phone lay in the gutter. Cracked screen, scratches, and a roach was prying at it.

I squished the thing.

It was Chewie's phone. He had the latest iPhone, with a sparkly case featuring a hologram of a pair of ten-sided dice rolling double zeroes.

We knew which way they were heading.

A car horn blared. Three long honks, three short, three long.

S.O.S.

I ran. "It's them."

Shadow's skeleton clanged after us as we made it to an intersection near the parkway. A small school bus was up on the curb, having run into a patch of landscaping and smashing a neighborhood watch sign. Laura and the others were inside, and it was surrounded by rats.

I activated Stealth and moved in. The rats were tearing at the door, the hood, and the windows. There were a lot of them.

Kermit was pressed against the door holding it shut, but the glass was already cracked and would give away at any moment. I targeted a rat and cut loose with a Stab. The blow demolished two of them, thanks to Whirlwind. The ability reset. I hit it again, and a third time, clearing six rats in quick succession.

"Get 'em, Bones," Shadow purred.

His skeleton sprang into the group at the back of the bus. It slashed and raked and took out three rats. Two rats jumped on the skeleton, their knives a flurry of steel on metal, sending up sparks.

A flash and a shock knocked me on my ass.

One was a Shock Vermin. Scratch that, there were three of them. The other two abandoned their deconstruction project and leaped to the ground in front of me.

I stabbed one. It didn't go down, but my whirlwind skill hit the vermin behind it. It blasted me and I nearly blacked out as pain surged through my body. My muscles clenched and my jaw locked up. The third one skittered closer, coming in for the kill.

Stab was ready. I slashed it.

Critical Hit! Twelve Damage!

The blow sliced off one of the vermin's arms, but it didn't go down. The attack also took out the already wounded vermin next to it. Stab reset. But the remaining mob pulsed, charged up, and fired before I could stab again.

I convulsed. Couldn't do much else. Picture the worst leg cramp, except surging through every muscle in your body.

My combat log related the details with all the passion of a cereal box listing its nutritional value.

You were hit by Vermin Rat (Level Two) for seven damage.
You have zero hit points.
You are unconscious.

6

Achievement: Stare into the Abyss. Lose all your hit points and almost die. Key word? Almost.

Kermit hovered over me as I fought to control my limbs. Motor control came back gradually, even as a dull ache echoed from fingertip to groin to my little toes.

Laura held two car window-breaking safety hammers, one in each hand. "I said keep that thing back."

"Suit yourself," Shadow said. He led Bones away to the other side of the street.

I motioned for Kermit to help me up. The rats were all gone, nothing more than scattered debris. But a line of roaches marched towards the school bus. A few were claiming the easy pickings of the rat and vermin pieces and carrying them off, no doubt to make more monsters.

One hit point back, according to my combat log and thanks to my meager health regen. Anyone could have knocked me down with a sneeze.

Laura had murder in her eyes. "Where were you guys?"

I realized Shadow had looted the rats. There was nothing left. "There were monsters."

"Tell me about it. But you're our only defense. You were supposed to be scouting."

I looked at Shadow for support, but he was fiddling with Bones where the rat had struck it.

"I'm sorry. There was a game object I needed to check out." From my back pocket, I produced the glasses. Fortunately, they had survived getting crushed. "Someone in the neighborhood was part of the game.

I don't think they made it. But their glasses were in a backyard, and Crimson Gauntlet wanted us to find them."

Bennett and Chewie emerged from the bus. Chewie had blood caked on his chin and nose, as if having taken a header onto the ground. Probably when he had lost his phone.

Kermit inspected the glasses as I held them. "Who should use it?"

"No one," Laura said. "If Janus is behind what's going on, those things are dangerous."

More roaches scurried our way. Laura stomped one, then another.

I took out my phone and slid it towards the line of roaches. One made a detour and climbed over the device. It dug in, cracking the case with a series of sharp blows using its needlelike proboscis. Two more of the bugs helped dismantle it.

I felt acid in my throat. "We need to get rid of our phones."

Bennett placed a hand on his pants pocket. "No. I can't. What if Kirsten calls?"

"If she got out of your house, where would she go?"

"Her sister's place in Davis."

Way too far. "She would have called if she could by now. If she made it to an aid station or a hospital, they might have trouble with the network with the power out. But the phones are catnip to these things."

"How do you know this?"

"It's everything we've seen. The little bugs are taking cars, phones, and appliances apart. It might also be how the bigger monsters find us."

That, and the glasses. I left that out. But Laura must have been thinking the same thing because she didn't look convinced. She held out a hand for Bennett's phone and powered it down before handing it back.

She next turned her own device off. "In case Eddie's right. But the phones are our only lights if we're stuck out here for another night."

Kermit followed suit.

I was tempted to start squashing bugs again, but we had been standing around for too long.

"Shadow?" Bennett called. "Turn your phone off."

Shadow had his phone out. He held up a finger before tapping at the screen. His phone pinged. He read for a moment. Laughed before offering me the phone.

"It's the game. It wants to give you all a message."

7

Welcome to Crimson Gauntlet!
Do you like fast combat, high stakes, and an immersive game world?
You've come to the right place.
You are cordially invited to the world premiere of the greatest massive multiplayer experience in history! Taste the danger, feel the thrills, and learn the secrets of the most engaging entertainment event ever!
If you're receiving this message, you are inside the live game zone. All efforts will be made to make sure your adventure is the unforgettable event of your life.
The developers realize not everyone wishes to play. If this is the case, please report to the game zone exits. While we hate to see you leave so soon, stepping outside of the zone will exclude you from all Crimson Gauntlet events.

Shadow leaned in as I read. "There's a map."

Laura joined us as I shielded the screen with my hand to limit the glare from the sun.

Two pins appeared on the map at the bottom of the message. One was labeled Tutorial Start Here. The marker lay to the east just past the highway. The other pin was ten miles west. Game Zone Exit.

Kermit, Chewie, and Bennett waited their turn for a look. Their fear of Shadow's pet skeleton had momentarily evaporated.

I looked at Shadow. "Why was this texted to you if you already have the glasses and an invitation?"

"It wasn't a text. It was a Nixle alert. This is the same way the evacuation messages were sent out."

"So the game's using the emergency message system to make sure everyone got this."

"Everyone with a phone that's powered on and signed into the network, yeah."

"Or that's still alive," Laura added. "This is too strange. This 'game' started with no warning. And now it wants people to come to a central location to play?"

I tried to visualize where the Game Zone Exit might be. "Or direct us elsewhere if we want to quit."

"How did it hack into the Nixle system?" Chewie asked.

No one had an answer.

"You think it's a trap, Laura?" Bennett asked. "It's probably a trap."

She shrugged. "I don't know what I think. But I want us all to get out of here before more rats, motorcycles, tanks, or whatever else comes driving through."

I took the phone back to study the map. "The game wants us to go either east or west. Which direction?"

"Neither."

She led us to the end of the street where we had no choice but to continue along Redwood Parkway. About a mile down past several condo and apartment complexes, the parkway crossed Country Club Boulevard. We snuck through a bank parking lot. A grocery store stood just across the four lanes.

My stomach grumbled.

Laura's plan was to get supplies and continue along Redwood Parkway towards the Merrydale neighborhood so Chewie could check on his wife. If she was there, we'd take her with us and continue south. There had to be a vehicle somewhere.

More blue game assets and quest indicators hung in the air in every direction. All were too far away. One more armor and I'd finish a quest. Might be enough for level four. The game was trying to tempt me and Shadow.

A waypoint to the east lit up. Crimson Gauntlet wanted me to head towards the tutorial. But I was hurt, hungry, and tired.

No cars in sight. We crossed the street together towards the grocery store and found shelter beneath the row of mulberry trees growing along the edge of the property.

Shadow and Bones kept their distance.

A dozen cars stood parked in the lot. They had been dismantled like every vehicle we had come across. It was like a locust plague of car parts thieves had overrun the area before moving on.

Where were the roaches?

"You see anything?" Laura asked.

I resisted the urge to hand her the spare glasses. "Uh-uh. They must be assembling the cocoons elsewhere. And if the monsters here are like the last ones, they're hiding until we get close."

"How do you want to do this?"

"I have a stealth skill. I'll sneak into the store and get what we need. Water and a few energy bars should do."

I turned on Stealth and stepped out from under the tree.

"I still see him," Bennett said.

Laura shushed him as I set out across the parking lot.

The label of the closest game asset appeared next to a soda vending machine.

Crafting Station.

I touched it. A menu appeared. I could build armor or weapons, or single-use items, like grenades and healing potions. My health bar remained at one. But I didn't have enough coins. Every option was grayed out.

The automatic doors to the grocery store stood ajar, with a rubber floor mat crumpled between them. Candy, dog food bags, and plastic bottles of water lay scattered throughout the entryway. Display cases were knocked over. The body of a clerk leaned against a checkout counter, one outstretched arm caught in a shopping bag rack. The dark stains told the tale, but it was impossible to know what kind of monster had murdered him.

With no light, the space beyond the registers stood in shadow.

I could collect water from along the front shelves beneath the windows and candy from the stands near one register, but energy bars were across the store in the same aisle as breakfast cereal. A game asset waited there too.

Did Crimson Gauntlet know what I needed? Like a worm on a hook, as if I had ever gone fishing.

I heard a squeak. Sneakers on tile. A hushed whisper.

The racking of a shotgun.

They came down two aisles, a group of five. Masks or motorcycle helmets, one with a baseball catcher's chest guard and knee pads, two in leather jackets. The closest pointed a shotgun and I stopped cataloging their gear.

"Who are you?" Shotgun asked in a rough voice.

A woman clutched a baseball bat. "And what are you doing?"

I had been sneaking, at least as far as the game was concerned. Now I felt stupid.

A scrawny kid wearing a full-face helmet that made him look like a bobble head approached me and patted me down. "What's with the weird glasses?"

Punch and Stab lit up.

I kept my hands raised. "I need water."

"Well, the store's ours," the scrawny kid said in an echoey voice.

"The shelves are full. You don't need it all."

Shotgun snorted. "This is what we call finders-keepers. World's ending, and we got here first."

The game painted them in a purple outline. Each received a label.

Enemy Player (Level Zero).

Unlike Shadow, Crimson Gauntlet didn't provide a name.

Helmet flicked my cheek. "Hey, I asked you a question. Why are you wearing those funny things?"

"They help me see."

The girl next to Shotgun guffawed. Her shrill laugh went on and on until one of the others, a man or a woman, I couldn't tell, told her to shut up.

I licked my lips and wished my voice sounded steady. "Look, it's us versus those things out there. Everyone who didn't evacuate is in danger. There was a Nixle alert telling people to head west."

"A what?" Helmet asked.

"He said Nixle, idiot," Shotgun said. "No one here has a phone. Those bugs were all over them in the breakroom, so we threw our devices outside. How many people are with you?"

Helmet remained in range. Would I even hurt him if I attacked? But I had no intention of getting blown in half finding out. "Look, I don't want anything from you. If you won't share a few bottles of water, I'll leave."

"Or you'll come back with reinforcements. How about you lie down on the floor?"

"I don't want to do that. We don't want your store. We're heading out of here. You could even come with us."

"So there *is* more than one of you. Trish, go look outside. And you? Get down. Preston, tie him up with something."

The girl ran to the door. "I don't see any—oh my GOD!"

Shadow's pet Bones crashed through the glass. The skeleton landed on top of her and smashed a bladed hand down with a sickening crunch. The others screamed. The shotgun thundered. I dropped to the vinyl tiles and crawled to the nearest display stand. Poor cover. It was made of cardboard and filled with bags of candy for an early Halloween.

The shotgun boomed again, the earsplitting blast deafening me. Bones leaped off the girl and out of sight. Someone shrieked as metal struck flesh.

Shadow appeared in the doorway.

"Call him off!" I shouted.

He stepped over the girl's body and strode past me. Hard steel feet clanged on the floor, and it was Shotgun's turn to scream. The rending sounds were followed by wet pops. I rose in time to see Bones tear Shotgun's arm away and his weapon drop to the floor. The body tumbled from the monster's grip. The skeleton paused, as if taking in the carnage. Its grin was spattered in red.

The scrawny kid in the motorcycle helmet was down, and the other two had vanished into the back of the store.

"Shadow! Let's get out of here!"

He glanced my direction. "Nah. I have a new quest to finish."

With a nod, he sent Bones down the canned fruit and vegetable aisle.

I hurried to catch up. "Let them go. We get our water and we don't have to hurt anyone else. I'm fine."

He ignored me. With a nod, he sent Bones to smash open the back swinging door into the storage area. One of them had thrown a mop across the door, but it snapped like a toothpick.

Bones closed in on the last two store defenders as they struggled to unlock a rolling loading dock door. Light spilled in from outside, but the door was only open by inches.

I grabbed Shadow. "Make it stop!"

He held up a warning finger. "Or what?"

Bones froze, its claws poised to shred the two.

One of them was younger than he had first appeared, with a pimply face and a mess of hair beneath the bill of a green Oakland A's baseball cap. The other had a wisp of a goatee and a black band T-shirt.

"They're just trying to run away. They didn't hurt me. We take what we need and get out of here."

The kid with the pimples was shaking. His trousers were damp.

Shadow popped his lips. "Okay. Take what we need. Fair enough. Bones here doesn't need anything else. Why don't you collect some rations for the team? I'll keep an eye on them."

I returned to the store. The stockroom door was still swinging when I heard the screams. I burst into the back in time to see Bones tearing the guy in the black T-shirt apart. The pimply kid shielded his face as Bones dropped his companion's lifeless body next to him.

"Leave him," Shadow said to Bones. "Hagar's right. It's time to go."

I was numb as they passed me. "Why?"

"I already told you. I *needed* one more to finish the quest."

8

As we left the store, I imagined I could hear the last survivor crying. My chest was tight. The bags of energy bars and water bottles felt heavy.

I had been ignoring my quest log, but the tab was lit.

Quest Available: Kill Five Enemy Players.

I hadn't accepted the quest. Somehow, Crimson Gauntlet knew the people in the grocery store were there. Had it expected they would be hostile? How could the game want us to kill other people?

Shadow had taken the time to collect loot on the way out. One crafting, one weapon, and an armor asset. Now he strolled along with his mechanical murder skeleton, as casual as can be.

How could he have so casually murdered them? Had he gone crazy? What kind of psycho had we been playing with?

Cry more, noob.

The dark thought reminded me of all the taunts we'd say when ganking low-level players in an open PvP zone. Sprites and pixels there, not flesh and blood.

Laura rushed from the cover of the trees to meet us. "What happened? We heard gunshots."

Shadow relieved me of a water bottle. "A successful supply run."

My breath came up short. "He…Shadow killed them."

"Correction: Bones killed a group of bandits about to take our boy Hagar hostage. They had weapons."

"Who were they?" Laura asked.

"Enemy players."

"What do you mean 'players?'"

"The game tagged them," I said. "Maybe because they had a shotgun. Maybe because we wanted what they had."

"How would the game know?"

"Because it's here, it's everywhere, and it knows where we are and what we're doing."

"The machines will have heard those reports. We should move."

Bennett had approached during our discussion. His wrapped hand remained tucked against his side. "If the game let us get this far, it's because Shadow and Eddie have been playing. You still have the extra set of glasses? I want to see what's going on like you guys."

"Eddie has them," Shadow volunteered.

I took out the spare glasses. "I wanted Laura to have these, Ben. No offense, but you're hurt."

Laura shook her head. "I don't want them. We don't know what they're doing to you. And if the monsters can find our phones, they can target us by us wearing them."

Bennett looked at her and nodded.

Chewie and Kermit joined us.

The faster Kermit spoke, the stronger his British accent sounded. "Laura's right. If Janus built the glasses and is somehow connected to all the monsters, it can't be safe."

"If no one else will wear them, give them to me," Chewie said.

"You don't know what that's going to do to your brain."

"Maybe it will help me get home."

"How close are we to your house? The road west is here. Eddie just told us that people died in there. We need to find the exit and get help. We can send someone for your wife after."

"We don't know if there *is* an exit. But from what I've seen, Eddie and Shadow have the only tools to survive this. Hand them over, Eddie."

I did as he asked. Chewie considered the glasses as if I had offered him a drink of unknown origin and ingredients. As if putting them on was a dare and we were waiting to see if he was chicken.

He slipped them on. "Woah." Gazed about. Looked at each of us. "I have two attacks. How does that work?"

"You can engage with anything in the world that has an enemy tag," I said. "Most are orange. But you can also destroy the blue game assets, so be careful. You're level zero. The first thing you'll need to do is choose where to put your first five attribute points. We'll need to talk about your choice of attributes once you hit level one. It'll happen quickly once we kill something. I'll help you. But let's get moving first. If everything goes right, we'll find your wife, get out of here, and we won't have to fight anything else."

9

Chewie stumbled. It was the third time, and I almost wanted to take his glasses away. Laura led us. We moved west along a bike path that followed Country Club Boulevard.

I held onto him until he steadied himself.

"'Please note,'" he said. "'Some players you may encounter are not equipped with resources to engage with the interactive experience. They will be marked in a manner so they can be easily identified as game assets. Fellow Crimson Gauntlet players will see you tagged as an ally once you accept the terms by clicking Accept at the bottom of the end-user service agreement and disclaimer.' Did you go through all this?"

"I skipped some of it."

"Maybe it's talking about the guys in the grocery store. 'Game resources.' Didn't you say they were marked as enemy players?"

"Yeah, but they were people, too. I tried to talk to them and get them to let me go. Shadow—"

I stopped talking. Shadow had been last in our little procession. He and Bones shuffled past. I tried not to think about the spattered stains on the skeleton.

Chewie waited for me. "So, when do I get one of those skeletons?"

"Level two, depending on which class you select."

"Shadow seems stronger than you."

"Maybe he picked better. Hopefully, it won't matter once we get to the exit."

"You haven't finished telling me what happened in the store."

I kept quiet. Didn't want to think about it. The dead people near Bennett's house had been bad enough. Seeing Shadow's minion tear four people apart in front of me was something I wouldn't be able to wipe from my mind. If I could get them to safety, I might put the nightmare behind me. We could deal with Shadow later once this was all behind us.

We ducked as a **Goliath (Level Ten)** raced past on the road. It had once been a large fire engine but now was busy with spikes, armor plating, and a dozen rats as passengers clinging to the back and side. It didn't appear to be chasing anyone. A patrol? Heading off to murder more people foolish enough to have remained behind? Even Shadow took cover, with Bones comically crouching behind him.

Kill Five Enemy Players.

The prompt remained on my quest tab. Still unaccepted. My uncompleted task? I still needed one more armor. But a box was unchecked at the bottom of the quest menu.

Find available quests?

With a blink, I could activate yet another game feature. Was I ready for more distractions? Get to the Game Zone Exit, hand the glasses over to the Army, Navy SEALS, Men in Black, or whatever alphabet government agency handles emergencies of this nature. Did anyone know what was happening to Bell Park?

I blinked.

The world was alive with quests. While the game dropped some in my lap, this opened the game landscape up and gave me a chill how far Crimson Gauntlet might have spread. None of the quest labels were close enough to read, and some of the distant waypoints appeared to be miles away. Most were to the east.

No wonder Shadow kept gazing off in that direction.

Chewie stopped at the next intersection. "This takes us to my house."

"I thought it would be closer," Bennett said. "I don't know how much further I can go."

From my job, I knew the neighborhood. "It's not that far, is it?"

Chewie took a few steps past the road sign. "No. Another thirty minutes. A little less. Maybe Bennett can rest up here. I need to keep going."

"I'll go with you."

"We're not splitting up," Laura said. "If Eddie and Shadow have the gas in case we run into more trouble, we're pressing on. Come on, Bennett. No one's getting left behind."

I had three hit points. They were regenerating a little faster than before, but sloooowly. "I'm fine. Let's do it."

Off to save Chewie's wife. Chewie, the man who would talk smack about her over guild chat. One of his gems? "I can't understand why she gets so annoyed about me playing online so much. An angry woman. Of course, her hobbies make her mad too. You should see how she glares at me when she vacuums."

Carol had been a gamer too. Played vanilla Night World to max level, but never ran instances, never grouped, and didn't want any part of our guild. Maybe she didn't want to play with her husband.

I wished I felt optimistic about finding her after what I had seen inside Bennett's home.

The Merrydale neighborhood was all two-level mansions close enough to one another you could poke your neighbor's house with a broom. Every home had a double garage and a postage-stamp backyard, which might fit a grill or a jogging trampoline, but not both. The monotonous taupe and beige color scheme made every house look the same. Each had a black mailbox, and only the occasional flag or front porch flowerpot differentiated one from the next.

The Dodge Charger parked on one of the first driveways had its doors off and its tires were flat. I could see holes in the metal and loose body panels as we got closer. More vehicles were parked further down the lane, and they were likewise disassembled.

The sidewalk had no hedges or cover. We were exposed.

I directed the group to the side of the street with the fewest cars.

A bright playground with benches and a dog run occupied a corner lot. The streets in either direction looked the same. More cross streets up ahead. The Merrydale neighborhood was a bland suburban maze.

I realized how much I needed my GPS to navigate. "Which way, Chewie?"

He pointed at the park. "Kill five rats."

Past the slide and main play area, several forms with orange tags scurried about. They didn't appear to notice us.

"You have a quest?" I asked.

"Yeah. You got to level one after killing just a couple of them back at the diner, right?"

"Something like that."

"How about we skip the monsters?" Laura said. "We're in no condition to run."

"It'll make Chewie stronger. I'll go with him."

"We're not splitting up again."

Shadow had fallen behind. He was across the street and peering through a front window. Bones towered over him and looked bored. I didn't see any game assets, but there might be many of them waiting behind closed doors. Monsters, too.

But we could handle a few rats.

"Laura, this will only take a minute. Besides, I'd rather not leave those things at our back."

She glared for a moment before shepherding Kermit and Bennett to cover beneath a row of bottlebrush hedges.

I patted Chewie on the shoulder. "Use your Shoot. Stay out of range, keep moving. I'll sneak up."

He nodded. Licked his lips. He dragged his feet as he walked along the sandy asphalt.

With Stealth on, I closed in on the rats. All level one. Were they here just waiting for us? It was very game-like behavior. The mobs had nothing better to do than stand around waiting to get murdered.

I looked back and gave Chewie a thumb's up. He responded in kind.

My mind screamed in protest as I slunk closer to the nearest rats past the playground. This was easily avoided danger. It wasn't in my wheelhouse to bungee jump, parachute, paraglide, or para-anything involving jumping off a perfectly safe planet in defiance of gravity.

Stab crit, and two rats burst to pieces. But my overflow damage evaporated as the other three were too far away. They bounced my direction, coming in from three sides.

"Chewie?"

Footsteps behind me. Chewie was running away.

10

Eddie Rush's First Rule of Winning? No plan survives intact after the start of combat.

One hit and I was toast. The three rats weren't waiting to see who first got a piece of me. I dove over a waist-high fence dividing the walking path to the play area. Climbed the ladder to the top of the slide. The rats massed beneath me. One sprang up and landed at my feet. I kicked it. It dislodged the thing, but I hadn't used a skill.

From inside the plastic slide, I heard a *click-click-click*.

A Shock Vermin stuck its head up and out of the plastic tube. I hit it with my Stab and destroyed it.

The three rats circulated beneath me as if deciding on a plan. They were sticking together. Stab reset, and I felt confident I could kill two, but the third would get a shot in. They began jumping and jabbing their blades between the faux-wood planks at my feet. They were the sharks and I was the ham hock on the life raft.

"Damn it, Chewie!"

Where was Shadow?

One of the rats' health dropped to a sliver. It turned and bounced off past a bench where Laura stood, comically thrusting her hand in the air over and over as if trying to shake off water. She wore game glasses.

"The cooldown!" I shouted.

But she didn't need the reminder. Her Shoot skill blasted the thing to pieces. I dropped next to the other two and finished them.

Laura walked along the edge of the play set, arm outstretched like an overzealous crossing guard and eyes on the perimeter. "We clear?"

"Yeah. The shock vermin was a surprise. They didn't touch me."

She removed the glasses, inspected them, and put them back on. "That...made my head hurt."

"You get used to it."

"Yeah? And when did you last take yours off?"

"I'll wait until we get out of the game. Did you take those from Chewie?"

"He practically threw them at me."

"He ran. But I'm glad you came. Thanks. Did you finish the quest?"

Her eyes darted as she read. "Credit for three of five."

She collected a couple of coins before we rejoined the others.

Shadow was nowhere in sight, and we couldn't go off looking for him.

Chewie huddled with Bennett and Kermit at the park entrance. Kermit had his hand on his shoulder.

"I'm sorry, Eddie," Chewie said. "When those things started moving towards us...."

"It's fine. Laura helped me. The rats are dead."

Laura patted him on the shoulder. "All right, pull it together. Let's get to your place and find your wife, okay?"

He nodded and we headed down the road. She didn't offer him the glasses.

Eddie Rush's First Rule of Winning? Don't suck.

11

Laura was level one. She took longer than I did making her selection, and wasn't sharing what she chose.

Did I mention my hit points ticked up to four?

A pack of three rats came for us from a storm drain. I took two down, and Laura killed the third before it made it close to her.

I looted a coin and a crafting asset. Laura grabbed an armor token from the gutter before I could snag it to complete my quest.

"Sorry," she said. "I didn't know the loot was free-for-all."

Chewie joined us in the middle of the street. "My house is right up here."

He and the others waited for us to take the lead, as it should be. I looked behind us down the street. Shadow hadn't returned.

We crossed a corner yard and stopped at the end of a row of bushes. Through a broken picture window, an **Asset: Armor** glowed.

I hissed for Laura. "There's something inside I need."

"You want to stop for another fight? You said it yourself, you're one hit from dying again. If there's anything harder than a rat after you go down, we're in trouble."

"Okay," I said reluctantly.

We moved to the next house when a notification opened in my interface.

Quest: Escort Ally Home.

I accepted it. A waypoint appeared above a house halfway down the block. A game tag marked Chewie.

"You get that, Laura?"

She waved her hand over Chewie's head. "Yeah, I took it. But I'm hating this more and more. How does the game know where we're going?"

"What's wrong?" Chewie asked.

I activated Stealth. "For better or worse, Crimson Gauntlet wants us to take you home."

With my head on a swivel, I took point as we crossed the road and stuck to the front yards along the opposite side of the street from Chewie's house. Each picture window had a coin or asset glowing just inside, candy waiting for a greedy hand to reach in to grab it. A dozen demolished cars near us, but no cocoons. Roaches streamed along the gutter. The lines of robotic insects vanished through the sewer grates.

No Dumping—Flows to Bay.

With each step, I expected a monster to appear. Every piece of rubbish was suspect. The last pack of rats had come from the sewer. What else might the roaches be building down there?

Laura kept the others huddled in front of a garage beneath the shade of a maple tree. Gave me a nod.

With Shadow no longer with us, it meant it was on me alone to go forward and trigger the encounter.

Eddie Rush's First Rule of Winning? Never start a fight unless you're ready.

I made it to Chewie's front walkway. It cut through a typical yard full of drought-resistant plants, with a spikey prickly pear cactus near the porch.

I tried the bell. No sound. Knocked softly. After a moment, I checked the door, but it was locked.

An asset glowed through the kitchen window. The windows wouldn't budge, so I crossed the driveway. The garage door wouldn't lift. I signaled to the others and motioned I was heading to the backyard. Laura gave me a thumbs up.

The side gate opened. A small door to the garage was likewise locked, so I headed to the back.

At the house where I had found the glasses, there were four skeletons. But Shadow had been with me. I couldn't assume the game would scale the encounter down because I was solo.

Find Carol, get her out of there, head for the game exit. I refused to think about what I might discover inside. The last thing I wanted was to find another body.

A raised vegetable garden with tomatoes and bell peppers was in the backyard. The slider opened.

To call out or not to call out?

The family room had a giant sectional couch around a fireplace and a monster-sized television. I counted three game consoles stuffed haphazardly into a cabinet beneath the screen. The kitchen was oversized, with an island and twin sinks and smart appliances all without power.

An **Asset: Weapon** waited in front of the fridge. I didn't touch it.

Past the kitchen, a pile of metal waited at the bottom of the stairs.

One step closer. Two. I waved my hand about, but didn't want to get closer.

The **Skeleton (Level Four)** wasn't fooling anyone. It rose and stood there, blind to my presence. My quest objective remained outside. Chewie needed to follow me in for the quest to continue, but I wanted to clear the place first. I stepped around the skeleton.

It swayed, as if being struck by a breeze.

Achievement: Sneaky Bastard. Avoid a monster using stealth.

The rest of the downstairs rooms were clear.

I returned to the foyer and the waiting skeleton. With my back to the kitchen so I could retreat, I hit Stab. No crit, but the damage was enough. The skeleton didn't have time to react as I sent its metal bones scattering across the carpet. A coin and a transportation asset dropped. I scooped them up and fetched the weapon asset from the kitchen.

A quick check of the front living room found nothing besides a recliner and an uncomfortable-looking stiff-backed set of dining room chairs around a massive table.

Something clunked upstairs.

I mounted the steps. Each creaked, as did the banister when I put my weight on it. I had Stealth up again, but the noise couldn't be missed.

"Hello?" a woman called.

"Carol? It's Eddie Rush. I'm Chewie, um, Keith's friend from the game. He's with us outside. I'm coming upstairs."

"What happened to that thing that got in the house?"

"It's gone. I killed it."

I pushed open the door to a bedroom. Carol was a middle-aged woman wearing purple pajamas and she had wedged herself into the corner by a nightstand behind an overstuffed mattress. Her frizzy brown hair dangled around her face, and she had streaks of eye makeup on her cheeks. She clutched a shotgun.

A game label hung above her.

Enemy Player (Level One).

12

Available Quest: Kill Five Enemy Players.

The game doubled down. Now it wanted me to attack someone I knew. I hadn't accepted it before. Wasn't going to do it now.

Carol lowered the shotgun barrel. "Eddie? Take me to Keith."

"Yeah, of course. Follow me. Just stay back in case something new pops up. Are you hurt?"

"I'm okay. It was a crazy night. Who else is with you?"

"The rest of the gang from the diner."

I realized her purple pajamas were hospital scrubs. Doctor or nurse? My brain was too fuzzy to remember all of Chewie's comments about his wife. But how was it she was a level-one player instead of level zero?

I stopped at the top of the stairs. "I know this is going to sound strange, but Keith received a pair of glasses like mine from a game company. It arrived today. Do you know where he might have put them?"

"What does it matter? Take me to Keith."

"It's important. They're key to what's going on outside."

"He was home yesterday afternoon. I'm sure he brought in the mail. He puts it in the office."

The office was downstairs, a tidy workspace with little personality except for the collector's edition dragon miniature from the original Night World edition sitting next to a closed laptop. No box, no glasses. Maybe Chewie hadn't brought in the mail. A cursory check of the kitchen and all the countertops confirmed no glasses there either.

Carol kept her weapon tucked against her shoulder. "There were a couple of those things outside the house earlier just after the power went out. I ran upstairs and got the gun. The phone was out and I didn't have a signal on my mobile. That's where I was all night. Tell me what's going on."

"It's hard to explain. If you saw the thing I killed at the base of the stairs, then you'd believe me when I say there's more of them. Some smaller, some much bigger."

"You look like you've been in a fight."

"More than one. It's the glasses that let me see them coming."

"Uh-huh."

The disbelief in her tone was impossible to miss. Also impossible to ignore was the fact she kept a pace or two behind me with her shotgun as we went out the front door.

"Carol!" Chewie called. He emerged from behind a pickup truck where they had been waiting and ran towards her.

When the two skeletons rose from the bed of the truck, I realized Crimson Gauntlet was running the escort quest identical to hundreds of other video games. It was the escorted NPC who triggered the encounter, not the player.

I was far enough away from the monsters to turn on Stealth. "Run towards me!"

Carol cried out as the skeletons leaped off the truck after him. She backed away, the shotgun in her hands idle. Chewie stumbled as he made it to his wife, his feet catching on themselves. They both went down.

Laura didn't hesitate. She blasted one with her ranged attack, but it barely scratched the thing. I scurried forward, willing Stab to light up before the skeletons tore Chewie and Carol to shreds. Stab was ready. I hit the wounded one. A crit. It blew to pieces.

Carol screamed. She and Chewie remained in the dirt next to me. Roaches crawled up her arms and legs. No time to help.

The second skeleton slashed at me as I fell back. Missed by inches. But then it changed direction and lurched towards Chewie.

"Come on!" I shouted at it.

Laura charged forward and punched it. Another feeble blow. "Don't stab it again, Eddie!"

"Why not?"

"Because you hurt Carol!"

The skeleton spun and nailed Laura with a backhand that sent her toppling. But she wasn't down.

I used Shoot. Hit the thing. It still had three-quarters of a health bar and stood poised to tear all of us to pieces. It bore down on Laura. She was up in time to deliver another blow, catching the skeleton in the hip. One of its legs buckled and it fell. I used my range attack, firing as fast as possible. Whittling away, but too slow.

"Carol? Chewie? Move!" I shouted.

They scrambled away, making it to the front of the garage. If I had hurt Carol with my Stab's Whirlwind ability to strike multiple targets before, at least she was out of range now.

The skeleton crawled at Laura while dragging its legs. She kept out of reach and was blasting it with her level-one Shoot. I caught up with the thing. My Stab took it to pieces.

Quest Complete! Your ally is home and reunited with their loved one.

Achievement: A Little Help from a Friend. Help an ally accomplish a task.

You are now...

Level Four

1

"Eddie? Look at me and tell me what's going on!"

I had never heard Chewie so angry.

Chewie, the first with a wisecrack even after our guild lost an encounter we had beaten before because people weren't focused. Chewie, the player who would make fun of his wife and call her a neat freak after she had been overheard on his microphone shouting at him to pick up his dirty dishes from his office because of the ants. And Chewie, the one who had asked aloud in the guild voice channel who was going to be our new lead healer moments after Laura had shared the news about Manabanana's real-world death.

But Chewie the Wag was now Chewie the Angry Husband. Carol stood behind him, using a tissue to sop up blood that ran from two long cuts along her upper arm.

He was in my face. "How did you hurt Carol?"

I minimized my level-up notifications and my new character class options so I could see him. "The game has her flagged as an enemy player."

"What do you mean, an enemy? Like the people in the grocery store?"

"Yes. I don't understand it. I also don't know how I physically hurt her."

"Well, she's bleeding."

"I'm going to live," Carol said. "It looks deep enough to need stitches, eventually. I'm going inside. I keep zip sutures in our first aid kit."

"You're not going back into the house, honey. I'm taking you out of here."

Laura checked Carol's arm. "It needs to be cared for. Tell me where you keep the kit and I'll get it."

Chewie was staring daggers at me. But his attention turned to Carol as he helped her sit on the pickup truck's back gate. She had recovered her shotgun. Kermit and Bennett watched the street and the surrounding houses. It had grown silent again.

I followed Laura inside. She led me to the garage where she found a go-bag with Carol's first aid kit.

"I didn't mean to hurt her," I said.

"Of course you didn't. But I saw what you did on my combat log."

"The game has her flagged an enemy. We need to find out why."

"Don't tell me you took that quest."

"I didn't. I want to get out of here alive, just like you. But this is a new curveball. The game's manipulating us."

"None of it will matter once we make it to the exit."

I hurried to make my character selections. Five more in Dexterity, raising it to fifteen. And I wanted Advanced Fade. Now I could pop out of sight even if in combat.

My health was full again. Small favors.

Laura was reading on her glasses.

"You're level two," I said.

"Big quest. Or the game's rubber banding me to catch up with you. That might be a two-edged sword. It means Crimson Gauntlet will throw bigger monsters at us."

We emerged through the side gate.

I stooped to pick up a coin I had missed. "What are your stat choices?"

"Health is fifteen. I just want to live long enough to survive."

Her class selection appeared when I inspected her label. Brute. The melee class featuring damage resistance.

She helped Carol with the sticky sutures. They cleaned up the wound with water and a swatch of gauze. Chewie looked like he was going to hurl as he watched.

I put the first aid kit back into the go-bag. "What's your class skill, Laura?"

Chewie tore the bag away from my hands and fought to zip it up. Spare socks and a bottle of Advil tumbled out. "Stop talking about the goddamn game."

Kermit helped him pick it all up and repack the bag.

Laura changed the subject. "Carol, are you dizzy?"

"I'm a little nauseous, but okay. I can walk. Nice job with the stitches."

"Not my first rodeo. You're wearing your scrubs. How was your shift at Kaiser?"

I listened as we got moving. Apparently, they knew each other, at least a little.

"Got off at seven."

"Anything unusual before the blackout?"

"No. It happened after work. The night was pretty quiet at the ER. A car wreck with a couple of people with soft tissue damage and rattled nerves. A pulmonary embolism. Pretty quiet otherwise. You guys met at Tasty's Diner?"

"We did. You know you're welcome to join us."

Carol laughed. "All that nerd might rub off on me."

"Were you home when the lights went out?" I asked.

"Yeah. Internet and cell phone too. I heard gunshots outside but didn't see anything. Then, about an hour later, one of the creatures appeared in our front yard. I thought it was Earl, our neighbor, in a Halloween getup. I called out from the kitchen window and he ignored me. When another showed up out back, I tried to call 911 but the landline was out. So I hid upstairs."

"And nothing came inside? You didn't kill any of them?"

Chewie scowled. "Enough with the questions."

"I'm sorry, but we need to know. The game thinks you've leveled. It also has you flagged as an enemy. It's the only reason I did damage."

"And enough about the game! You didn't 'do damage'. You cut her. Keep your distance, Eddie."

"I'm not carrying any weapons. I don't understand how it happened."

Laura motioned for me to let it go. Chewie walked Carol ahead of us, while Kermit and Bennett brought up the rear.

"I'm not off-base for asking," I grumbled.

"It's not the time. Give it a rest."

"It would have been an easy fight if Shadow had been here. Should we leave him a sign which way we're going?"

"Shadow seems to have his own plan. He knows where we're heading."

"True. You know Carol had to have done something to hit level one. And why is she an enemy player?"

"We don't know anything. It could be the game's messing with us. It could be a bug."

"Yeah, that's probably it," I said with little conviction.

After a few minutes, she leaned closer. "Heal: Level One."

"What?"

"My Brute class skill. I figured if you keep getting hurt, someone needs to keep you alive."

2

The Merrydale neighborhood let out onto Riviera Avenue. The secondary artery would eventually hook up with Redwood Parkway. We could get to the game zone exit, but we had been walking for hours. And Riviera Avenue had no easy sidewalk or bike lane. Following it meant being exposed, with a wooded creek along one side of the road. Single-family homes with large yards lined the opposite side.

The sun hammered us.

Bennett wasn't the only one flagging. Kermit and Chewie plodded along, and I was feeling it too. My throat felt parched and I was light-headed.

"Let's take a break," Laura announced.

The front drive to a mansion provided shade beneath a large redwood tree. A spiked gate on rollers stood closed. A brick driveway led to a vine-covered home with a gabled roof. An intact-looking white Range Rover stood parked near the front door.

Laura wiped the sweat from her brow. "Don't even think about it."

"I could get us water. Maybe even ice from the freezer. And what if that car runs? We could even look for bikes. Anything would be faster than walking."

"A car would have AC," Bennett added hopefully.

"We're not walking through the Sahara. Another few hours and we're safe. No more risks."

Kermit found a place to sit near the base of the tree. "Anything on your game radar?"

An enemy player. The notification marked Carol's location and her every move. But I kept it to myself. "Looks clear. Doesn't mean there isn't something there. But we're further from the dense homes back in Merrydale. Maybe the roaches haven't made it this far."

Chewie went to the rolling gate. "Carol needs water."

Laura took off her glasses and rubbed her temples. "Then we send Eddie. Can you look without aggroing everything?"

Eddie Rush's First Rule of Winning? Skip unnecessary battles. Raids take long enough without fighting every trash mob in the instance.

"I'll be quiet," I said.

The gate was an easy climb, even with the spikes. I had Stealth up and I walked slowly, even as I guessed I could approach the house normally with no monsters noticing. No roaches, and the Range Rover had no damage to it. Locked doors. The thought of plush leather seats, a soft ride, and climate control almost made me swoon.

The home had solar panels. It hadn't occurred to me someone might still have power. I mounted the steps and hit the camera/doorbell combo. Heard no chime or tone. I knocked at the door. Pounded.

"Hello? Hey! Anyone there? We have someone hurt and need help!"

I rounded the house in search of an open window. I didn't fancy getting shot by someone hiding in their home, but the idea of having a car was too tempting.

They had a skylight on the second floor propped open. A side window had an alarm sticker. I rattled the gate in case of dog, but the latch worked. There was digging in progress in the spacious side yard. A hill was getting a new retaining wall. A swimming pool and a tennis court occupied an upper terrace replete with big plants and steel free-form sculptures.

"I'm in your backyard. We need help to get to a hospital. Anyone there?"

I went to the rear patio. Nicer furniture than my apartment. Outdoor pizza oven, a gas firepit, and a cornhole game set beneath a grapevine-covered pergola. Empty beer and wine spritzer bottles filled a bucket. I discovered a small fridge next to a grill. Beer and hard lemonade inside.

A water spigot worked, and I drank from a hose, ignoring the tongue-coating rubber flavor.

A back slider stood open. No dog dishes.

I knocked on the glass. Called out again. The door slid effortlessly as I chanced to step inside.

The kitchen looked like someone had done a poor cleanup after a big dinner. A dozen plates stacked in the sink, the garbage compactor open with food scraps and flies, and cutting boards and knives in need of washing.

While I was sure they had central air conditioning, a flick of a light switch confirmed the power was out. It was cool enough, though. If I couldn't find keys, the house might be a place to rest. I tried the garage first. No cars, but plenty of supplies. Two mountain bikes, too, hanging from overhead racks.

Where did they keep their keys? No key peg, no key dish, no front desk where mail and keys got dropped. A formal dining room and a sunken TV room were tidy but yielded nothing useful.

I went upstairs.

Six bedrooms, and only one appeared in use, with an unkempt bed and a closet that appeared tossed, with clothes halfway off the hangers and blouses and shirts scattered on the floor. The main bathroom had an electric toothbrush rack with no brush.

Someone had packed and left, perhaps in a hurry.

I was searching the last bedroom when the view out the back caught my attention.

A crafting station stood in the center of the tennis court. While

I hadn't climbed to the upper terrace, I would have seen the crafting station as I entered the yard. It hadn't been there before.

A cold lump wormed through my guts.

I checked the window to the bedroom across the hall and stared out at the front. I couldn't see past the gate. But the game knew we were here.

Abandoning my search, I took the stairs two at a time and nearly slipped as I took a turn and ran through the foyer. Stopped.

My inventory had five Crafting Assets. Enough for a turn in. I couldn't remember all the crafting options, but one had been a healing potion.

I unlocked the door, swung it wide, and whistled for the others.

3

I left Laura in charge of getting everyone settled. The thought of a nap and a meal almost made me feel giddy. Crafting first, rest later.

The tennis court lacked the cracks and weeds that filled the community courts near my place, not that I played. Its green and white paint looked pristine.

The crafting station held the ethereal blue glow of a game asset. It sparkled, as if anticipating my approach. Yet I hesitated before setting foot on the court. Beyond the fence stood a hill covered in oak trees. How was this game asset here?

With the glasses off, the crafting station vanished.

Once again, Crimson Gauntlet was broadcasting its signal and allowing me to see something that didn't exist.

I went to the station and checked the menu to see what I could buy.

Grenade (Level One), Invisibility Oil (Level One), and **Health Potion (Level One)** cost five Crafting Assets each. So did a weapon and armor upgrade, each requiring their specific asset type. I had four apiece. But then I checked a purchase tab. Five coins would get me any asset. I had eleven coins.

Doing business with the virtual machine was as easy as touching the item I wanted to purchase.

I bought a weapon asset and an armor asset with the coins and a health potion with my crafting assets.

Achievement: A Coin Spent is an Asset Earned. Spend Five Coins.

Achievement: Ride the Hobby Horse Without Getting Your Feet Wet. Use a Crafting Station. It's more of a vending machine, but you like the idea you made something, don't you?

The achievements were getting weirder.

Quest Complete: Collect Five Armor Assets.

Nifty. More experience without having to face down an enemy.

The crafting station had two new selections ready. I purchased armor and weapon upgrades. A flash, and my armor was now plus five from zero, and my attack had a plus five damage bonus.

I flexed my hand. My virtual twin claws had serrated edges and had grown slightly longer. My shoulders were wrapped in light and looked beefier as if I wore shoulder pads. Pauldrons, I corrected myself. My wrists and legs likewise held a sheen, as if wrapped in translucent silver.

Hopefully, it all would improve my survivability.

The crafting station had no options for Transportation Assets. I only had two and wondered what they would buy me and where I could redeem them.

"Hey there."

The soft voice came from the far end of the tennis court. A young man in his thirties, muscular, wearing a camo collared shirt and khakis, along with a backpack, had just come through a gate. A purple label hung above his head.

Enemy Player: Level Four.

He wore sleek game armor, which shimmered over every inch of his body. Plate chest piece, open visor helm with a brush plume, spiked kneepads, and studs along his waist, all made of light. His right arm was a small cannon. Blaster class, I guessed.

He waved. "I didn't want to startle you. I was hoping to use the crafting station."

"Where'd you come from?"

"Cutting through the hills to avoid the things on the roads."

A quick check confirmed I was alone. The others remained inside the house.

"Anyone with you?" I asked.

"Yeah, but I thought I'd come down here alone so I don't freak you out. We're trying to find our way south to Tracy where my folks live. You?"

"I've got a group. "

He came closer to the net center court. "I see you're playing. How many with you are in-game?"

"Enough of them. You want to put your weapon away?"

"Of course. Apologies. Things tend to jump out of nowhere, so I like to be ready."

"Of course," I said agreeably. "There aren't that many of us playing. How'd you get into the game?"

He tapped his glasses, as if it answered everything. "What's your name?"

"Eddie. You?"

"Peter."

"You local?"

"Sacramento. Tried following 80 south, but the freeway got too hairy. We lost our ride. We should have tried for I-5, but there was too much craziness up in Sac."

"The game is up there too?"

He wore a bemused expression. "At this point, it might be everywhere. How far have you made it?"

"Been on foot the whole time. I keep hoping to find a car so we can make it to the game exit."

"Yeah, I saw the notification. Wonder if that's legit."

The polite thing would be to invite him and his friends to join us.

He forced a smile and gestured at the crafting station. "You mind? There aren't enough of those things."

I stepped away, moving back to the gate. "Help yourself. You finding a lot of assets?"

"They're out there. You just have to look. The game tucks them away in the craziest places. Inside mailboxes, up in trees, under cars. Sometimes they don't show until you're right on top of them. You having luck locating stuff?"

"Just spent the last on my upgrades. What happened to your ride?"

He worked at the crafting station. The game wouldn't tell me what he was purchasing or making. "Those vipers. They zip between the wrecks on the road and catch up with you. You saw them?"

"Yeah. The goliaths, too."

"Big boys have more trouble navigating the freeway. But out there you'll see Reavers, Shredders, and Plague Riders. It's actually quiet here. Nice place, by the way. We've been on the move since midnight. Maybe my friends and I can catch some Z's here?"

"That's not a good idea."

"Why not? We're on the same side. It's us versus the machines. I'm exhausted. Any food and water you can spare?"

"What I've got are friends who aren't as chill as me."

He appeared finished with the crafting station. "Then how about an introduction? Let them decide."

"I think it's best you left."

He considered me for a moment, as if sizing me up. He still hadn't put his cannon away. Then he looked past me and his tone brightened. "You've got a swimming pool and everything. Shade from the sun. And like I said, we've been going all night. How about you let my friends and I kick back on those chaise lounges and take a little nap? I promise we won't disturb you."

When he took another step towards me, I made a fist. My claws appeared and I activated Stealth.

"Whoa, hey! We were just talking. Eddie—it's Eddie, right?—I'm not looking to hurt you. I'm just exhausted. I haven't slept. My group is short on supplies. We're thirsty, and we want to survive this. If my being here is going to upset you, then I'll leave."

"That would be for the best."

His eyes darted about. Still couldn't get a fix on me. He turned.

Hesitated. "You know there isn't anything in the game world that can't be taken."

"You have dozens of homes to choose from. This one's ours."

"Not trusting people is how the bad guys win."

"The game has you tagged in purple. What did you do to earn that?"

He looked up as if noticing his label. The game wouldn't let me see mine.

"Machines aren't the only thing out there keeping us from getting home," he said. "You haven't had to defend yourself against other people yet?"

"I haven't hurt anyone."

He dismissed his blaster. "Stealth is a funny skill. Means I can't target you. Bet you have a nasty alpha strike. The game told me about you. Dropped a waypoint here as if it wanted me to pay you a visit. Said I was being hunted. A new quest: Hunt the Hunter. But then here I am with my cheese in the breeze, and you let me craft. What's the deal with that, Eddie?"

"I never took the enemy kill quest."

"Too bad. The experience is good. But there are two sides to the game. It wants us to play one way, but it works with us when we improvise."

He removed his glasses. From the small of his back, he pulled a pistol. Pointed it vaguely in my direction, as if having trouble focusing on me.

I raised my hands while easing through the open gate of the tennis court. "Hey. There's no need for that."

"Isn't there? I asked nicely for a drink and a place to rest for me and my friends. And one of you is out to get us. I say let's find out who. What do you say you introduce me to your group and we sort this out?"

I considered running. But game stealth wouldn't save me from getting shot. Would the game give him experience for murdering me with a gun?

We descended the terrace stairs to the back patio together.

I spoke loudly, hoping Laura and the others would hear. "Look, there's a car out front that's intact. I haven't found the keys yet, but you take it. Is it the house you want? It's yours too."

"Why don't we see what's what first? How many other players with you?"

I stopped at the back door. "This is stupid. We should help each other. The game exit is a short drive away."

"Maybe I'm not ready to leave yet."

A branch crunched. The crisp snap of ivy. The wisteria along the nearest fence shuddered.

Two metal hands appeared. Shadow's pet Bones pulled itself up to the top of the fence.

Peter raised his pistol. "What the hell?"

He squeezed off a few shots, maybe a dozen. I didn't know. As soon as the shooting started, I dove to the concrete and crawled to the cover of the pizza oven.

Bones crashed on top of a patio umbrella near me. However many times he had been hit with bullets, he was still up. Peter must have had his cannon up again. He blasted the skeleton. The blow toppled Bones, severing one of his arms. A second fiery bolt took off his head.

I did a combat peek. Peter had dropped his pistol and was moving to loot the fallen monster. Priorities.

I crept forward. Stealth remained activated. When he was in range, I hit Stab as I clawed at him.

My strike tore at his back. He shrieked and pulled away from me. He had at least two-thirds of his health. His hand shook as he raised his blaster. It flared as a small sun brewed inside its barrel, but at the same instant I used Fade and ducked out of the way.

The blast burned the air where I had been standing. Thank you, thank you, thank you Fade. He swept his weapon about as I flanked him. Could he not see me?

Stab lit up. I punched at him, driving my blades deep into his arm and shoulder. The second blow was a critical hit, knocking him down to a third of his health. Blood flew. He sprawled on the stone patio deck. My Fade wouldn't reactivate as it began a long cooldown.

His hand flashed orange-yellow as flames enveloped me. The heat burned me and the pain replaced everything. I was on fire, screaming, and running in whatever direction would get me away from the agony. I couldn't breathe. My skin cracked as I stumbled and tripped over a deck chair.

And the next instant, the fire was gone. I had lost over half my health.

Achievement: Burn, Baby, Burn! Disco may be dead, but you survived your first taste of fire damage.

Peter's hand held a growing ball of flame. "Hadn't fought a Hellion before. Nice trick."

Nowhere to hide. He was out of Stab range and I could barely move.

"Why are you doing this?" I asked.

"The First to Level-Five quest. The game takes care of those who play."

The flame ball darkened. He spun it on his palm, grinning and clearly enjoying the display. Purple and black streaks ran up the blistering sphere to its crown.

The green glob that struck him came from the direction of the fence. Peter's weapon arm blistered. A second and a third hit his face and leg. He stumbled back, swatting wildly as his fireball vanished. His health bar ticked downward with every second.

"I knew you'd turn up," Shadow called. "The game had two people on top of the local leaderboard. I took care of one. Maybe you got the notification. You're next."

The burning blisters faded as Peter again summoned the fireball. No monkeying about this time. He cocked his arm like a baseball pitcher. Before he could fling it, a shambling humanoid figure of metal galloped towards him on all fours.

Acid Zombie (Level Six).

The creature was a mass of parts. Bicycle gears, a lawnmower engine, and pulleys and wheels from a weight machine. Woven between the cogs and metal joints were lumps of dripping flesh. It left a trail of bubbling footsteps along the terra cotta stonework.

The zombie latched onto Peter and yanked him close. Peter's skin smoldered. With a rattly growl, the zombie slammed him to the ground. A massive mouth opened, the jaws a bear trap of jagged steel shards.

Peter screamed. The zombie bit down, its maw clamping on Peter's head and neck.

I tried to rise, fell again, and crawled to the glass slider. I turned in time to see Shadow's pet tear Peter to pieces.

Shadow grunted as he dropped from the fence. He was limping as he closed in on Peter's remains. Crouched to pick something up. His Acid Zombie stood there stupidly, looking as if it would fall apart if struck by a stiff breeze.

I turned on Stealth.

He glanced my direction. "I know you're there, Hagar." But he looked from side to side as if he actually couldn't see me. "Let me guess. You were going to have him in for a beer and a sit-down. You miss the fact he's an enemy player?"

My heart jackhammered. I had no spit in my throat. "He was a person."

"Who was going to murder you. You think the game gave him that tag by mistake? He's a player killer."

"Yeah, I get it. I asked him to leave. Then I tried to stop him. Where were you, Shadow?"

"A couple of quests popped up nearby. You guys were doing fine. It didn't take long to catch your trail. Maybe I made a few stops along the way. How do you like my new pet?"

His zombie kept dripping.

I gingerly touched where Peter's fireball had burned me. The skin was tender beneath my shirt. My clothes hadn't been touched. And then I considered what was left of Peter. Shadow had used his skills against him. Unlike his skeleton pet tearing the gang apart in the grocery store, it was the game that had somehow killed Peter.

Virtual spells and weapons meant actual injuries.

Zero hit points meant death.

Shadow turned the chair near me upright. "So, hey, how about a grats on level five? Quest complete. First in our zone. That creep did it for me. Excellent experience with the enemy player quests. How many have you gotten?"

"I didn't accept it."

"Your loss. Too bad about Bones, though. But I'll find another pet. I get two now, you know. Plus, there's some level-six and -seven vipers with some new abilities cruising the streets. We could team up and grab one. Knock out the others for some easy loot."

He opened the fridge and grabbed a hard lemonade before walking up to the tennis court. Unlike Bones, his zombie wasn't tagging along. It gazed my direction and sniffed the air noisily.

I worked up the will to crouch next to Peter's body. The virtual hand cannon and armor had vanished, and Shadow must have looted the glasses. I touched him. His skin was pasty and already cool. The blood on his shirt was sticky. He stared off into nothing. I closed his eyes before wiping my fingers clean on the concrete.

Shadow had killed him like he had the people in the grocery store when he completed his first PvP quest. The quest remained in my log, waiting for me to take it. It even offered me a credit of one out of five players I needed to kill. I had a hand in Peter's murder.

Self-defense, I thought lamely.

Shadow gave a "woo-hoo" as he worked at the crafting station. "I do love me some armor."

Four more people and I'd start to catch up to Shadow if I accepted the quest.

I called out, "You finished your first PvP quest at the grocery store, right?"

"Yeah, why?"

There had been four people inside, not five. Shadow had found someone before then. The realization made my stomach go sour.

Bennett's wife. The blood on his pet viper. Had the viper gotten bloody *after* Shadow had tamed it?

"What's wrong, Hagar?"

"Nothing. I need to get out of the sun. Don't bring your pet inside. It will scare everyone."

I dropped Stealth and opened the slider.

The family room led into a large industrial kitchen with four ovens, two refrigerators, and other appliances I couldn't identify. Wine bottles lined a wall wine rack. Bananas moldered on banana hooks. A waffle machine stood open as if awaiting a dollop of waffle batter.

Laura peered from behind the granite island. "What's going on out there?"

"Where are the others?"

"Hiding in the front room near the door. Carol found keys to the Range Rover." Her face creased as I got closer. "What is it? What's wrong?"

"Shadow's back. He just killed another player. But Laura? He may have also murdered Bennett's wife."

4

We exited out the front door.

Carol handed the keys to Laura while keeping her shotgun ready. Laura thumbed the fob, but the car didn't unlock. The key worked on the driver's side door.

Kermit and Bennett piled in the rearmost seat, with Chewie and Carol waiting at the passenger side for someone to unlock it.

I kept an eye on the house. No sign that Shadow knew we were leaving. Hopefully, he was still in the backyard with the crafting station. Laura squeezed into the driver's seat. Whoever had last used the car must have been short, and she was having trouble getting the seat to move back.

"You said Shadow was out back," Bennett said. "Why are we running?"

Laura pushed with her butt to slide the seat back. "We can't trust him. Come on, stupid thing."

"No dome light," Kermit said. "Battery's out."

She stuck the key in the ignition. Turned it a few times before slamming the steering wheel with her palms.

A Transportation Asset appeared in the Range Rover's cargo space. It hadn't been there before. I leaned over Kermit and grabbed it. A roach skirted around my foot and scampered towards the front tire. A dozen of its buddies trailed along behind it. The game was here.

"Get out. Everyone."

The Acid Zombie smashed open a side gate and strode towards us. Shadow limped along behind it. His health was full, but he remained injured.

"What's the rush, guys?"

Carol turned her weapon on him. Her grip was less than steady.

He raised his hands. "Woah, hey! I'm with them. You're Carol, right? Chewie's wife?"

I got between Shadow and the Range Rover, with Stealth up for good measure. He still appeared to have trouble seeing me.

"Stay back, Shadow. And keep that thing with you."

"Will you relax? We're on the same side here. You want to bring everyone to the exit? Great, let's do it. But taking that SUV out on the road will only get you killed. You'd know that if you paid attention to what Crimson Gauntlet is telling you. It wants us on foot unless we earn our wheels."

"What did you do to Kirsten back at the trailer park?"

His face clouded. "Why, Hagar, whatever are you implying?"

"Tell me it was an accident."

"How about you show yourself and we talk? What's with you guys running off without telling me? And where's the gratitude? I just saved your ass."

Laura was out of the car and took the shotgun from Carol. Her hands were rock steady as she aimed at the acid zombie. "Is what Eddie said true?"

Shadow's pet cocked its head and pivoted towards her.

A ball of green energy appeared in Shadow's hand. "Don't point that thing at me, Rosette. It didn't go well for the scumbags in the grocery store."

He was calling her by her game name too now.

I readied my fist. My claws were out. "Why'd you really come and find us?"

"This is where the quests take me."

With a mental command, he could send his machine in and murder the others. Laura might get a shot or two off, but it would be over.

I accepted the PvP quest.

Quest Progress: Kill Five Enemy Players. (1/5 Complete).

Group up to increase your experience points earned. Would you like to group now?

Invite Player: Shadow? Invite Player: Rosette? Invite Player: Chewie?

Shadow hadn't bothered to offer to group up with me. I wasn't an ally. I was prey. So was Chewie, even if he no longer wore the game glasses.

He moved a few paces, getting his zombie between him and Laura. "I won't argue with you while you have a gun pointed at me. I don't know what happened to Kirsten. Why would I hurt her?"

"Bennett's glasses," she said. "Are they quest loot? Maybe you attacked her because you couldn't control your viper minion."

"What do you want me to say? I didn't do it. Hagar—Eddie—is wrong."

"Then call off your zombie and send it away."

His pet tensed up. Shadow was about to command it to attack.

During their exchange, I invited Player: Rosette aka Laura to group. If the game had group chat, I couldn't find it. What I could do was select a target. I chose the zombie.

"I've got the add," I whispered to Laura. "Take the boss."

I was rewarded by seeing Laura's target icon appear over Shadow.

Eddie Rush's First Rule of Winning? Trust your teammates. And: a classic strategy is hard to beat.

Countless boss fights featured spawned minions, also called adds. They usually had to be managed and sometimes killed first, depending on the enemy.

"What are you whispering, Eddie?" Shadow asked.

I hit the zombie with Stab. The creature faltered as I took out a leg. Critical Hit! Still alive, still with almost half of its health, which meant more hit points than the skeletons.

Laura fired the shotgun. The *ba-BOOM* deafened me as I backed up, vanished using Fade, and hit the zombie again. No crit. A wedge of health remained. And I was visible, with no more tricks.

Shadow dropped to the driveway and crawled towards the corner of the house. The zombie clambered towards me, hand over hand, dragging its single leg behind it. Its claws clinked and scraped against the concrete. It swung at me. I hurried out of its way, keeping my distance.

A Corrosive Blast blossomed my direction and struck me dead on. Searing pain erupted along my left hand and arm. A green blob clung to me. My health dropped and kept dropping. I tried to shake it off but couldn't. The agony spread to my shoulder, neck, and chest.

I was about to die.

Achievement: Sizzler! Take acid damage. Duck next time, eh?

My health potion. The thought brought up my inventory. A mental command, and I "consumed" it. A cherry cough syrup taste coated my tongue. My health spiked, but continued to dwindle.

Laura strode forward and delivered a series of shotgun blasts into the zombie. It wavered and finally toppled.

I furiously swatted at the blob of energy eating away at my flesh.

Laura's hand glowed. **Heal: Level One.**

Instant relief as the pain evaporated. My health level stabilized. Four hit points left. My new armor had saved me, acting like a buffer bar of health points. The armor points replenished before my eyes without me having to do anything, but my health didn't regenerate.

"Where's Shadow?" I croaked.

She kept her eyes on the side of the house where he had vanished. "I don't see him."

"He'll be back. He might have also taken an invisibility potion, so be careful."

"You said he killed Kirsten. Did you mean that?"

"I can't be a hundred percent sure. But I was with him until the grocery store. He needed five kills to finish the quest. The math works."

"So the game can apparently tag anyone as an enemy player."

She hit me with another Heal. Cool fingers dispelled the remaining discomfort on my tortured skin, even as she never touched me.

Kermit helped me to the Range Rover and got me seated. "Should we go after Shadow?"

"We don't know who else or what else is out there. He said he can charm two pets. We barely survived one and I don't want to wait around to see what else he tames."

"Carol, you have more shells?"

"Just what was in the shotgun," Carol said.

Laura stowed the weapon in the back of the SUV. "Then we're out."

I squashed a roach. It had dropped from the wheel well with a length of wire in its pincers. More followed. Kermit joined me. Soon we had twenty or more roaches dead beneath our feet, but more were coming.

Laura popped the hood. "Keep killing them. It's our only chance right now."

"There was a battery jumper in the garage," Chewie said. "It had power."

He led Laura into the house again. They were gone for a minute, but it felt like ten. Finally, they appeared again with a shoebox. During that time, Kermit, Carol, and I squashed bugs. Four streams of mechanical insects were marching towards us now, undeterred by the slaughter we were inflicting.

Laura popped the hood and appeared to know what she was doing with the battery booster. In the engine compartment, the damage had begun. Wires and a hose had been severed. Once she finished connecting the booster, a green indicator winked on.

I flung out a roach that had escaped the purge. "Try to start it."

She got in the car. The engine whirred. Finally, it chugged to life, but green fluid dribbled from beneath the front bumper.

"We won't get far with that," Kermit said. "There were bikes."

"Enough for all of us?" I asked.

"No."

The lines of roaches were twice as thick as before. Some streamed towards the remains of the Acid Zombie. Whether recycling or rebuilding, I didn't want to be around to find out what they were up to.

"Everyone in the car now," Laura called. "Let's drive this thing as far as it'll take us."

5

"What were you talking about out there with Shadow?"

Bennett's question lingered as I squirmed to get comfortable on the center row seat next to Carol and Chewie. He was in the rear of the SUV by himself, his injured hand tucked beneath his arm like a bird with a broken wing.

Laura drove, with Kermit in the front next to her, eyeing the road ahead. The Range Rover engine labored like a shop vac trying to suck up a bowling ball. The suspension had a shimmy to it and I questioned whether we had removed all the roaches.

"Eddie?" Bennett prompted. "Why won't you answer me?"

I didn't have the mental bandwidth to lie. "I think he killed your wife."

"We don't know what happened or what he did," Laura added.

Bennett leaned forward, his voice soft. "But you suspect he did something to Kirsten. What did you find at my house?"

I turned to face him as best I could. "There was a lot of blood. One of the machines had gotten inside. I...didn't see her body. There's a chance she escaped."

"A chance. Don't bullshit me. You think she's dead and you think Shadow did it. He was controlling one of the motorcycle monsters when you fought the goliath."

"You received a pair of glasses. Shadow knew that. Somehow, it made Kirsten a target, just like the game directed us to the house off Mt. Lassen Drive where I found the game rig. And Shadow finished the PvP quest at the market where he killed four people. Kirsten may have been the first."

He slumped back into his seat. "Oh, god. Oh, god."

Laura shot me ice daggers in the rearview mirror. "Eddie's guessing."

"I am guessing," I continued. "But the game was ready for us at Bennett's place, too. Easier monsters, the goliath was only level four, and Shadow had creatures he could tame. Same with the place where I found the extra glasses Laura's wearing, and again at Chewie and Carol's house."

Carol scowled. "You mean I was bait?"

"Bait implies you were passive. But you were armed, and not just with the shotgun. Chewie's glasses were inside your house. That means the game considered you a piece on the game board. And you might have done something for the game to consider you an enemy player."

"Hey!" Chewie snapped. "Don't call her that. Knock it off, Eddie."

Bennett rocked on his seat and fought back a sob. "I...I can't take this anymore. Stop calling it a game. Kirsten hated me for playing so much. If I had only quit. If we had evacuated. She'd be alive, and I wouldn't be stuck here...."

"You're going to be okay" wouldn't cut it. We all kept quiet.

Laura drove down Riviera Avenue, keeping to the center of the street. We passed a couple of wrecks and a home on fire. She kept checking the rearview mirror. I was guessing she had the pedal down, but we weren't going much faster than forty.

If the car could hold out, we might make the game exit in thirty minutes if the road was clear.

The vehicle shuddered. A clattering sound rumbled through the floor. Red lights blinked from the dash and the engine quit.

She coasted to the right and pumped the brakes. "That's all we get."

Bennett had distracted me. I checked my mini-map. It had a drop-down list of filters. The quest tab gave me what I was looking for. The quests lingering on the edges of my HUD were distracting. But having them restricted to the small map felt natural and manageable, a view I was accustomed to after thousands of hours of gaming.

My PvP quest didn't mark enemy players. Too bad. No doubt Shadow would pursue us. It would be good to know if there were others like Peter. If only Crimson Gauntlet would scoop up all the bad eggs and drop them in an arena so they could tear each other to pieces and leave us alone.

We walked.

Bennett was slower than ever, with Kermit and Carol on either arm helping him along.

A quest hung in the air above the next intersection. Cascade Avenue ran roughly east-west, a local shortcut that rounded the dry reservoir and the farms and larger properties on the outskirts of Bell Park. It could take us most of the way to the game exit where it would connect with Redwood Parkway.

Available Quest: A Free Ride?

The quest dangling in the air ahead of me had no further instructions.

Several vehicles had crashed or pulled over around the four-way stop. Even from fifty yards away, it was obvious they had been picked apart by roaches. A white Ford van waited in the center of the intersection. It looked intact.

"I accepted the quest," Laura said.

I did too. "I'll scout. Keep down. If anything pops, run. I'll catch up."

As I closed in on the first wrecked car, an **Asset: Armor** glowed from behind the steering wheel. Another car had a weapon asset, and another had a coin. Picking something up momentarily broke Stealth. I collected it all, taking a moment to pause and see if anything was going to spring at me.

The air was still.

A transportation asset hung above the wreckage of a scooter ahead of me. I walked a wide circuit around the van towards the scooter. My breath caught. A body of an older man was sprawled by the driver-side door in a pool of drying blood. A key on a smiley face keychain lay by his outstretched hand.

I grabbed the transportation asset, activated Stealth, and watched the van.

Common sense told me to get out of there. We could carry Bennett if we had to. But the van was the quest objective. Could it be this easy?

Another **Asset: Transportation** shone blue from inside the van. With it, I'd have five. If the game math held, it meant I could cash it in for something, although the crafting station hadn't told me what they might buy.

Too tempting to pass up. I went to the van and tried to collect it without opening the door, but couldn't. The driver-side door looked unlocked. It meant stepping over the body.

Laura approached, her hand flexing as if holding back on an attack. "Anything?"

Chewie followed close behind, with the others breaking cover and coming closer.

I motioned for them to hold up. "Might not be safe, but I don't see any monsters. There's a body here. May want to keep back."

The dead man's eyes stared blankly at me as I moved around the van and opened the door. The van was clean inside, as if it had been detailed. I reached in and collected the asset. But the quest didn't finish. What else was I supposed to do?

A text appeared above the dashboard. **Would you like to claim this vehicle? Cost: Five Transportation Assets.**

No way to know if it had gas or if the key outside would work.

Laura peered through the other window. "You have enough assets to claim it?"

"I just got my fifth. But I'm wondering what's the catch? And the quest has no instructions. Not sure what it wants us to do."

Chewie came up behind me. "There's a key."

"Yeah, I saw it." I stepped into the van and sat. Was about to finish the quest when Chewie crouched and picked up the key. "No, don't!"

The van shuddered. As the steering wheel pulled away from me, arms with blades detached from the van ceiling behind me.

The game gave the vehicle a new label.

Mimic (Level Five).

6

Before I could move, the driver's seat tilted forward, shoving me against the dashboard. Each blade finished unfolding and hovered like a scorpion tails poised to skewer. The walls of the van shifted. The entire machine shuddered as if the mimic was wriggling with anticipation of my impending murder.

A girlish titter erupted from the radio speakers.

I shoved to move the seat back. Strained with all my might. It had been ten years or more since my last pushup, and the seat wouldn't budge.

"Get me out of here!"

Chewie tried to put the key in the door. He dropped it. The others were running closer, but I couldn't see what they were doing. The knife arms moved. But instead of coming for me, they passed through gaps in the mimic's body and appeared outside.

One shot towards Chewie. He didn't move in time and went down.

Carol screamed. The others screamed, too.

I slapped at the dashboard, tried to kick, and wriggled every way possible, but the chair held me fast. It kept pressing against me. Inch by inch, it squeezed. If I let out a breath, it would crush me.

The arm that struck Chewie rose and prepared to plunge down again. Laura appeared and knocked the blade aside with her fist before grabbing it and bending it. I couldn't process what I was seeing. But then I reminded my panicked brain I was in a game.

With my Stab skill, I punched the chair seat. It bucked and the pressure relented. I could inhale.

A mewling cry erupted from the speakers.

It took a moment for me to hit it again, and, with a second blow, the chair completely broke. I was free.

The mimic had a health bar and remained as strong as a Night World were-ox under a full moon. I couldn't Stealth. Made sense, as I was standing inside the thing.

Outside, Laura had snapped off the damaged blade arm, but the second one dodged, weaved, and kept trying to stick her. The van vibrated like a paint mixer.

Carol dragged Chewie away. He clung to her desperately, his legs pushing at the ground. His shirt looked as if it was stained with fruit punch.

I tried the door handle. It wouldn't open. I used my Stab against the door, expecting it to explode. It didn't. My knuckles hurt from punching metal. I tried the passenger-side door, and then the slider. They wouldn't budge. As I went to the back door, a hissing sound gave me pause.

Snot-yellow droplets rained down on me from tiny nozzles. They burned! My combat log flashed a notification.

You suffered two hit points acid damage from Mimic (Level Five).

Like Shadow's Corrosive Blasts. The mimic stopped whining, chortled, and was making a yummy-yummy sound. I was being digested.

Two more damage.

Forgetting my earlier lesson, I slapped at the back door even as my skin blistered. My Stab skill was useless.

Laura banged on the side door. Must have busted the second blade arm. "Eddie? Eddie!"

"I can't unlock it!"

"Check all the doors! Try the unlock button!"

The mimic laughed, as if Laura had cracked a joke.

I coughed and choked on the fumes. A splash of acid on my face had me wiping my eyes. Searing pain across my retinas. Half-blind now, I felt my way back towards the front of the van and the wrecked chair. With every passing second, I took more damage. I was below half my health.

I spammed the unlock button on the driver's door. Nothing happened.

A clunk reverberated through the monster. It shuddered. I didn't want to find out what else it could do.

More caustic mist belched over me. A fog clouded the windows. Every inch of exposed skin hurt. You know the tooth pain when the dentist drills too deep and you're insufficiently numb? My skin felt like an exposed nerve ending. My health ticked ever downward.

I pressed against the spray spewing from the ceiling above me, ignoring the searing agony on my hands. I couldn't stop it.

Laura had given up trying to open the door. She pounded on the side of the van with her fists. If my Stab barely hurt it, her Punch wasn't going to do squat.

I focused through the pain. Nothing on the dashboard. Touching the radio only seemed to tickle the machine as it giggled with every press of a button. And the key was outside.

I leaned on the horn. "Let me out!"

The mimic guffawed. Made a *nom-nom* sound.

It's a game, it's a game, it's a game, I kept thinking, as if the mantra would permit me to bust out of the creature. Something in my mini-map? My combat log? Attacking the chair had hurt it, but now my attacks barely scratched it.

I found my inventory and crafting tab.

Would you like to claim this vehicle? Cost: Five Transportation Assets.

I screamed, "Yes!"

The acid stopped. As if disappointed, the mimic sighed. The door locks popped. My skin continued to bubble and hiss as the damage-over-time of the acid kept burning me. I opened the slider.

Laura grabbed my wrist. "Eddie? Come on!"

She dropped a heal. The acid effect vanished and the burning stopped. My health went up a smidge. She tried to pull me away from the van.

"Wait, Laura. It's over. Look at it. You see? It's mine now."

Civilian Vehicle. Owned by Player: Eddie Rush.

7

Quest Complete: A Free Ride?
Achievement: Devil in the Details. Fight a mimic.
Achievement: Cool Set of Wheels, Friend-O. Purchase a vehicle.

Carol was doing her best to comfort Chewie. A long slash ran crossed his chest and stomach. It bled like crazy, but it wasn't deep.

"I'm not getting closer to that thing," she said. "It almost killed him. And we're definitely not getting inside it."

Laura used her Heal. His bleeding stopped.

"How is that possible?" Carol asked.

"I don't know," Laura said as she examined Chewie's wound. "It appears to work. How are you feeling?"

Chewie grimaced as he touched the cut. He still appeared to be in pain and didn't get up.

Kermit and Bennett remained next to my new ride and apparently had been with Laura as she had tried to break into the mimic. Bennett peered inside as I climbed in and studied the dashboard.

I pressed the virtual start button.

The mimic's engine purred even with no key in the ignition. The driver's seat was ruined. I wasn't sure how I was supposed to control the van if I couldn't sit at the wheel. I wasn't sure I wanted to. But it was a vehicle and it belonged to me. I had paid my five transportation assets and the mimic ceased to be a monster.

Civilian Vehicle was now in my inventory.

Laura returned to the open side door. "Need another Heal?"

"I'm fine."

"Carol's right; this is a bad idea. What's to stop the game from turning it back into a monster once all of us pile in?"

"Because that's not how Crimson Gauntlet works."

"How do you know? It's not like we have a manual. And if it turns on us and kills us, what are we going to do? Post a bad review?"

"If the game only wanted us dead, that would have happened by now. It keeps giving us a chance."

"It keeps throwing things in front of us. I thought when we got rid of our phones, we'd opt out."

"That's what the game exit is for."

"Assuming it's for real," she said bitterly.

"If you don't want to drive, then we walk. But that runs the risk of Shadow catching up with us or us running into a goliath or anything else roaming the streets. The guy who attacked us mentioned other creatures roaming the highway. The game says this is my vehicle. Bennett can't walk much further, and Chewie doesn't look like he's at one hundred percent. What other choice do we have?"

"I can walk," Bennett said.

Laura's jaw clicked as she glared at me. "Carol? Chewie? Come on. We can't stay out here any longer."

The two spent a moment in a quiet argument. Finally, they got up and joined us. Kermit helped Chewie into the van. Blood dribbled from a still-bleeding slice on Chewie's wrist. It dripped onto the floor of the vehicle.

"Mmm," the mimic said from the radio. "Num-num-nummy."

Carol had been about to sit with Chewie against the wall of the van. "No. Absolutely not. We're getting out of here."

Laura was about to close the slider. "We're out of options and out of time. I can't force you to go with us, but it's our best bet."

Carol sat and checked Chewie's wrist. "Can you do your heal thing again or should I use the first aid kit?"

Laura healed him.

Carol inspected his wrist and shook her head in disbelief. "All right, Eddie. How does this work?"

I still hadn't figured it out. "Close the door and hang on."

The doors locked. I grabbed for the driver's side door handle. It opened. I closed it again and kneeled while gripping the steering wheel. There was no way to work the pedals at the same time.

I touched the radio. "Are you there? Are you listening? Let's roll."

The mimic sighed with delight.

The engine revved and we lurched forward. We topped out at 30mph, the same as the speed limit. I was steering but it felt wrong having no control over the accelerator or the brake. It slowed when I asked and sped up when I told it to go faster. We were heading down Cascade Avenue and passed Dixon Catholic High School.

Laura leaned over my shoulder and inspected the dashboard. "It's still alive. It has a health bar."

"Yeah. But can you see its label changed? It's not a monster anymore. I don't think it can turn back into one now that I own it."

"You 'think.' That's comforting. I leveled, by the way. Bought Damage

Resist and upped my Health again. I considered Advanced Heal, but for now I want to avoid any of us getting hurt."

The engine continued to hum. The mimic warbled over the speakers in an attempt at harmony.

"Stop it," I said, and it went quiet for about thirty seconds before resuming its song.

Despite the heals and my health once again being at full, my eyes still burned and my skin itched.

The game takes care of those who play. Peter's words, and he had no doubt believed them until the other part of the game, the PvP side, hit him like a freight train. Had Shadow killed Peter's companions? Had they all been willing to bushwhack anyone they came across in order to survive?

The road was empty ahead. I dared hope we might cruise past the farms and the west side of town and leave it behind us. I scanned my quest tracker. They waited on either side of the road beyond the handful of estate houses and barns. We passed the Bell Park Creamery. A group of cows watched us lazily from beneath a buckeye tree beyond a line of barbwire fence.

I knew the road well enough. Past the creamery was the Memory Rock Cemetery. I drove the residents of the Golden State Care Home there enough times for services. No respawns yet shambling from the graves. That was a different game, I thought darkly.

"Ah-hem." The mimic paused its humming to make a throat-clearing sound. Motion in the rearview mirror. A motorcycle was coming. **Viper (Level Five).** A second one joined it.

Shadow hung on to one of them. On the second viper rode a woman in black motorcycle gear. A purple game tag hung over her, too.

She and Shadow were both **Enemy Player (Level Five).**

8

Shadow and the mystery player would overtake the mimic-van in seconds. I forced the wheel to the left to straddle the lanes. The van resisted me.

"Uh-uh," the mimic murmured.

"Come on, you stupid thing! Keep them from passing us!"

The steering wheel relented. I swerved from side to side. The van ran across the bumps in the center of the road but the vipers were too fast. They pulled up around us before speeding ahead.

"Is that Shadow?" Kermit asked.

"Yeah, and he's got company. Hang on."

I directed the van along the shoulder, but the mimic wouldn't go fast enough to bump Shadow's viper out of the way. The road took a long corner. My passengers in the back of the van fought not to tumble about.

Shadow let go of the handlebars and turned on his seat. He was riding backward. He launched a Corrosive Blast, which detonated against the hood of the van.

The mimic yowled.

The woman likewise turned around and hopped up to crouch on the seat of the viper. Violet claws appeared on her fists. And then she vanished.

A Hellion. Just like me.

Her viper decelerated. The mimic almost rammed it before likewise slowing down. Shadow threw blast after blast, each hitting their mark.

The van was fighting me again as I tried to steer past it. A thump on the roof. Then claws pierced the top of the vehicle.

Weaving now, and the mimic screamed.

The mimic's health bar plummeted. Another Corrosive Blast sizzled against the windshield. The glass melted before my eyes. I had a hard time seeing the road.

If we crashed, we were dead.

"Heal it!" I said.

Laura was crouched behind me. "What?"

"Heal the van!"

She raised a hand. A white glow shimmered from her fingertips. The mimic mewled and sighed with relief. The mimic's health rose a bit, but the Heal barely outpaced the damage over time from Shadow's blasts. Claws ripped into the roof. Another sharp dip in the van's hit points.

I tried to see the woman above us through the gashes in the roof. My Stab wouldn't light up. I needed to get her off.

My window refused to roll down.

I banged on it. "Open up!"

The mimic obliged and rolled it down. Another blast took out the last of the windshield. Above us, the woman tore open a fresh gouge in the metal as if cutting through crepe paper.

The floor split beneath our feet. Bennett, Kermit, and Laura moved to not fall through to the street as Carol and Chewie clung to hooks along the walls. The front of the van remained stitched together, but the rupture kept growing. My mimic shook and slowed. It was dying.

Laura hit it with Heal after Heal. An all-too-human sounding groan rose from the engine.

I activated Stealth and climbed out the window. I took a breath and got my feet under me and stood so I could reach the roof. A luggage rack helped, but the van's vibrations threatened to throw me to the asphalt. Miraculously, I kept my balance.

The purple player had her claws plunged into the roof of the van.

She was just in range. I made a backhand motion and hit Stab. The slash caught her across the side and she tumbled off the vehicle. She plummeted into the weeds along the shoulder of the road. But she didn't stay down. A moment later, she was up and running after us.

It was like watching a cartoon character, or a figure in an anime movie. Too fast. Yet somehow the game let her perform like a world-class athlete. Or a superhuman.

"Eddie..." Laura said.

The viper without a rider braked and spun. A cloud of dust and rubber smoke erupted as it changed shape and sprang for us. It landed hard against the hood, where it pounded a spike appendage into the engine. It then latched onto the dashboard through the gap where the windshield had been and began to climb inside.

I dropped back into the van, reactivated my Stealth using Fade, and thrust my claws into the thing. Its blade arm tore free from the hood and shot towards me. Laura appeared next to me and took the hit. She cried out as the viper's blade sank through her armor.

Shadow nailed me with a Corrosive Blast.

I ignored the pain, made a fist, and drove my claws deep into the viper, piercing its engine. Critical Hit. Its health vanished and it crumpled to pieces. A loot box appeared and I swiped it away too fast.

It vanished into a spray of light. Crap.

Asset Destroyed. Chaos Level: +1.

The mimic was holding it together by inches. The purple player kept pace behind us even as Shadow launched one green blob after another, hitting Laura and the mimic, with more to come. He could stay ahead of us, out of reach, and snipe until we were dead.

An uphill driveway to our right. A metal rolling gate with fancy scrollwork stood open.

Memory Rock Cemetery.

I cranked the wheel. The van sections nearly separated as it bottomed out and raced up the turning driveway.

Shadow and his viper had overshot.

We crested the hill and raced towards a roundabout with a dry whitewashed fountain, a flagpole, and an office. I drove us straight at the front door. Slammed the steering wheel. "Stop here!"

The mimic obliged with a sigh.

"Everyone out now. Get inside!"

I stumbled from the van and waited for the purple player. She appeared at the opposite side of the fountain and wiggled an index finger as if beckoning me towards her. I flipped her the bird.

Laura was next to me. Her health was way down. She healed herself. The upward bumps to her health weren't large, but her bar inched up steadily as she spammed the skill. My Fade was no longer on cooldown. I vanished. So did the enemy player.

Laura tilted her glasses down. "I don't get it. Why can't I see her?"

"It's the game. It's the same way we get hurt even if nothing actually touches us. And It's how you can heal."

"That doesn't make sense."

"It's what's happening. Be ready."

The electric hum of an oncoming viper preceded Shadow driving up to the fountain.

The others had found an unlocked door and ran inside the cemetery office. Kermit remained outside and stepped off the curb. "Leave us alone!"

"Not interested in you," Shadow called. "But Hagar and Rosette are a prime catch. Too bad you're not playing. Could always use another DPS, since Hagar isn't interested in the game."

I waved Kermit off. "Go inside. The other player is here, too, hiding."

"What are you talking about?" He gestured off to his right. "She's right there."

No glasses, not part of the game, I realized.

"This is stupid," he continued, his accent thicker than ever. "Shadow? What are you even doing? We have two people hurt and we almost died because of those machines you're riding."

Shadow got off the bike. Stroked the handlebar as if caressing a lover. "Remember your War Caster named Morticia? You knew how to kite adds without having to be reminded in the Blighted Downs. What happened to you?"

"Oh, bosh. Morticia was a character in an online game. This stopped being amusing when Bennett got hurt at the diner."

"If you say so. At least Morticia was interesting. I guess there's nothing left for you but to leave."

Kermit looked to his right. Backed up. "What are you—"

The purple player appeared next to him. She swiped with her claws and tore a gash up his front and along his neck. Kermit went down. No glasses, not part of the game, but his blood was everywhere. His body gave a last spasm before he was still.

I attacked her, nailing her with a Stab, popping Fade, and Stabbing again. Her health was cut in half from the first strike, but the next one missed as she leaped away, impossibly fast, and landed on the edge of the fountain.

Prudence, according to her game tag.

Shadow was powering up a ball of yellow goo as Laura ran to Kermit's side. She was healing, but it didn't appear to be doing anything.

I closed in on Prudence, willing my Fade cooldown to go faster. Shadow's viper rose, standing upright on its rear tire. Four spider-like legs steadied it. Its two blade-arms extended into the air. It strode towards the fountain as Prudence did a reverse somersault and landed next to Shadow and his pet.

I was ready for his Corrosive Blast. This one he was nurturing. It grew and grew.

One on three, and they out-leveled me. At that moment, I didn't care. Fade would be up in seconds. Take Prudence out, get in a lucky shot on Shadow. He and the viper would kill me. But before that happened, I wanted to hurt them.

The sharp, long blast of an air horn reverberated around us. Both Shadow and Prudence looked surprised.

It came from the rear of the cemetery office. The throaty growl of a big diesel engine grew louder as something clanked and ground towards us.

A yellow bulldozer on metal tracks and a raised front blade tottered around the corner. Black smoke erupted from its vertical exhaust pipe. It blasted its horn again, almost deafening me.

Heavy Behemoth (Level Twelve).

9

The imposing machine had company. A throng of rats bounced along behind it. Ten, fifteen, maybe thirty of them.

I vanished.

Shadow's eyes darted about, as if searching for me. "See you soon, Hagar."

He jumped onto the back of his viper as it dropped onto its tires. Prudence joined him and they made a sharp turn and raced down the driveway.

Another blast of the air horn. The machine was almost at the roundabout. The rats spread out. I hurried back towards the office entrance. If a rat touched me or if the higher-level behemoth got too close, Stealth would break.

Laura was dragging Kermit inside, the door slamming behind them.

I hurried around the first of the rats, careful not to bump against any of them. Neither rat nor behemoth paid me any mind. The enormous machine wasn't stopping. Had it aggroed on Shadow? If so, it wasn't going to catch up. It led its procession past the fountain.

Inside past a reception hallway, the group had gathered around Kermit. His slack expression was locked in a grimace.

Laura kneeled beside him. She was no longer healing. Next to them, Bennett sobbed as Carol crouched next to him with an arm on his shoulder. Chewie leaned against the wall and chewed a thumbnail. His shirt was soaked pink.

Shelves and display cases featured decorative urns. Floral watercolors hung on the walls. I caught a whiff of an antiseptic smell that reminded me of a dentist's office.

I watched the monsters outside through the front window. Some twenty rats remained. The behemoth had vanished, but its engine occasionally growled and the noise from its treads was unmissable.

Eyes bloodshot, Laura's voice barely rose above a whisper. "How?"

"How what?" I asked.

"How did she do that? She had claws like yours made of nothing. She killed him."

I made a helpless gesture. "The game. It can hurt any of us, whether or not we're playing."

"He never even tried on the glasses. I knew the machines could harm us, but what I saw isn't possible. It's like her claws were made of actual steel."

"They are, as far as we're concerned. Wearing or not wearing the glasses doesn't matter. Crimson Gauntlet has somehow infected all of us. I don't know if infected is the right word. But we're part of it because we're here, whether or not we agreed to play."

She brushed the hair from Kermit's face.

Carol fished in her back pocket of her scrubs and produced a set of game glasses. "So the only way to get out of here is by playing,"

"Honey? You had those the whole time?" Chewie asked.

"They showed up yesterday morning. I opened the box and saw who it was from."

"It's my mail."

"It was another computer game accessory, controller, haptic glove, or VR goggles, with you spending money on stuff you don't use anymore and we can't afford!"

"Goddammit, Carol, they're mine. Plus, they were free."

"How was I supposed to know that? It looked like more junk, and then you tell me you're meeting your game friends instead of staying home for dinner. I almost smashed them, but then those machines showed up at our house."

"Give those to me."

Carol inspected the glasses. "Laura, you and Eddie understand what's happening, don't you?"

"We're trying to," Laura said.

"These give someone else the power to do what you guys do. I don't want to die like Kermit."

"Then put them on. We'll help you."

"The first time I did it, I broke the game items inside my house. It gave me experience and got me a level which didn't make sense. That's also what made me an enemy player, isn't it? Maybe someone else should take them."

Laura looked at me. "What do you think?"

I hadn't considered Carol as a player. But how to undo her enemy status? "She's the right choice. Chewie ran away from the rats. No offense. And Bennett's hurt. I don't think you're up for this, bud. I vote for Carol."

Bennett nodded, only half listening.

Chewie looked like he wanted to murder me. "I don't want her fighting those monsters."

"We're not facing off with anything we can run away from. Just deciding who gets these so we have extra tools to handle whatever Crimson Gauntlet throws at us."

He shook his head in disgust.

I took the glasses and opened them and handed them back for Carol to try on. "I'll help you through the game interface."

She let me place them on her face. Blinked. Took them off and put them on again. "They make my head hurt."

"You get used to it, kind of," Laura said. "But Eddie's right. You're our best choice. Let him help you. He's good at explaining game rules to people."

Chewie's face was flush but he kept quiet as I led Carol towards the front door.

"How do you feel about rats?" I asked her.

10

We waited until evening.

Laura and I moved Kermit's body to a back room. The place wasn't a crematorium, funeral home, or morgue. They didn't directly handle the dead. So no refrigerator, either. The storage room was the best option for the moment. No one else came with us.

"Last words?" I asked her.

"My parents' church didn't allow for women to talk. You?"

"Wash the body and sit with it and watch it until it gets buried. Not that I ever did it. Kermit was a good guy. When he first joined our guild, we would always try to guess how old he was. Finally seeing him, we were surprised he wasn't older than forty, always talking about bands no one heard of and eating weird food and traveling. Didn't think he'd last as long as he did playing with us, but he learned his class, got good at the fights." I struggled to add something of importance. "Solid DPS."

"Lord Almighty, please let there be someone who can actually speak show up after I die. Amen."

My cheeks grew hot. "You're welcome to say something. I'm no good at this."

"Relax, Eddie. It's a bad joke. We're going to get out of this and he'll be put someplace more dignified than a room full of stacked chairs."

"No wife or kids, but he has to have some family."

"We're it for now."

We shared a moment of silence. After about thirty seconds, we looked at each other before closing the door and joining the others.

Carol was at the front door, keeping watch with Chewie.

My mimic van remained where I had parked it just outside. It looked like a stiff breeze might make it fall to pieces. Two flat tires, the windshield gone, and gouges everywhere.

Bennett was asleep on a couch in the first office. We had placed all the food we could find on the desk. A mini-fridge had a large container of pasta salad with peas and pepperoncini that didn't smell off. Add to that some granola bars, fossilized Valentine's Day mints, and a few overripe bananas, along with tea and an urn of cold water, and we had a feast.

"All clear except for the rats," Carol reported. "They're milling about the driveway."

Chewie had lines beneath his eyes, and his face was visibly pale even in the poor light. "I don't like it. It's like they're waiting for us."

I checked the window and confirmed no other visible threats. "They're waiting. It's just like monster game behavior in Night World. Maybe it's because we have a new player. Carol, did you accept the quest?"

Carol adjusted the glasses. "Kill Five Rats."

"You're not actually thinking about going out there," Chewie asked.

"It's our only option if we want to get past Shadow," I said.

"I wasn't talking to you, Eddie. Honey, give me the glasses. Let me do it."

"We talked about this."

Chewie held her hand for a moment before shuffling past me without another word. Laura joined him and they went to a second office across from the one where Bennett slept. I could hear them talking.

"Your husband's right to be nervous," I said to Carol. "You don't have to go outside. I'm sorry if I pressured you."

"Keith ran. Bennett's in poor shape. I'm the logical choice, so let's do this."

"Okay. Are you getting used to the UI? There are a lot of menus that can get in the way. Don't be afraid to dismiss them to unclutter your vision. We're going to focus on your two attacks. Shoot is the one I want you to use. It's ranged and you won't need to get close. I'll be next to you and will kill anything that comes after you."

"Yeah, I think I got it. I've been reading through the menus and tutorials."

Tutorials? I kept my mouth shut. The game had wanted me to head east to a location to begin what might be a tutorial quest chain, and I had ignored it when we decided on the exit. But I also had never revisited the tutorial tab.

She made a fist and looked at her hand. "So I ignore my Punch unless something is close. Easy enough. I accepted the quest. It's like the starter zone in Night World except there's no cut scene."

"Yeah. We're living it."

The rats hadn't gone anywhere. If they had, we could sneak out. They were scattered in packs around the fountain outside the front of the office. Not as many as had first appeared with the behemoth, though. With Carol and Laura to back me up, I felt good about thinning their ranks.

I pulled up my quest tracker. Three quests hung just outside the front door, but I didn't have to move to take them.

Escort to Game Exit.

Taunt the Behemoth!

Collect Five Armor Assets.

I guessed the armor collection quest was repeatable.

"It's evolving," I murmured.

"What?"

"It must want you to level faster. Probably trying to lure me and Laura out. It also doesn't just want to kill us while we take shelter. All of this points to the game pushing us back outside."

"You talk like the game's alive."

"I don't know what to think. But I'm pretty sure if we stay put, it will throw things at us until we leave."

She took a breath and nodded. "Okay. Lead the way and let's kill some rats."

"Laura? We're leaving."

She emerged from the second office alone and joined us at the door. We stepped outside into the warm air. Laura and I stood in front of Carol as Carol raised an arm. Fired at the closest rat.

One at a time, she took the level-one machine critters down like a pro. Laura and I used Shoot and polished off two that hadn't died immediately. Four down.

I was worried the behemoth might come, but I didn't hear it.

We stepped closer to the fountain.

"One more, and you're done," I whispered.

On the next pull, Carol had three rats bounding in at her. I was careful in my ambush so my damage wouldn't hit her. She remained an enemy player. I could hurt her with my Whirlwind Stab, as she might count as my extra target.

She took down one of them, damaged the second.

The two rats were too close to Shoot. I played it conservative and used Punch. Single target, base attack, but it did more damage now that I was level four. Punch liked to crit, as it did it twice in rapid succession.

Achievement: Rat Catcher. Kill twenty rats. You're the scourge of the rat population.

A final rat surprised me, appearing out of nowhere and brushing past, making a beeline for Carol. She swatted at the thing, not using a skill, and it sliced her arm before Laura slammed it with her fists, sending it to pieces.

Laura went to heal Carol. Her hand glowed, but the cut on Carol's arm remained.

"It's not working."

"The first aid kit's inside," Carol said.

"That's not the point. My skill should help who I want it to."

I moved to help Carol back towards the cemetery office. "File a ticket and take it up with management."

Chewie was at the door and holding it open. "What happened? Honey, you're hurt."

"It's not that bad, dear. Stings like the devil, but the game says it's just one hit point. And now I'm level one and have points to spend on my attributes. How do you want me to do this? And when do I choose my class?"

11

We talked it through, Laura, Carol, and I. Chewie had retreated to the second office and slammed the door.

Carol finished fixing a bandage on her arm. "He'll be fine."

I felt a twinge of jealousy. Here was a fresh player and she wouldn't waste her attribute points by allocating them accidentally. "Don't even think about spending them until you're sure."

"You've told me twice already."

Hacker sounded too complicated even though Carol had played a Beast Master in Night World and understood the concept of having pets. Brute meant running front and center, tanking and healing. We had Laura for that.

I drank some water from a bottle. "Don't bother with Charisma or Strength. Hellion will allow you to sneak. The class works well with Dexterity. Probably the Move attribute, too. I'm guessing the purple player upped her Move to be able to do what she did. But I like the idea of you choosing Blaster."

Laura used a damp paper towel to wipe her face. "Health will allow her to survive. We just need to last long enough to make it out of here."

"'Dexterity governs your chance to hit and dodge,'" Carol quoted as she read on her glasses. "Dodging means avoiding damage altogether. I like the sound of that. What can a Blaster do?"

"Shoot things like the guy back at the last house did," I said. "Fire, ice, electricity. All ranged."

"That sounds like it will give me time to pick my targets. Plus, you don't have to worry about hurting me in combat."

She mercifully left out the word again.

"And the woman with Shadow?" Carol asked.

"Hellion class."

"That means I can sneak like you. But then I have to get close to the bad guys. I'll take Blaster."

"I'd like to find out how we can get rid of your enemy player status," Laura said.

Carol looked at her hand. "I'm purple to you?"

"Yeah. Just like Shadow and his new sidekick."

"Teaches me for messing around with Keith's mail."

It wasn't that funny but we laughed.

She chose Dexterity. If she made it to level two, she'd go with Blaster. I went to check on Bennett. He was snoring. I went to the second office and knocked softly. The door hadn't shut completely so I pushed it open.

The small office had a window. Moonlight glowed on the white fountain.

Chewie sat on the carpet with his back against a wall and was looking outside. His tone was acid. "Get your party organized?"

"Just doing what we have to do so we can survive this."

"Don't give me that. This is your bread and butter. You love this. Ben and I are hurt, Kermit's dead, and you've got my wife lapping up your sage gaming advice."

"If there was another choice, we'd make it."

"Of course, there's another choice. The big machine's gone. We have some food. We hide here. There's a basement downstairs with a solid metal door. Instead, you're getting us ready to go out there again, aren't you?"

"After we rest, yes. Crimson Gauntlet says there's an exit."

"You told me that. Why should I trust you or the game?"

My cheeks were burning. I was woozy. "I'm not Shadow. This sucks. I don't want to be here. I've also got family I want to get to."

He looked at me. "You never talk about them."

"There's enough cross chatter in raid without me going on about my parents. My mom's in Colma, my dad lives in Orange County. I visit my mom every Saturday morning and we go for breakfast. We've gotten along better lately since she accepted I was never going back to college and wasn't going to temple. I don't talk much with my dad since the divorce."

"So maybe you want to get out of this. I'm...I'm just...wound up. I just wish it looked like you didn't enjoy this as much as you do."

"I'm going outside to look around. Be back in five. Maybe then you can get some sleep and I'll keep watch."

My mimic was crooning. I couldn't identify the warbly wordless song. Loud enough to hear when next to it, but not so bad it would attract attention.

I patted the thing on the hood. "You did good. Now get some rest."

My van cooed.

I stepped out from under the overhang and studied the night. A breeze promised a cooldown. Maybe we'd get fog from the delta. The stars above glowed brighter than I had ever seen them. No freeway or city lights. It also meant the dark places were inky pools where anything might be hiding.

I didn't like the idea Prudence could sneak about anywhere. But she and Shadow had fled from the level-twelve behemoth. Once I got back inside, we could lock the door and barricade it. Shadow might send in a minion to break in, but at least it wouldn't be a surprise.

A half-dozen rats remained at the far side of the roundabout. I left them alone as I made a circuit around the office.

A purple curtain hung in the air to the east. It vanished when I took my glasses off. It reminded me of the Aurora Borealis. I had seen it once when visiting my aunt up in Vancouver. The wall of light bent and shimmered, but stayed in place. It was marking something, but the game gave it no label.

The purple color was enough of a hint. An enemy zone, I guessed. So

Shadow and his friend Prudence had a place to go. There must have been more bad guys to warrant a game zone marker like that. The thought chilled me.

I lingered out front and spent some time with my interface. With my quest tracker, I could orient myself. All but the escort quest remained out of reach, but the game dangled them in front of me.

The **Escort to Game Exit** quest was tempting. We were heading there anyway. But I didn't want to start a game event.

When examining the frustratingly brief quest description, it provided a waypoint. West, consistent with the announcement over Nixle. But traveling at night meant risking falling and breaking our neck with no complications courtesy of Crimson Gauntlet. The quest target? Bennett.

Somewhere beyond the first ring of gravestones, the **Taunt the Behemoth** quest waited. I guessed starting the quest would summon the thing. No, thank you. None of us needed to wrangle with a level-twelve beastie.

Collect Five Armor Assets took us further uphill into the cemetery. That one might be easy, but I was certain the game would have a surprise in store.

I had a previously accepted quest in my log. **Kill Five Enemy Players (1/5).**

No waypoints, no pings on the mini-map. The game wasn't going to make it easy to know where Shadow and Prudence had gone.

"See anything?"

I hadn't heard Laura come outside. "Two quests here in the cemetery. The armor one might be easy, if we want to get Carol her next level."

"Let's get some rest, since it seems nothing's out to get us at the moment."

A helicopter raced past overhead. The percussive beats of its rotors were both frightening and comforting. Someone with the government, be they police, Coast Guard, or Army, was still out there. But my first reflex was to confirm I had my Stealth up.

The flying machine had no game tag. It vanished to the south.

We went inside to wait out the night.

12

Using a flashlight from Carol's go-bag, Chewie studied a map on the wall inside the office. The map labeled each area within the cemetery. Remembrance Hill. Mountain View. Skylark. Orange Blossom Walk. He pointed to the top left edge of Memory Rock Cemetery, where a property line ran across the length of the map. Beyond it lay county open space.

Carol slept on a pile of coats found hanging behind a door. Otherwise we were alone.

"That's part of Foothill Regional Park," Chewie said. "That lets out near Redwood Parkway. You said the game exit's near there?"

I knew the park, but not the off-road terrain around it. "Yeah, it's a few miles west. How'd you know about this?"

"Mountain biking. You need to get out more."

"You think that's better than following the road?"

"Cutting through a jungle would be better than facing more monsters. The cemetery has a water department easement that connects to a fire road. We take that, go uphill a little way, and it's a stroll down to the park."

"It means going through the cemetery. The game has assets there."

"About now, I'm guessing it has assets everywhere. So what do you think?"

It was a few minutes to six. The sky was brightening. I didn't want to hang out at the cemetery office any longer than we had to.

"I'll wake the others up," I said. "And Keith? Nice work."

I woke Laura first. She had settled in near the front and rested on top of a pair of seat cushions. She nodded when I explained the plan. Chewie and Carol spent a moment talking. They roused Bennett, and soon we were ready.

By the time we left, the sky was a smear of maroon clouds. Laura and I took point, marching up along the paved road that wound through the tombstones. We had both accepted **Quest: Collect Five Armor Assets**. So had Carol. If they were going to be lying around, we may as well benefit and getting her another level and picking a class would help.

Bennett had a spring in his step. Bleary-eyed, but alert after having downed an energy drink discovered in an abandoned cooler. He hadn't said much since getting up, but at least he was moving.

Carol appeared content to walk with Chewie, not that he needed help. He no longer looked like he wanted to murder me. We were once again fellow survivors, now that I was no longer trying to drag his wife off to fight monsters.

But the monsters were there.

We passed a golf cart, a hearse, and a backhoe, all of which had been picked clean, with no roaches or cocoons in sight.

Remembrance Hill was the cemetery centerpiece. A mausoleum for ash urns and a few free-standing crypts. The largest grave markers stood here too, with angels, scrollwork, and lengthy epitaphs declaring pithy wisdom to the bereaved.

Three armor assets were visible and there for the taking. We would walk right by them.

Laura pointed them out. "We should get those."

"Get what?" Chewie asked.

"Game assets right here. Eddie and I can grab them."

"What happened to skipping unnecessary battles?"

My rule. Well played. I said, "The assets are necessary. They keep us from getting hurt."

Discussion over. Laura and I would grab them, but Carol stayed behind with Chewie and Bennett. They waited by a section of small, in-ground grave markers that needed weeding.

We collected three armor assets apiece. Too easy. The mausoleum had two more just inside a glass door.

"You get them, you have enough for a turn in," I said to Laura.

The three **Skeletons (Level Four)** rose from a pile of dirt. One knocked aside a wheelbarrow and the fiberglass shell of a riding lawnmower.

We went to work, with Laura wading into them and dropping Punch after Punch. I didn't hesitate to hit Stab, knowing Laura would be safe from my Whirlwind effect. My first blow knocked out one of them and hurt a second. Fade, and I did it again, demolishing the injured one, with my spillover damage hurting number three. Laura demolished the last one after suffering a backhand rend across her forearm. After a Heal, she was as good as new.

"Carol should be here," I said. "She'd get experience and wouldn't have to do anything."

"Their choice. Leave it."

We went inside. She collected her three armor assets. But there were three more, one at the end of each wing of niches. It meant I could finish the quest a second time. Two more skeletons, and one **Acid Zombie (Level Six)**. But they popped one at a time and we had no problem taking them down.

The zombie was the toughest, with a big health bar, but it didn't hit much harder than the skeletons, if you don't mind the damage over time because of the acid.

Laura hit me with a Heal where the zombie had mauled me.

I checked the wound. Pink skin, but I've had worse rashes. I collected the last piece of armor and a few coins. **Quest Complete!**

"All we need is a crafting station."

I felt the rumble in my bones before I could hear the behemoth's engine. "Let's get out of here."

We met the others on their way into the mausoleum. The behemoth wasn't slowing down as it barreled towards us, smashing through gravestones and crushing the remains of the golf cart. Its shovel dropped like a jouster in a Middle Ages tourney using a battering ram.

Bennett was the slowest inside.

I grabbed him. "Run!"

We made it to the center of the mausoleum when the building shuddered. Glass windows burst inward as the machine shoved itself halfway inside the front wall. Its engine shuddered and roared. It worked the shovel and loosened a cascade of debris from the ceiling before backing up.

Laura was halfway down one hallway. "There's two fire doors. We split up and run for it."

"Hold on," I said. "The game wants us to taunt it. We just need to accept the quest."

Chewie's eyes darted between us. "We're not going outside with that thing!"

Carol was reading on her glasses. "Eddie's right. It's going to come in here if we wait. Or it brings the place down on top of us."

"I'll go," I said. "Wait here until I lead it away. If the game wants us to taunt it, I'll taunt it."

The behemoth punctuated my statement with a blast of its horn before it tore away a swathe of glass and metal from the entryway.

Leaving that direction would be fatal. I used one of the emergency exits, wincing as the door clicked shut, as if the behemoth could hear me above the racket it was making.

Stealth on, I crept around the side of the mausoleum. It rammed the building again, taking out a corner. Black smoke spewed from its exhaust. Seeing the thing in action froze me in place.

How do you taunt a fifty-ton earth mover?

As soon as I accepted the quest, the behemoth backed up, revved its engine, and pivoted my way.

Despite Stealth, it knew I was there and lurched towards me. My ability to hide in plain sight had limits and now I was running to avoid getting smushed. I headed downhill, not thinking, darting and weaving between the tombstones. The behemoth took the direct route, crushing everything in its path.

I made it to a lower paved road, cutting laterally through the section of the cemetery. Headed left.

The quest wasn't satisfied. What did it mean to taunt the behemoth?

"Come and get me! My mom drives faster than you! Pretty pokey for a level twelve!"

The only thing my shouting accomplished was to rob me of precious breath. While it was slow, it wasn't giving up. I was running towards a dead end. I headed uphill.

A pair of level-one rats bounced along next to me and were closing in. Two more launched my direction from behind a grave. One almost caught me, but for a lucky backward Stab that shredded it. The others weren't close enough for Whirlwind.

I was winded by the time I made it to an upper lawn replete with more headstones. The behemoth lumbered on, having fallen behind by fifty feet. The rats circled me. They were a distraction, but one of them cut my leg before I killed it.

Saved by my armor, but I took a point of damage. The other two charged. My Stab crit and they both died.

A new object appeared in my HUD in front of a small crypt. **Quest Item: Behemoth Food.**

It looked like a big lizard-on-a-stick. I grabbed it. The item was virtual and had no weight. What was I supposed to—

An electric jolt knocked me ass-over-teakettle. My health bar took a hit. At first, I thought the behemoth food had done something, but as I fought off the tingling from my limbs, I realized what had happened.

The behemoth finished the climb and rumbled in my direction. A cannon on a turret on the giant machine's canopy swiveled about before fixing in my direction.

I tumbled behind the crypt as a second blast sizzled the air. The machine would be on top of me in seconds and the crypt wouldn't save me. Quest item in hand, I bolted from cover. I kept my head down and ducked and weaved between the tombstones.

What did the game want me to do? The behemoth didn't appear to have a mouth or any game asset besides the ranged weapon. Tossing the food and hoping it would nom-nom it up would be a mistake if it meant I needed to circle back to pick the object up.

It rolled after me, its weapon firing anytime I hesitated. I ran out of tombstones. The lawn before me was an expanse of in-ground grave markers. A granite wall stood nearby with niches for flowers. The behemoth-sized stone circle in front of it glowed.

I crossed the circle and the behemoth food vanished from my virtual grip. I didn't stop. The ground shook as the behemoth headed for the circle. I scrambled up a slope and paused when the behemoth cut loose with a blast of its air horn.

Behemoth Taunted (1/3).

My moment of victory was short-lived. It fired its cannon. The lightning blast exploded on the ground in front of me with a flash.

I wasn't done.

Two new quest items appeared in opposite directions. More behemoth food. The machine was once again heading for me. Too much open space to easily avoid more of the blasts. But it wasn't shooting at me as long as I moved.

The thing chased me as I hit Stealth and jogged forward. A sharp ache burrowed into my side. Phlegm in my throat choked me. I was barely moving faster than the behemoth and I wanted to stop and dry heave.

Had enough time passed for the others to have slipped away?

The next quest item waited atop a plastic trailer loaded with gardening equipment. Just before I reached it, it vanished.

"What the hell?"

Prudence appeared with the lizard-on-a-stick in her hands. She sprinted off in the circle's direction, which had reappeared before the granite wall. She stopped and waved. The behemoth blasted her but she jumped, rolled, and never slowed despite being hit. By the time the monster turned in place, she brought the quest item into the circle and planted it. She pumped her arm and gave a howl before vanishing.

The behemoth rolled into the circle and blew its horn.

My quest changed.

Quest: Beat the Opposing Player to the Last Behemoth Food and Taunt the Behemoth.

Achievement: Bury the Competition. Compete against another player in completing a quest.

One quest item left, and I was closer. It was perched atop a canopy tent shading rows of foldout chairs near a freshly dug grave.

Stealth had slowed me down as I tried to reach the second objective. I turned the skill off and jumped grave markers. I had to get it first. Where was Prudence? As my eyes scanned the graves, I stumbled. The air burned right above me from a lightning blast. A mad laugh erupted from my lips as I sprang to my feet and ran.

I was going to beat her there. I was going to win.

My heart sank when I heard the electric whine of a motorcycle. The viper shot up the road towards the tent. Its blades and arms were folded, but even a brush with the machine would be lethal.

Where was Shadow?

No choice. I hit Stealth, but not before nailing the viper with my Shoot skill.

Whatever programing Shadow's pet obeyed, self-defense topped its list of priorities. It braked, pivoted and rolled towards my last location. Swords extended from either side of it. Even if it couldn't see me, it was hoping to scythe me down.

I used a gravestone as cover. This earned a lightning blast from the behemoth, which detonated against the stone. The viper shot past, oblivious to my location. I guessed the monsters weren't sharing information. Once the motorcycle was past me, I again hurried forward towards the objective.

The behemoth charged on my left. The viper was behind me. Prudence was out there somewhere, but she'd have to be careful, too. Getting run over by a motorcycle would hurt, regardless of game armor, and the behemoth could no doubt see through her Stealth too.

But if I picked up the behemoth food, my Stealth would break and the viper would be on me.

Eddie Rush's First Rule of Winning? If your plan blows, change it.

I changed direction and approached the behemoth when it pivoted away to navigate a set of steps in front of a large memorial. Its cannon kept aiming at me, waiting for me to pause.

"Don't suck," I wheezed.

With a screeching war cry, I hit it with a Stab. Barely scratched the level-twelve beast. Its cannon spun and fired. Missed as I ran around its back and shot at the viper as it buzzed past. The viper was once again heading for me, but the behemoth blocked its path.

Now both monsters were trying to kill me. Too many gravestones for the viper to do more than zip back and forth on the grass. The behemoth steamrolled everything as it pivoted about.

"Come on, come on, come on!" I urged. But the viper wasn't stupid enough to hit the behemoth, and the larger monster was only interested in me.

We were close to the tent. But now I was stuck. If I tripped, if I hesitated, I'd be rolled over, crushed, stabbed, or all three.

Then my heart sank when Prudence appeared, leaping and claiming the third lizard-on-a-stick. She still needed to run it to the circle.

The behemoth shot her.

The quest item flew from her grip and I snatched it up. Couldn't Stealth, and now I had the gigantic machine's attention. I bolted through the tent as it tore after me, crashing the canopy down and pulverizing plastic chairs and a wooden lectern.

It faltered, hung up at the open grave. Maybe it was blinded by the fabric over its cab. I didn't stop to ask. The quest circle lay ahead. I was cutting through the tombstones, praying the viper couldn't get to me in time.

To my left, an engine roared.

An off-road vehicle with a roll cage and balloon tires bounced and swerved in my direction. Shadow was behind the wheel, with the windows down. He flicked a Corrosive Blast at me and it struck me in the ass.

The jolt of pain caused me to stumble. I hit the ground, my chin striking stone. The lizard-on-a-stick sprang from my grip. Shadow veered off to avoid the behemoth. The machine's shovel smashed into the ground. It was scraping gravestones and dirt as it rushed at me.

I had no choice. My backside burned and my health bar eroded. I stealthed, sprang to my feet, and dove aside as the behemoth clattered over my last location. Its horn trumpeted, deafening me. The viper crossed the lawn behind me. Shadow raced ahead and was coming around again. The lizard-on-a-stick might as well have been on the moon.

Empty-handed, I moved towards the quest circle by the granite wall, watching and waiting. The viper tagged the behemoth, drawing its ire. The machine trundled after it.

Shadow had stopped his vehicle and was getting out next to the behemoth food. "Come on and try for it, Hagar!"

I didn't know if I could survive another hit. The behemoth was heading the opposite way, its attention locked on the fleeing viper.

A row of gravestones still stood. Just enough cover that I could get close to the lizard. But Prudence had to be nearby.

Run, my instincts screamed. Staying was stupid. But if Shadow and his new ally finished the quest, they'd be that much stronger. I crept forward.

The lizard-on-a-stick snapped up into my grasp. Stealth went bye-bye. I flinched when Prudence materialized next to me, slamming me with a Stab. White hot pain up my spine as her blades cut deep. The blow tore away another chunk of my health.

I let go of the quest item, activated Fade, and nailed her with a Stab of my own. She shrieked, scampering out of range. If she had hit me any harder, I'd have gone down. I hit the grass as a Corrosive Blast missed my head.

The lizard-on-a-stick was inches away.

Something clanged on top of a grave marker and scampered towards me. A mechanical insect the size of a retriever. It had claws, long back legs like a grasshopper, and a maw that took up the front half of its body.

Blood Locust (Level Five). Player Shadow's Pet.

Shadow had found a new friend.

13

I scrambled back. Fade was taking too long to reset. I didn't dare fight the thing. It was all talons and rusty fangs and looked like the kind of monster that was all damage, all the time. As I scurried on all fours, it landed on a grave in front of me.

I raised my hand to ward it off. "Shadow? Take the behemoth food. It's yours."

"So generous. I was planning on it."

The blood locust teetered on the stone, a command away from tearing me to shreds.

I needed to buy a few more seconds so I could Fade. "Where'd you find your new friend? Haven't seen one like it."

"That's what happens when you turtle up and don't play. You could have beaten me to five."

"No one here's looking to stand in your way."

"Yeah, well. You know I've got my own set of rules. Never turn down easy XP."

I Faded. The bug stopped twitching. Its antennae moved about as if hoping to sniff me out. I rose on shaky knees and backed away, keeping it between me and Shadow. He picked up the lizard-on-a-stick.

At the far side of the lawn, the behemoth abandoned its pursuit of the viper. But Shadow was too close to the circle. Casual as can be, he walked it in.

The lizard-on-a-stick vanished. The behemoth rolled towards us and into the circle. Once there, it blew its horn and clanked to a stop.

Quest Canceled: Beat Opposing Player to the Last Behemoth Food and Taunt the Behemoth.

I used a fallen stone angel for cover. For the moment, the behemoth idled and didn't appear interested in any of us.

Shadow returned to his vehicle. The viper and the locust heeled on either side of him. "Come on out, Hagar, and I make it quick. No? Never works in the movies, either, but it was worth a try."

Prudence appeared at the passenger side of his car. "Shadow, let's go. The others will get away."

With a theatrical wave, he got in and they left. But his pets stayed put. I didn't dare break Stealth as they drove down the hill towards the cemetery office.

A timer over the behemoth began a countdown.

Quest Restart: 59:04. 59:03.

A little less than an hour on the behemoth. If Shadow was leaving, I could take the quest again. Maybe hit level five. But one more wallop from the behemoth and I'd be finished. I also couldn't wait that long.

I found a vantage point at a pool of remembrance that had been drained. It gave me a view of the lower portion of the cemetery and the farms beyond.

Shadow had parked around the front of the office and Prudence was nowhere to be seen. His pets joined him. The viper raced around the back and tore open one of the fire doors. The locust bound inside.

Ice fingers clutched my stomach. My friends were about to be slaughtered and I was too far away to even offer a chance at a last stand. But a moment later, glass shattered and the viper appeared out front. The locust followed and they rejoined their master.

Prudence materialized and consulted with Shadow. They both looked in my direction. I was effectively invisible, but ducked anyway. Shadow gunned his engine and they drove uphill along one of the cemetery roads. I recalled the map inside the office. Did Shadow or Prudence know where they might have gone?

I felt sick as I ran after them.

The top of the cemetery had a chain fence with barbwire. Keep the kids out and ward off the deer from nibbling on the flowers.

Shadow was rolling open a gate. He wasted no time in driving through.

The earlier breeze was gone. The day was getting hot and I was soaked with sweat by the time I made it to the gate. A dirt road lay beyond a wide culvert. Even if my mimic van was working, it could never cross the ditch. And on foot, I'd never catch up before Shadow overtook the others.

Trust your teammates.

Laura was smart. So were the others. Surely, they'd hear his off-road vehicle's engine and hide. The grassy hill had plenty of gullies and rocks and oak trees.

Time to gird up the old loins and back up my guildmates.

14

A sable-colored cow chewed its grass as it stared at me from the opposite side of the barbwire fence.

Did the game not care about animals? Or were the machines only prioritizing murdering humans before coming around to the rest of God's creatures?

I was surprised to see a couple of quests nearby. It meant moving even slower, but I went to the closest marker on my HUD.

Quest: Gather Five Crafting Assets.

I accepted it. They appeared on the surrounding hill. If Prudence was there somewhere, she'd have me cold. But I dropped Stealth and collected the first four in minutes. The game assets up in the hills left me wondering again how Crimson Gauntlet could project virtual objects in such a remote area. How far would we need to travel to be outside of the game's signal? Were the local cell phone towers part of it? Or even the glasses I was wearing?

I headed for my last crafting asset. A second and a third cow stood next to each other. I avoided piles of droppings before I froze.

Both cows watched me with little interest. Then they both lowed as something streaked through the grass. Shadow's blood locust. It moved like a shark through the weeds.

I hit Stealth just as it appeared beside a patch of blackberry bushes. It shifted from side to side, its antennae spasming. I hadn't heard Shadow's vehicle. Was he parked nearby? What was the range on his pet, anyway?

The quest item was within reach. I could grab it and vanish and leave.

At the crest of the hill, a water tower stood in the middle of a grove of dry pines and oak trees. A woman screamed. The robot bug moved, bouncing over the nearest fencepost, and headed for the sound.

I let Stealth drop before taking the fifth crafting item. The expected congratulatory notification filled my display.

Quest Complete: Gather Five Crafting Assets.
You are now...

Level Five

1

Ever try reading while climbing a barbwire fence? Don't do it.

A wire spur slashed my hand and another tore my pants. Enough rust to give my lapsed tetanus booster a run for its money.

I was running uphill, pushing through anise and thistle and twelve types of weeds I didn't want to know.

The scream had cut short even before the bug vanished into the tree line. Carol or Laura? Had to be.

Too many level-up notifications to ignore.

I had five attribute points to spend. Placing them in Move was too tempting. I didn't believe for a second it would help the stitch in my side or the shortness of my breath. Dexterity felt like a no-brainer. More dodge, more crits. I committed the points.

Achievement: Arise from Mediocrity. Hit level five and stop being a scrub. Crimson Gauntlet is watching you closely now.

I didn't want to waste time thinking about the vague, creepy threat at the end of the notification.

New Skills Available: Blind, Detect Weakness, Misdirect.

I could only choose one. Each had an explanation as I skimmed. All of them sounded good.

Blind was an offensive strike that would rob my target of their vision. It had a long cooldown.

Detect Weakness would give me and my allies a substantial bonus on attack for a marked target, bypassing 80% of armor and negating 50%

of dodge. Powerful. But I didn't like the idea of going toe to toe if I didn't have to.

Misdirect was a distract skill to get a target off my back, I guessed, but I was wrong. It would transfer an attack to another foe. Negate an incoming strike while damaging another enemy?

Yes, please.

I chose it, immediately second guessing myself. Blind would be an escape tool allowing me to wait out Fade's cooldown, giving me three back-to-back alpha strikes during one combat if up against a single foe. And Detect Weakness? Who didn't like a debuff that could benefit the group in a big fight?

But this wasn't a raid. Misdirect it was, and I couldn't return it.

There was more information, but I had already slowed down to make my attribute and class selections.

The air within the grove was cool. Pine needles cushioned my every step. I couldn't see the blood locust. Up ahead, a water tower stood in a clearing. It had a fence and a fixed ladder leading to the top of the tower.

Two people were up there, a man and a woman. Both were covered in blood and wearing torn clothing.

Around them swarmed a half dozen level-one rats with a couple of shock vermin in the mix. A collection of backpacks, camping gear, and a ripped-up tent were at the base of the tower. I slipped into Stealth and crept closer. Two bodies in the weeds. The rats had cut them into ribbons.

The blood locust was out of sight. It had to be nearby.

One rat bounced halfway up the ladder. It gripped a rung and climbed using its blade arms. At the top, the man kicked it in the face and dislodged it. Before it tumbled, the rat slashed, just missing his foot.

This was the source of the scream. I didn't know these people. While my health was full, thanks to leveling up, taking on a mob of rats and possibly Prudence, Shadow, and his minions wasn't smart.

Quest: Recruit New Player.

The quest object was directly in front of me. Both trapped hikers were my targets. I wasn't sure what the game meant by 'recruit.' Neither wore glasses. I didn't see any dead rats. I hated the fact Crimson Gauntlet wanted me there, either by design or by some dynamic quest creation. Two murder victims and two terrified people trying to survive, and the game was using it all to tempt me with another dollop of experience points.

Another rat made an assault on the ladder. It failed to make the top, slipping at the last moment. The other rats hopped about gleefully when it landed, as if excited about the sport of killing their prey.

The robotic critters were tireless, and the trapped hikers looked exhausted.

I approached the group of monsters with my virtual claws extended. My Stab obliterated three rats and one shock vermin. I Faded, hit the closest live rat, and four more went to pieces as I swiped wildly at them. I roared.

Letting loose like this wasn't me. But I turned and faced the three remaining creatures and couldn't stop grinning. The shock vermin blasted me and I used my Misdirect. A rat went down. The second rat slashed, but I jumped out of the way and it only struck air. I tore into it and its fellows, slashing, chopping, howling, and not even sure if I was using an ability as the metal animals went down.

My loot? Three coins and a transportation asset. A quest item appeared inside the ribcage of one shock vermin. Not virtual and it took some bending of wires to free it. It was a circlet of wire mesh construction or a metallic tiara made of scrap metal similar to my glasses.

I instantly understood what the quest wanted me to do.

After a check of the perimeter, I considered the two hikers. "It's safe to come down now."

The woman nearly fell as she was only wearing flip-flops. The man wasn't faring much better as he was missing a boot.

We were exposed. Shadow's minion could be anywhere and he might have the same quest as me.

Both survivors had cuts on their arms and legs. The woman was sunburned. The man wheezed as he breathed. They looked about at the remains of their camp and the two bodies. Finally, they approached me.

"Th-thank you," the man murmured.

"How long were you up there?"

"Yesterday morning. We ran for it when we realized no one was coming to help. But those things followed us. They're everywhere."

The woman sobbed and clung to him.

It was obvious they needed a moment, but I felt eyes on us. "Look, we can't stay here. More rats will come."

"Rats?" she asked.

"The monsters. Those are the little ones. There's bigger things roaming about, and some bad people too."

"How did you even do what you did?"

"It's...complicated. Do either of you play MMOs?"

2

Marcus and Andie weren't gamers, as it turned out.

He owned and operated a hair salon. She was an accountant. The two dead hikers with them were neighbors and they had sheltered together in Andie and Marcus' house during the first night.

We stuck to the grove as it followed part of the ridgeline. I still had the quest item in hand.

"So you played a 'game' against those 'rats' and you won?" Marcus asked, making air quotes with his fingers.

"Not exactly. We're all in the game now. The game is everywhere and is controlling the machines. It's running on a set of rules that gives people the ability to kill the monsters."

He nodded, unconvinced. "I think I get it."

He didn't get it.

"Look, I've got a device I need to give to one of you. It will help you see parts of the game world and let you use those abilities. There's a bit of a learning curve. Either of you use virtual reality software?"

They stared at me blankly.

"I have Instagram and my own Discord server," Andie said. "I sell scented oils."

"It's not like that."

I offered her the circlet, anyway. She gave it a casual examination but didn't put it on. I held back on pushing her. Her eyes were glazed. They both marched like zombies and had cracked lips. At least they were helping one another to move, as both looked ready to keel over.

And here I was, trying to give them a crash course on gaming.

Andie turned the circlet end over end. "So this will let me kill those machines."

"It will help. You'll have to put it on."

"It doesn't make sense."

"It won't, at first. Getting used to it takes some time. If you can't figure it out, then let Marcus have a shot at it. But one of you should try it on."

We came to the top of a trail that descended into the west-side valley. It's the direction Chewie suggested we go to make it to the game exit.

Andie put the circlet on her head. Blinked. "Whoa."

We waited a moment as she scanned the sky, the hills, and the surrounding trees. Apparently, the circlet was as good as my game lenses. She looked at her hands.

"I'm level one? This is a lot better than Second Life."

"Second Life doesn't try to murder you. See the selection menu for attributes? Take Health for your stat. Shoot will be the skill you want if we run into more rats. It's ranged. Just raise your hand and it will light up. But I don't want you to stop and fight anything. We need to get you both out of here. I'm with a few people but we got separated. There's a game exit and we're heading there."

They needed no further encouragement.

Quest Complete: Recruit New Player.

Achievement: Headhunter. Bring more sheep into the fold.

Andie had a red label with her name. Marcus, as far as the game was concerned, remained anonymous.

Reward: Recipe: Crafting. Crimson Gauntlet Key.

Ingredients: One Crafting Asset. A Crimson Gauntlet Key grants new players access to Crimson Gauntlet.

A small picture of a circlet hovered next to the recipe. So I could recruit new players. Wasn't sure how I felt about that.

A steep path intersected a fire road. From there, we followed it to a gate at the end of a street. My heart sank as I saw a Volkswagen sedan in a state of disassembly.

"We need water," Marcus said.

The first house had a frosted window next to a front door. I smashed it in with a flowerpot. Beyond lay an atrium and a sliding door. My new companions were reluctant to follow, but I was too tired and hot to be shy. Stupid, really. I should have knocked or called out. Someone might have been home.

They were. The stench struck me like a wet rag across the face. They had died in their living room. It looked like the rats or whatever machines had broken in had come through the backyard, as a window was shattered and glass lay scattered everywhere.

"Stay out there. I'll get supplies."

There was a plastic bottle next to the sink. I drank my fill before filling it up again. The cupboards had food. My stomach rumbled despite the smell. A bag of bread, a box of puffed rice, and some blackening bananas, and I was out of there.

We ate in the shade near a covered boat on a trailer parked in the driveway. Bees swarmed about the lilacs hanging from the corner of the garage. A squirrel inched across the power lines above. Up in a pine tree, a piebald crow nattered as another crow preened its neck.

Had Laura led the others here? They might have come down the ridge to several other streets like this one. Assuming they had survived.

I used a water spigot and splashed cold water on my face and neck. The two pieces of bread I had choked down made me want to gag. I drank some more, but was too restless to sit.

"We should get going."

Marcus and Andie were just starting on their bananas.

"We need a few minutes," Marcus said.

An engine whined from somewhere close. I held my breath and

listened, but the sound died and I couldn't tell which direction it had come from.

I might have been Shadow's target, but now that Andie was officially a player, she was a potential target too.

Andie wiped her fingers on her jeans. "Is anyone home?"

"Not alive. The machines have been through here."

"Maybe that means they've moved on and it's safe."

"It means the game controls the area. The rats and other monsters get stronger."

We left the shade and headed down to the corner. From there, a nearby street led to Redwood Parkway. No way to know if the others had come this way or were waiting for me.

Across the way, a weapon asset collection quest hovered, with a kill five rats quest a block over. And Marcus now had a game marker above his head.

Quest: Escort to Game Exit.

Andie stared at her husband. "What does that mean?"

"It means we're close to getting out of here."

3

A traffic jam blocked the road leading to the last big intersection a couple of miles before the freeway. Cars and trucks had tried to bypass it, but they had crashed or been stopped and now clogged the road in both directions. Some had gone into the dry creek that ran along the south side of the road.

The roaches were thick, running in streams from every vehicle. I stopped counting cocoons after thirty. The bundles of gestating monster machines were tucked in the hedges and tree line. The car decomposition process had an awful organization to it, with the roaches possessing all the tools inside their electric brains to know which nest to contribute their bit of scrap. Within hours or minutes, the eggs would split open and spill out scores of new monsters.

Many of the vehicles still held their victims. These had died listening to their car radios, begging their children to not panic while no doubt suffering their own overwhelming tidal wave of anxiety, trying to get a signal on their devices to communicate with loved ones, all while waiting for the blacked-out road ahead to let more cars through.

Then panic and a mad rush of drivers taking to the shoulders of the road as the assault of rats, vermin, and skeletons overtook them, turning the parkway into a highway of death.

Larger monsters, too, I reasoned with a chill. Lines of rubber led to several vehicles having been forcibly shoved off the asphalt and through a row of fences. Several cars lay on their sides or upside down amongst trampolines, swimming pools, lawn furniture, and back decks.

This was the only way out of the valley. We walked along the side of the street with the fewest obstructions. It meant being out in the open and in the sun. Both Marcus and Andie looked sick and kept their eyes looking forward. They held hands.

"Eddie, this quest?" Andie said. "It keeps prompting me to take it."

"Don't. It will start a game event."

"Can I just take the thingy off my head? It's uncomfortable."

"No. Keep it on. You're better protected that way. If it's off, you might lose your boosted stats."

She waved as if swatting away a fly. "Oh no. I took the quest."

I held up a hand for them to stop. The engine sound again, closer this time. And once again it went quiet before I could pinpoint a direction.

No point sticking around. "Hurry."

A hundred feet later, three skeletons popped up from the wreckage of the cars on either side of us. They pulled themselves free in moments.

I turned. Yelled, "Get down!"

Then the world went black.

4

Combat Log: You've been affected by Blindness.

Prudence. She had been waiting and we walked right into an ambush. Without hesitating, I hit Stealth and touched the nearest car, crouching and feeling my way to its back bumper.

Marcus and Andie were screaming.

If I appeared again, Prudence would get a free shot. I accepted the Escort to Game Exit quest. Marcus popped on my mini-map ten feet away as a quest goal. But the Blindness obscured the skeletons.

Why had Prudence used the skill on me? Why not just take me out?

"Marcus? Andie? Move past me!"

I stood upright with one hand out and walked towards Marcus. Glass broke ahead of me. Metal bent and tore.

Marcus' dot wasn't moving.

"Marcus?" I called. "This way!"

Andie shrieked.

I didn't dare move faster. I took off the glasses and tried to blink away the darkness around my eyes. It only made my game UI vanish. I was truly blind. Glasses back on, I felt my way to the side of a large pickup. Kept moving. I made it to the next vehicle. Listened.

"Marcus? Andie? Where are you?"

A sharp electric snap. Andie's Shoot ability. Her level-one attack would barely scratch a level-four monster. She screamed. There followed the sound of rattling and scraping metal.

"Run!" I cried.

Just ahead of me, Andie howled in pain.

I moved closer with my claws out but something caught my foot and I went down. A hard knee landed on top of me, pinning me to the asphalt.

"Looks like you found your own pets," Prudence said.

"Prudence? Let me up!"

Pain as something sharp lanced into the small of my back. When I tried to move, she pushed the blade deeper. I was helpless.

Andie cried out again before her scream cut off. Metal on stone, and a wet sound. Marcus groaned before a heavy thud impacted against the vehicle closest to me.

Quest Canceled: Escort to Game Exit.

"Oops," Prudence whispered. "That's going to leave a mark. Found new friends so soon? Too bad, too bad."

When I squirmed, she pressed down. Skin, muscles, and bone gave way to the scalpel-sharp weapon, tearing me open. I screamed.

"Tut-tut. Even though I can't see you, you make enough noise. Big mistake. Hey, Shadow! I got him!"

Shadow called out, "Hold him there for me."

Steel footsteps on asphalt moved about nearby. The ambushing skeletons, no doubt. Did she not hear them?

Somehow, the game allowed me to remain stealthed despite having taken damage. But my health bar hadn't moved. She had found me and attacked when I had called out. I realized whatever blade she had struck me with wasn't a game item. Not that it mattered. I was pinned. The pain was indescribable. With a wiggle of the knife, she'd tear me open and I'd die for real, virtual hit points notwithstanding.

"Why are you doing this?" I croaked. "They...just wanted to leave."

She pressed her lips to my ear. "Experience points, dummy. No wonder Shadow ditched you."

"He'll screw you over too."

"Who do you think invited me to the game? Save your strength, Eddie. Shadow wants a piece of you because you hurt his feelings."

Tall silhouettes above us closing in. Had it been seconds or minutes? The blindness was clearing. When the skeleton slashed her, she cried out and tumbled off me. It lurched forward, hitting her again. I crawled away, one arm paralyzed, the pain in my back white-hot agony.

My vision returned.

Shadow was crouched over the bodies of Marcus and Andie. Looting quest or game assets I couldn't see, no doubt. His blood locust and his viper stood guard.

Two skeletons closed in on Prudence. She turned to face them, slashing at the closest of them and taking it down to a fraction of health. No critical hit and she didn't have Fade, apparently. The downside of spending her attribute points on Move.

I needed to escape while I had the chance. That was the smart thing to do. My hands trembled. I swallowed hard and blocked the lingering pain as best I could. While Shadow had two guardians blocking my path, Prudence had her back to me.

I didn't need to perform a flashy move to use my attack. I got to my knees and hit her with Stab, used Fade, nailed her again, and sent her health plummeting. The two skeletons nearly finished her as she fell away from me.

She took down one of them as she retreated. "Shadow! Help!"

The viper dropped on its wheels and burned rubber as it accelerated towards me. It veered past an open car door and extended its blades. I stumbled back, bumping into the remaining skeleton, and flashed the viper with my Misdirect.

It gunned its engine. Its closest knife arm raised to neck height, ready to decapitate.

I braced for impact as it darted past.

Prudence cried out as the blade cut her nearly in half.

Quest Progress: Kill Five Enemy Players (2/5 Complete).

Achievement: Shell Game Short Con. Use Misdirect, Beguile, or Charm to trick an opponent into attacking someone.

A quick Stab and I killed the skeleton. A blue box appeared over Prudence's body. I grabbed it.

Asset: Enemy Token. Enemy tokens may be redeemed at faction headquarters for special armor, weapons, and skill and experience boosts. You must be level five to collect enemy tokens.

Achievement: Go Through Their Pockets; They Won't Need It. Loot a dead player.

The viper pulled to a stop.

"What did you do, Hagar?" Shadow shouted.

His blood locust leaped to the roof of a nearby pickup truck. It shivered, ready to spring at me.

I backed away. "Where's Laura and the others?"

"I was hoping they were still with you. It's a target-rich environment and I got distracted. But then my bug saw you had new friends."

"They just wanted to leave."

"Like you, right? But you took the quest and you led them here. You made them part of our game. What happened is on you. So what's next?"

Was he trying to stall? Worked for me. I needed just a few more seconds for Fade to be ready. At any moment, I felt like I was going to collapse. "I don't know what you mean."

"You don't get to walk away. Not anymore."

"Why? Because I wouldn't play this game your way? Don't lie and tell me you cared about Prudence."

"Every guild needs its officers. We're at the start of something new here."

I stealthed. "I don't want anything to do with it."

The locust jumped. It bounced about, hurling itself through the air where I had been standing. But I was on the move. I made it to the shade above the creek. My strength gave out and I fell into a patch of thistles. The pain from where Prudence had stabbed me ran from my neck down to my legs. Every move made it worse. Weakly, I pulled at my shirt in my effort to dislodge whatever was sticking in me.

A bloody pocketknife fell to the dirt. Prudence had filed the blade to a spikey point. It was my blood on it. My shirt on my back felt sticky. A wave of dizziness almost overwhelmed me.

Shadow lingered over Prudence's body. Then he climbed on his viper and sped off, his blood locust scurrying after him.

Alone. I couldn't draw in enough air. The world swam but I couldn't faint. I crawled to the road. Stood. Looked both ways and listened, but Shadow was gone.

In the back of a wrecked Honda minivan, I found a few bottles of water. I poured one over me and felt a pang of guilt at how good it felt to let the water wash over my face and head. I drank down a second one.

Stale, bath-water warm, plastic-flavored ambrosia.

There was nothing else worth taking. I made myself look at the two bodies of Marcus and Andie. They trusted me to get them out of the game, and I saved them both. But I had failed. In Crimson Gauntlet, there was no instance reset, no retry following a mass resurrection, no replanning session over chat.

Permadeath and hardcore mode, with no room for newbies.

"People," I corrected myself.

Shadow and his minion Prudence had chased us down and murdered them in cold blood.

West and the exit were where I wanted to take Marcus and Andie. Shadow was heading that way to continue his hunt. It wasn't personal. Me, Laura, Carol, Chewie, and Bennett were quest targets. Experience points. Enemy tokens so he could progress in the game.

Judging by the traffic, it's where everyone wanted to go.

A target rich environment, Shadow had called it. I couldn't fault the cold logic of going where the easiest opportunity for a level-up waited.

I followed.

5

The blue curtain rose above the haze in the overpass's direction. It wasn't there one moment, and there the next.

Redwood Parkway had a last big intersection with four gas stations, a Wendy's, a Starbucks, a Peet's Coffee, and a Black Bear Diner.

Beneath the curtain, several Humvees waited.

I had climbed onto the bed of a flatbed truck. The last mile had been clear of vehicles, but here was another bottleneck and gridlock of abandoned vehicles. Monsters moved about beneath the traffic lights. Not rats or vermin but vipers, acid zombies, blood locusts, and level-six creatures the game called Ice Ghouls.

A helicopter buzzed past on the opposite side of the highway.

I was at the city limits. The curtain was the game exit.

Home free, once I got past the pack of monsters. And those were the ones I could see. Nests lay everywhere. Roaches foraged the ground.

I could just make out a few soldiers at the roadblock carrying rifles and wearing taupe camos. They were hopelessly outnumbered. The last stretch of road between the intersection and the overpass appeared clear, as if the game or the military or both had agreed to a no-man's land.

I ducked as something swooped by. A propeller kicked in with a sharp hum, boosting the gliding machine higher.

Harpy (Level Seven).

It appeared content to stay on my side of the curtain.

No sign of Shadow. He could have turned off at several side streets or driveways. I hadn't used Stealth for most of my walk to make time. Had he seen me?

I dropped to the street and crept across a nursery parking lot with my Stealth up.

Two dead women in the rows of bags of mulch, manure, and potting soil. The sliding doors to the inside of the nursery stood open. Several nests inside, with roaches on the counter taking apart a register.

A rolling staircase for restocking the high outdoor shelves stood among the potted palms and roses. I maneuvered it towards the side of the store and climbed to the roof. From there, I had a view of the frontage road.

If I couldn't see my friends, maybe the game would help. I opened my quest tab. Several quests in range. I found the one I was hoping to find.

Quest Available: Escort to Game Exit.

While Laura and Carol were active players, and Chewie had leveled to one before surrendering his glasses, Bennett wasn't a player, just like Marcus. He still needed an escort out, and Crimson Gauntlet wanted me back in action.

Using the quest to guide me, I exited the nursery. A goliath rumbled past, forcing me to duck behind some bushes. Past a medical office, I found a swimming pool supply store. The escort quest directed me to the back lot.

Bennett appeared from behind a shed and a pallet of yellow chlorine crates. "Eddie!"

I joined him and found the others huddled beneath a metal shelter in an outdoor storage space. Pumps, filter tanks, pool robots, and plumbing supplies crowded the area. The roaches had been through, but hadn't bothered with most of the plastic pipes and fittings. A rusty fence had a section peeled away. Beyond lay a hedgerow of blackberry bushes and a dirt trail that led behind an apartment building.

Chewie eyed me listlessly as Carol leaned next to him as they sat on a stack of empty pallets.

Laura's eyes looked sunken. "You made it. What happened in the cemetery?"

I told them about everything: my escape from Shadow and the behemoth, my encounter with Andie and Marcus, and their deaths. I let them know Prudence was out of the game. Laura nodded with the certainty of someone who knew what that meant.

Laura healed me. It felt a little better, but moving and breathing still hurt.

"What happened to you guys?" I asked.

"We took the first fire road down over the hill," Laura said. "It put us at the top of the valley. We waited for a bit, but you'd have no way to know where we were. We stuck to the side streets because we kept hearing monsters on the parkway. We found a drainage ditch and another walking trail and made it here."

"You saw the monsters on the road?" Bennett asked.

I nodded. "Yeah. There's a lot of them at the last intersection. I also saw soldiers on the overpass."

"You could go for help."

"I don't know if they'd come. The game has a line in the sky. The machines don't appear to want to move past it."

"Want to or can't?" Laura asked.

"No way to know. If you saw the intersection, you'd see there's a pack of them, the biggest I've seen. But there's a quest. It involves bringing Bennett across the goal line."

"I see it too but I've been ignoring it. I'm worried about what will happen if we take it."

Carol shook her head in disbelief. "What's the point? I mean, why bother with a quest? We're here. We just have to find a way over the freeway and we're out."

Laura faced her. "We consider it because the game is dangling it in front of us. We ignore it? We're faced with the situation of an obstacle we can't clear. The quest might provide a way through them. It's game logic. But if we take it...."

"Crimson Gauntlet throws us a curveball," I finished. "It has every time. But there's always a way to win."

Chewie scoffed. "Tell that to Kermit. The only reason either of you is considering it is because you're hooked on this bullshit. It's our lives on the line, and you're willing to roll the dice that taking a quest is going to make things easier."

"What do you suggest?" Bennett asked.

"Forget the overpass. We sneak across the frontage road and the highway. If there are army guys on the bridge, there's more beyond that. Screw the game. We're not playing anymore. At least not Carol and me."

"Any chance you can make another vehicle?" Laura asked me.

"Not enough transportation assets. And then I need to find another van or car. How about you? Any loot?"

"We didn't fight much since the cemetery. I have a few more coins, some more armor, and one transportation asset. Five for a turn in?"

"Yeah."

"Then I don't have enough."

I looked out beyond the pool store's parking lot as a goliath barreled past. "Maybe Chewie's right. We don't have to take any quest to get out of here. Getting close to the big pack at the intersection is suicide. I'm guessing the next overpass down the road will be likewise guarded. How's everybody feeling about a run across the freeway?"

6

Two goliaths patrolled the frontage road every four minutes. One was a semi-tractor and the other a school bus. They rarely showed up at the same time, no doubt having a long route, and the timing wasn't exact. But it was rarely less than a 250 count, so I rounded down to keep it safe.

We were gathered by the side gate to the pool store. Only Bennett wasn't with us.

"Where is he?" I whispered.

He hurried from the supply shed where they had been taking shelter. He busied himself with his belt.

The high whine of the school bus engine grew louder.

I waved him down. "Hide. Now!"

He took cover behind the pallet of chemicals. We all ducked.

The school bus had its back windows blown out. Scorch marks marred the front of the vehicle as if its engine had been on fire. A figure leaned on the steering wheel, but the windshield and bi-fold door obscured the body. It had to be a body. It hadn't moved the last three times it had driven past. A fresh wave of revulsion rolled through my guts as I imagined what the driver might have been through during their last moments.

It streaked past, kicking up a swirl of litter scattered about on the street.

"Go. Now. Come on!"

I led them to the concrete barrier with the mesh metal top. An easy climb, but Bennett was limping and taking forever just to make it out of the gate.

We all ducked when the harpy swooped past overhead.

Laura gripped my arm. "It saw us."

"It kept going. We can only hope the game doesn't have the monsters sharing information."

"You think it plays fair?"

I waved Bennett towards us, hoping my impatience wasn't showing. "In its twisted way, yes."

"Then let's hope it doesn't cheat."

I was the first over the barrier, landing on the trash-strewn shoulder of the highway. Abandoned and picked-apart vehicles were scattered in either direction. Haphazardly, I thought at first, but then realized they had been shoved either to the shoulder or against the center divider, as if bulldozed out of the lanes.

Had the army or the game done this?

Laura and Carol were helping Chewie up and over. He moved stiffly, jaw clenched, his face bathed in sweat. Despite the heals to his injuries, he struggled.

A figure dropped onto the shoulder of the highway a couple of hundred yards down in the opposite direction of the overpass. Slight frame, long hair, gray trench coat. Shadow.

I raised a hand to the others. "Hold up. Trouble."

Shadow stood erect and brushed himself off. His game tag burned bright purple and was impossible to miss. His viper appeared next, moving upright and easily clearing the barrier. It dropped onto its tires and was once again a motorcycle. The blood locust followed and bounced to the handlebars.

The engine revved even before Shadow mounted the bike and sped towards me.

"Everyone back over!"

I shoved Chewie back over and into the arms of Carol and Laura before joining them. We got Bennett turned around and hobbled back across the street and through the side gate to the pool store property.

Laura pushed the back door to the store open. "In here. I found it open when we checked earlier."

We were inside and hiding behind a hot tub filled with water. A display stand had brochures and proclaimed the benefits of an ozone system.

"Shadow's here with his pets," I said.

"Did he see you?"

"Yeah. Let's hope he missed us ducking in here."

Laura's voice took on an edge. "We can take him, can't we?"

"I don't know. I'd rather lose him."

"How long can we wait him out?"

"The goliaths aren't his friends. He'll have to deal with them."

It didn't take long before the viper's engine whined from outside before cutting out. Shadow appeared outside at the mouth of the parking lot, straddling his viper while leaning on the handlebars. The blood roach was nowhere in sight.

Laura leaned on my shoulder to look. "It's like he's asking for it. Let's oblige him."

"He's not stupid. He's got to have a play."

"You guys inside?" Shadow called. "It's been a long run getting here. I thought we could bury the hatchet. You want out of the game, the exit's here. We go together. I'll get you out safe."

"He can't be serious," I whispered.

A whirr and a thump as Shadow's blood locust slammed against the store window. Carol cried out as the big bug climbed along the awning.

I activated Stealth. "He's one level higher than me. If I open up on him, you come out and get ready to heal your ass off."

"You sure?"

"We can't wait around forever. He's here. We fight."

Eddie Rush's First Rule of Winning? Start the encounter when you're ready before someone in the raid has to go for a bio break.

"What do you want us to do?" Bennett asked.

"Hide." I crossed the showroom, slipped outside through the door, and stalked towards him.

Shadow smirked. He hadn't moved from his bike. "There you are, Hagar. Game won't let me see you, but that door didn't open on its own. No chit-chat? Straight to duel-sies?"

The roach was on the roof now. Its wings and legs clicked and snapped. I'd have to dodge it, the viper, and Shadow. But Shadow's class relied on Charisma. I doubted he had put a single point in health. I might get three Stabs off before his pets could take me down, and it would be over.

Laura would get a few heals in and we'd win.

I approached his left flank so my back wouldn't be exposed to the locust.

Was I ready to do this? Kill him? I conjured the image of Kermit. Bennett's wife Kirsten. Andie and Marcus. How many others had he slain? Yet my mouth was dry and I couldn't get enough air.

Five more steps and he'd be in range.

A cold prickling brushed my neck. Not nerves. As if an icy breeze washed over me. I suppressed a shiver.

Before I could move closer, Shadow's bike raced in reverse.

Shadow spread his hands. "Too slow, buddy." Twin balls of green energy formed in his palms.

The phlegmy gurgle next to me made me jump as an **Ice Ghoul (Level Six)** materialized next to me. A stretched and misshapen scarecrow of a human form made of mesh, rebar, and gears. Its back legs dragged behind it as if unable to hold its form upright. Torn clothes, rags, and trash were stuffed into its limbs. It caught me with a meaty swap of its oversized hand.

I was knocked against the fence bordering the lot. Felt the world go bleary. Tasted copper on my tongue. Stealth had broken, but I hadn't attacked. What was going on?

"Eddie, Eddie, Eddie. I made a new friend I wanted you to meet. I know you're wondering how it is I have three pets." He patted the viper. "I turned Wheels, here, into my mount. Tamed one of these guys to see what they can do. 'See Invisible' is a nifty trick when you're up against a Hellion."

When the blood locust landed next to me, I hit it with Stab. **Critical Hit!** The blow took it halfway down. The ice ghoul leaped on top of me. It was about to slam my head to paste when I cued Misdirect. The hammer blow crushed the blood locust. The locust popped, its pieces scattering everywhere.

Laura sprang from the front door. Hit me with a Heal before punching the ghoul. It spun on her as Shadow hit her with both blasts. She cried out as her back erupted in twin plumes of smoking flesh. I stepped back and hit Fade. My instant ambush took the ghoul down to a quarter of its health. Laura swung and missed and I finished it with a final Stab.

A squishy monster.

Another acid glob struck Laura. Her health bar was melting away.

I limped ahead of her towards Shadow. "Get inside!"

She made it to the door, where she collapsed.

Shadow backed up further along the street and was doing something with his hands. "I learned a few new tricks. I thought I could practice them on you."

Chewie and Carol were dragging Laura inside.

I sprinted towards him before he could conjure another bolt. I had to end it while his pets were dead. From down the frontage road, the school bus was coming. Did he not hear it?

He flung a game asset on the ground before making a tight turn and pulling away. Out of combat range. I used Stealth and stayed put. What was the purple hockey puck he had dropped?

He stopped the viper fifty feet away and was staring intently as the Goliath sped closer. But then it came to a rapid stop in front of me and on top of the purple puck. The sudden braking caused the dead driver to lean forward against the steering wheel.

My interface identified the item. **Monster Bait.**

Shadow hurled a second bait puck, which landed at my feet.

You have been afflicted with Monster Bait!

The goliath's engine revved. The thing did a five-point turn in the narrow lane and rolled into the lot. I scampered away, retreating to the shed. It kept coming. Either it was too high of a level for my Stealth to work, or the Monster Bait debuff overrode it. The bait must have been a new skill or a reward for the Taunt the Behemoth quest.

The goliath stopped next to the pallet of chemicals. Unlike the transforming monster we fought at the trailer park, this one didn't change its physical shape. What it did was sprout brilliant blue tentacles the size of firehoses from every broken window.

The limbs thrust towards me as I ducked around the back of the shed. The arms bent the aluminum shed as if it were cardboard and crashed through the branches of a tree encroaching from a neighboring property before slamming down at me. I made it through the gap in the fence as the chain links and one of the posts were crushed. I tumbled into the creek. Thorns and brambles scratched and tore at me, snagging clothes and hair and skin.

I couldn't see what the goliath was doing, but the shed was now the object of its fury. It was tearing it to pieces. I pulled sections of berry bush off me as I made it to the bed of the dry creek. My heart was hammering and my head rang. I touched my scalp and found I was bleeding.

I didn't know what to do. Low on health. The monster was too powerful. Judging by the engine's sound, it was moving, but not far. Glass shattered. It was attacking the store.

You are no longer afflicted with Monster Bait.

Shadow must have switched targets. Or the goliath had caught a whiff of the others.

There was no easy place to climb out of the creek. I used the exposed roots of a bay tree. My arms were rubber and I fell. I tried again and made it to the narrow trail, only to collapse. I couldn't catch my breath.

Run. It was the only smart thing to do.

Someone was shouting. A second round of shattering glass and tearing metal drowned them out. The pool store was being ripped apart.

I made it to the cut in the fence, almost forgetting to Stealth.

The behemoth had smashed its way into the showroom. It backed partway out before sending in its tentacles. Wood splintered. A scream followed.

Attacking it would be suicide. One more hit and I was done. If I even got close to the thing, it would see me.

Shadow was still on the street. He had come closer. He hurled another bait ball into the pool store parking lot behind the goliath. It backed up on top of it. Its tentacles retracted, its engine idled, and there followed a slathering, smacking sound as if it were eating.

"Send out Eddie, send out Laura, and the rest of you run free," Shadow called. "Or your new friend tears the place down around you."

Had he thought I went inside?

Eddie Rush's First Rule of Winning? If your opponent is making a mistake, don't correct them.

It was my mistake to make. There'd be no winning here. Shadow was at full strength. I couldn't take him down alone. And with the goliath nearby, I couldn't even get close to him.

The school bus continued to busy itself with its virtual chew toy, judging by the sounds. Shadow tossed it another one.

"Shadow?" a voice called from the store. "It's Bennett. We surrender. There's no reason to do this. Laura's hurt already."

"Where's Eddie?"

"He's not here."

"Don't lie to me, Ben. I'll know. Of course, there's another way we can do this. You come out to me. I'll bring you into the game. You'll be strong."

Something clattered from inside the wrecked storefront. Bennett must have knocked something over. The goliath stirred, its tentacles reaching towards the sound. Shadow threw another bait ball into the far end of the lot near a disassembled pool service truck. The goliath chased it down, drove on top of it, and was once again absorbed in its delicacy. Did Shadow have unlimited monster treats?

"You see, Ben? We can be masters here. You won't ever have to run from anything or anyone. You don't have to be weak. I'll show you how."

I snuck forward. Gambled that if the goliath was ignoring Bennett, it would ignore me.

Bennett stepped to the breach in the store where the window and door used to be. Was he considering the offer?

"Go back inside," I hissed. "And don't look at me. Shadow can't see me."

"Laura's hurt pretty bad," he whispered back. "We can't move her."

Shadow had a corrosive bolt rolling across his hand and fingers like a magician with a coin. "Limited time offer. What's it going to be?"

"Ask Shadow why he's offering this now," I whispered. "Will he let Laura and the others go if you stay with him? And what class would he recommend?"

"I get it, I get it. Keep him talking."

Shadow rolled his bike up to the lip of the parking lot. "Oh, Ben? What's your answer?"

Bennett sounded out of breath. "How do I know you don't want me to just come out where your machine can grab me?"

"The machine, as you can see, is busy. And alas, it's not mine. Come here, and I'll give you your own game rig. That missing finger and all your aches and pains will go away, just like *that*." He snapped his fingers. It was more of a *thib* of fingers rubbing together. "Health potions are a thing now."

"I don't want any of them to get hurt."

"You always were a softy. No stomach for PvP? Doesn't matter. This is a limited time offer."

During their exchange, I walked towards Shadow. He was in range. I knew I could hit him with a double tap before he could react, but at the moment he might take me down with a sneeze.

His eyes darted about as if looking for me.

"We're so close to getting out of here," Bennett said.

"The game's not done with any of us. There'll be no quitting."

"Hmm. What class do you suggest? You seem pretty powerful."

The goliath revved its engine. The monster bait was gone.

Shadow backed up the viper. "Chit-chat's over, Ben. You could have made it." The viper revved as it turned, before racing away.

"Get to cover!" I called as I ran out of the parking lot.

I took the sidewalk and hurried through the front hedges of the neighboring property when the goliath rolled onto the street. It paused, as if considering which way to go. Sweat stung my eyes. Had it seen me? But it turned the opposite way down the frontage road and rumbled off, resuming its patrol as if its encounter with us hadn't happened.

No time to ponder what role it played in the game. Not chasing down players, it seemed.

And Shadow? He was gone, but he'd be back. He had been heading for the last intersection. More monsters, new pets, and the hunt would continue.

Ignoring the cramp in my side, my aching ankle and myriad injuries, along with pains in parts of my body not properly exercised since my physical education class in my second year of high school, I went after him.

7

Why tame one ice ghoul when you can have two?

Shadow lured the grotesques away from the pack one at a time. They slithered towards him, their fingers digging into the street as they hauled themselves along. Intent on murder until Shadow's Hacker-class skill switched their label from monster orange to purple.

They were his now, and they both vanished from sight.

Two invisible pets, and they'd have no problem breaking into the pool supply store's back office. With Laura down, two ghouls were more than I could handle. And with their cloaking skill, Shadow had the perfect defense against my class.

He drove beneath a tree and appeared to be busy on his interface.

I could leave. Cross the overpass and make it to safety. The soldiers could send help. But whatever border they were manning as defined by the curtain bisecting the highway, the military appeared content to keep on their side.

Which meant they wouldn't help.

Eddie Rush's First Rule of Winning? Do your job. Everyone's counting on you not to suck.

Shadow finished up with whatever he was doing and drove slowly down the frontage road.

My interface had enough tabs to be distracting. I had gotten good at ignoring them. Combat log, class abilities and stats, inventory, quests, notifications. So far, nothing I couldn't keep track of.

No new skills to bring to bear, no quests I hadn't seen, and the combat log was a sad list of attacks that hadn't landed hard enough to make a difference. If I only had a day to level up.

No cool toys in my virtual backpack, just my transportation item.

Civilian vehicle. Would you like to summon your ride?

I didn't know what that meant, but I hit yes.

A dot appeared as my mini-map zoomed out to accommodate a wider view. A friendly looking dot ambled my way from the direction of the cemetery. It was much closer than where I had left it. I wasn't sure how it was possible, considering the mimic's condition, wrecked, with two flat tires. Had the game directed it to keep pace with me? I wondered how it would get past all the monsters. But the dot never stopped as it headed my way.

What had been an overland trek and brutal hike for me was only a few miles on surface streets. The dot was speeding up. I wasn't sure what this meant. My ride, even functional, wasn't going to save the others from Shadow.

The goliath appeared. The charred school bus drove up from the direction of the pool supply store and took a turn just before the intersection. Hopefully, it had caused Shadow to take cover, delaying him.

The dot on the mini-map slowed. I wanted to crawl out of my skin in frustration as the vehicle got closer, took a turn, and appeared to be heading away again. But then it course corrected. It was heading straight for the monster-infested intersection. I'd need to dismiss it unless I wanted a tidal wave of killer machines on top of me.

Do you wish to remove Civilian Vehicle from your inventory?

I hesitated. It was the one game asset I hadn't accounted for in contemplating my fight with Shadow.

My mimic van appeared. It looked worse than before, with its shredded top smashed in and both front doors dented. Somehow, it had replaced its flat front tire, but the back tire flopped and dragged noisily as it slalomed through the pacing monsters. It nearly clipped an acid zombie.

The monsters paid it no mind.

My corner was clear. I stepped off the curb and hailed it as if the mimic were a ride share. Felt instantly stupid. The driver's door wouldn't open. The side slider obliged with a delighted squeal from the mimic's sound system, but only halfway. Enough to slip inside. Still no driver's seat, so I kneeled behind the wheel.

"Go."

I didn't like my plan. Couldn't think of a better one. I made a 180-degree turn and drove straight at the pack of monsters. Ran over a Blood Locust. Didn't kill it, judging by the irritable chitter that erupted from beneath the tires as we bounced over it.

Achievement: Beep! Beep! Run Over a monster with a vehicle!

The mimic tittered.

If my shape-shifting van hadn't aggroed the pack before, it would now with me inside it. I had every monsters' attention within thirty yards.

The whole intersection faced me. Zombies, vipers, and ghouls slashed, spat, and stabbed at the van as I sped past in a wide arc, driving up onto a curb and making a hard turn onto the frontage road. At least two locusts had leaped on top of the roof. We left the acid zombies behind, but not before they rained down sizzling blobs of corrosive goo. A viper raced along on either side. One tore a gash into the van. The other slammed it and nearly knocked the steering wheel from my grip.

The mimic didn't have a health bar, but the steering column wobbled precariously. A shudder ran through the floor and a moan erupted from the engine.

"Drive. Drive faster. Come on, come on, come on!"

I cranked the wheel and took us onto the sidewalk. The vipers weren't fast enough to correct, and they fell behind. The locusts above me worked in concert as they pried at the metal above me. They must have missed the fact they could have climbed in through the missing windshield.

When the first one stuck its head into the van, I rose and hit it with a Stab. It blew apart. But there were three more outside. The vipers drove through the landscaping behind me as we bounced down the curb and back onto the street.

The pool store lay ahead.

More sections of roof tore away as the locusts cut an even larger hole above the rear cargo space. The mimic bawled like a toddler with a scraped knee.

A locust dropped in behind me. It shivered in anticipation of carving me to pieces.

The vehicle shuddered and felt like it was about to fall to pieces as I made a wide turn and took us into the parking lot without slowing. The locust tumbled against the wall of the van.

Shadow stood next to his bike near the store entrance. One of the ice ghouls was visible inside.

Even as I was about to get torn to pieces by blood locusts and vipers and probably die in a crash as my dying mimic raced for him, it was all worth it just for the look on Shadow's face.

8

Stop me if you've heard this one. It's controversial.

I've never posted it before because it would only cause a flame war. Plus, I believed our raiding guild needed to learn the fights as intended.

But every now and again, a game will throw you a bone in the guise of a glitch or exploit.

Eddie Rush's First Rule of Winning (unpublished)?

Use every advantage you have, even if it breaks the game.

Achievement: Pied Piper. Get over five monsters on your tail.

Crimson Gauntlet didn't have a programed snap-back distance on the monsters. Something I had noticed back when fighting the first rats around the diner. Every game in recent history included a point-of-return so a player couldn't round up a map full of nasties and drag them over to a player starting area, an auction house, or an enemy city.

I saw the realization in Shadow's expression a split-second before the mimic plowed into his parked viper. He dove aside at the last moment. The viper was crushed against the wall and we came to a jarring stop. I was thrown into the dash and smacked my forehead.

The mimic buckled and sagged. It let out a pained sigh.

I caught a lucky critical hit and killed the locust inside the van before throwing the slider open to my ruined vehicle.

Shadow was extricating himself from a collapsed stack of empty chlorine cases. His hair hung over his face. His mouth twisted into a snarl as corrosive globs formed in his hands.

"Is this taking the game serious enough?" I said.

Then I used Fade and vanished.

The two vipers pursuing me raced into the parking lot. Shadow nailed one with a bolt. It screeched before deploying blades and gunning straight at him. The second viper was hot on its tail. Three zombies loped along after them. Shadow launched blast after blast, using the front of the van as cover from being run over. He was surrounded.

I circled the back of the van, careful not to bump into any of the zombies.

The rest of the mob of creatures I had picked up from the intersection appeared disinterested. I was no longer in combat with them now that I was invisible. They stopped in the middle of the street before beginning their trek back towards the intersection.

Griefing Action. Chaos Level: +1.

So the game didn't like me dragging monsters onto other players. Tough.

I wanted to hit Shadow while he was busy, but I couldn't risk engaging him with my Fade timer out.

Shadow retreated into the ruins of the showroom as the vipers, locusts, and zombies swiped and clawed at him. Then his ghouls attacked. One delivered a haymaker to an already-hurt viper and killed it, while the other tore a zombie to pieces.

One viper, two locusts, and two zombies left.

I hurried around them, ducking under part of the collapsed ceiling as I headed for the back. A solid door stood beyond a service center littered with plastic parts belonging to several dismantled automatic pool cleaners and robots.

I pounded on the door. "Bennett? Carol? It's Eddie!"

Laura opened the door and pulled me inside. "What's going on out there?"

"You're...alive?"

"Carol looted a health potion and used it on me. What happened to you?"

"No time to explain. Shadow's busy for the moment. We need to leave."

No one argued. The back of the store comprised a break room, billing office, manager's office, and bathroom. There was a rear exit, but the door was bent inward and the fanny bar didn't work.

We hurried into the showroom and stayed low behind the service counter. Shadow was still up and fighting, judging by the noise.

A fire door led to the alley along the side of the building. Here was the gate that led to the street.

Carol cracked it open. "We couldn't risk leaving with Shadow and the goliath around."

I edged past her and looked both ways. "Let me go first."

The goliath was coming. We stayed hidden as it chugged past.

Rending metal and heavy thuds reverberated from the opposite side of the store. The pit in my stomach grew. Could Shadow survive? I wanted to go back and help finish him. But it would mean once again abandoning the others.

"What are we waiting for?" Chewie asked.

"Over the barrier," I said.

Our group didn't move fast. Bennett remained the slowest, but Laura was limping along despite having her health restored. We all helped shove Bennett over before making the climb. Laura failed her first pull up.

I gave her an awkward push on the rump. "I thought you healed yourself up after taking the potion."

Laura pulled her legs over the highway wall one at a time. "The game can't fix everything."

We were back on the shoulder of the freeway. Carol and Chewie led Bennett along by his arms. We were moving too slowly and had barely made it over the wall. The divider between the north- and southbound lanes was higher and the small-loop mesh fence on top of it had no fingerholds. No way we'd clear it.

Too quiet. The fight at the pool shop was over. A gnawing queasiness squeezed my gut.

"This way." I led them towards the closest on-ramp and the overpass.

The pack of mobs had stuck to the intersection and hadn't been on the ramps leading on and off the highway. We'd be exposed. Couldn't be helped. Hopefully, we'd be out of range and could get off the highway before anything big happened upon us.

Motion behind us. I had my Stealth up again and waved the others forward.

Shadow dropped to the shoulder of the highway. A single ice ghoul flopped onto the asphalt next to him. It reared up and howled. The yowl was a cross between a horse whinny and a wolf's bay. It disappeared.

"Hurry. We need to hurry."

Bennett stumbled. One of his shoes had lost its laces. Carol and

Chewie did their best, but he was moving slower than ever. We'd never make it. I was out of tricks. I had no way of knowing if Shadow had his second ghoul. One was bad enough. Would he send it in for an attack or hold it in reserve with the hope I'd be stupid enough to face him?

My mimic's dot remained blacked out.

Not a lot of choices.

I pulled up the quest tracker. One still hung directly over Bennett.

Quest: Escort to Game Exit.

This time, I accepted it.

"I'm okay," Bennett said as I took over for Chewie.

I didn't let go. "We can't slow down."

Yet we did. Some of it was Bennet's flagging strength. Some of it was me. If Chewie, Carol, and Laura could make it up the on-ramp and get onto the overpass, at least some of us might survive. Doubts raced in my mind. Accepting the quest might only have killed us faster. Getting the timing right meant being lucky.

Besides the occasional critical hit, my luck hadn't been noticeable, despite it being part of a Hellion's class description. Trusting luck got smacked in the face by Eddie Rush's First Rule of Winning. Skill trumps blind chance every time.

Shadow was catching up with us at a steady run.

I was surprised when Bennett jerked his arm away from me.

He turned to face Shadow. "Shadow? We surrender! I'm not in the game. Leave us alone!"

Shadow slowed to a march, a Corrosive Blast prepped. He'd be in range in moments and didn't appear interested in chit-chat.

Ahead of us, the others had stopped and were watching us. Laura headed back.

Chewie tugged at Carol. "Come on!"

No more threats. No more flourishes. No more showing off. Shadow had murder in his eyes as he launched a bolt straight at us.

I cast Misdirect, and the bolt veered, striking the air next to Bennett. Not air. A ghoul howled as it materialized a few feet from us. I was visible too, having just engaged in a hostile action against an enemy player. No choice. I laid into the thing with a Stab, dazing it. I hit Fade, slashed it again, and took it down to a fraction of its health.

It retreated towards its master as the Corrosive Blast melted away the last of its health before dissipating. But just before it hit zero, the monster's health bar moved upward.

Shadow was healing, and it appeared to require all his attention.

I got Bennett moving. "He's distracted. Come on!"

Laura met us at the foot of the on-ramp. I handed Bennett off to her so I could go after Shadow. But just up the incline, Chewie and Carol had stopped.

"Why are you stopping? What's wrong?"

I didn't see them before they were on us. Two level-six acid zombies lumbered up from beneath the overpass. They had used the cover of a mangled Cal-Trans street sweeper to get close. We all backed up.

Carol raised a palm as she prepared her Shoot skill. "Where did they come from?"

"Did you start a quest?" Laura asked.

"God damn it, Eddie!" Chewie said through clenched teeth.

I stopped retreating. "Carol? Chewie? Get Bennett out of here. Laura, I need you for this. Go straight at them. We both hit the one on the left. I attack first."

Shadow was watching us. I didn't have time to check his ghoul's health bar in my UI, but I guessed it was at full strength.

The zombies were veering towards Laura.

I had Stealth up and nailed the left one, ripping across its midsection and taking off a sizable chunk of its health. Laura socked the thing, her fist pulsing. It didn't die. Both zombies swiped at me. One hit me, sending me sprawling and leaving a damage-over-time acid burn across my shoulder blades that left my flesh blistering. The second zombie missed, but with a sudden burst of uncharacteristic speed, shambled past us.

Before Laura could react, the remaining zombie swatted her and sent her off-balance.

The others had barely moved. Carol screamed as she unleashed her Shoot skill. It didn't scratch the incoming monster.

Our zombie pounded on Laura. Only her big Health score saved her as she tried to ward off the blows. I was up and I drove my claws into it. It fell to pieces.

Laura grabbed me and her hand flashed. It felt like heaven as the acid wound stopped burning. But we couldn't wait. The second zombie was about to overtake Bennett. He was the quest target.

Carol kept her distance, using her level-one Shoot over and over. I ran after the thing. Another good hit, and it might kill me. Fade wasn't ready. The zombie was about to swipe at Bennett, who was cowering in front of it. I fired off Misdirect. The zombie swung and hit the ground. It groaned sorrowfully as I pulled Bennett away from it. Laura got in front of the creature, and was swatted aside a moment later.

She bought us seconds, enough to get Bennett hobbling beside me as we hurried up the on-ramp towards the overpass. The zombie followed. But once again, Bennett drooped.

I fired off my weak-as-a-moist-towelette Shoot at the zombie. "Come on, Ben. Don't stop!"

Carol closed in on the monster's back, blasting it over and over. The thing had been ignoring her, but it caught her with a surprise blow that took down almost all of her health. Level six versus level one. Laura taunted the thing off her, her hands waving in the zombie's face as she shouted.

I left Bennett behind and rushed towards them. My Fade was ready. I vanished and lunged at the thing. Critical hit, but it didn't die. It switched targets again, slashing at me. I had its undivided attention. It staggered at me as I backpedaled.

Laura slipped away and helped Chewie with Carol. Carol burned from the zombie acid. Laura healed her as they ran to Bennett. They moved as one away from me, and just in time. Shadow drew closer. He was in range again. I kept the zombie between me and him, using it as cover. It clawed at me. Dexterity or luck, you pick, but it missed twice.

"You think I'm going to help you, Hagar? Trying to get me to take the quest?"

"We were on the same team once."

"The ship's sailed. You had a good run. But you're too many experience points to let slip away."

I almost backed into the guardrail. The zombie kept looking away from me, as if I had lost its attention. I used Shoot and it once again focused on me as I led it up the on-ramp. Fade and Misdirect were taking an eternity to finish their cooldown. I kept just outside of the zombie's melee range.

Shadow followed us, his ice ghoul on his heels. "Enough fun." With a motion of his hands, he got the zombie to spin and face him. The monster snorted and sniffed. Its name tag went purple.

Acid Zombie (Level Six). Player Shadow's Pet.

He sent his ghoul after me. The two monsters charged as Shadow kept his distance. Just before it made it to striking range, the ghoul vanished. A quick glance behind me confirmed the others were almost at the top of the on-ramp.

My Fade popped. I activated it.

"Them or me, Shadow?" I said, as I disappeared.

9

I headed straight for him.

Each scrape of my shoe was a giveaway. But he didn't appear to hear me coming. If he had recalled his ghoul, I would only have a moment before I was torn to pieces. Shadow's health was at 60%. No self-heal, and the pack of monsters had taken their toll.

When Carol screamed, I realized I had miscalculated. Shadow wasn't holding the ghoul back; it had charged forward stealthed and was attacking them.

I hit Shadow with a slash across his face. The blow staggered him and sent him reeling. My second Stab missed as he stumbled away from me. A Corrosive Blast almost took my head off.

Disengage? Hide? Wait for Fade? But judging by the screams, I didn't have time.

I ran straight at him, my fists back, my virtual claws up.

For the first time in maybe ever, Shadow looked scared. He flung a blob of green I couldn't dodge. It clung to my arm, melting skin. He didn't have time for another as I tore into him. I lost track of what skill I was using. Stabbing, punching, driving my fists down over and over, I ignored the pain exploding from my split knuckles. Tears burned down my cheeks. I blubbered and laughed and cursed, knowing at any second he'd sear the last sliver of my health from me, or his zombie would grab me and tear me in two.

My flurry of blows weakened as I realized Shadow was no longer moving.

Experience earned, my combat log said.

Quest Progress: Kill Five Enemy Players (3/5 Complete).

Achievement: Can I Borrow Your Slingshot? Take down a higher-level player.

His purple label vanished. All that was left of him lay before me in a bloodied heap. My knees barely supported me as I rose. The zombie was gone. So was the ghoul at the top of the on-ramp. As dies the Hacker, so go their pets.

Everything hurt. The burns on my skin were raw wounds even as I willed myself to believe the injuries were make-believe. My virtual claws had meat clinging to them.

"Eddie, get up here!" Laura called.

What now? I could barely walk. If anything jumped me, I was toast. I needed a heal, but Laura was kneeling over someone. I forced myself to move faster.

It was Carol. She lay sprawled against the curb. She clutched her throat and looked pale. Chewie had his hands on the wound and was trying to staunch the flow of blood.

He turned towards the soldiers at the Humvee. "Help us! Why won't you help us?!"

They remained in place halfway across the overpass.

"Why won't they come?" Bennett asked.

"Because the game won't let them," I said. "Some kind of truce. A no-man's land. We have to go to them."

Somehow, I found the strength to help Chewie pick up his wife. She nearly slipped from our hands as we brought her towards the soldiers. Bennett and Laura did their best to help.

"Help us!" I cried. "She's dying!"

Bennett still had the quest target on him. Moving into the blue curtain triggered something.

Quest Complete. Escort to Game Exit.

I was now…

Level Six

1

I couldn't clear my UI fast enough.

Still, I was careful not to make any hasty decisions. We were about to get out of the game, yet I wanted to make sure I'd be as strong as possible in case of any curveballs. There were always curveballs.

My head ached too much to remember whether I had a rule covering this.

Carol had fallen limp in our arms. Laura was right behind us, as Bennett needed her help again.

Game Exit.

The blue letter banner hung across the opposite end of the overpass. We were inside the curtain, but it covered the width of the highway.

As Chewie and I carried Carol towards the soldiers, they climbed into their Humvee and raced away. They pulled to a stop in the intersection past the game exit.

Chewie faltered. "Where are they going?"

Laura caught up with us. "Wait, let me help. My Heal is up again."

I had most of Carol's weight on me. I kept checking behind us to make sure there wasn't a ghoul, a behemoth, or a revived Shadow bearing down on us. The street was empty all the way back to the intersection.

Laura kept a glowing hand on Carol as we continued to approach the exit. "We're almost there. I have you. Stay awake, Carol."

I couldn't see whether the bleeding stopped. Carol's health bar went up a smidge to 8% but she remained unconscious.

"Why aren't they helping?" Bennett asked.

I was curious too. "It doesn't matter. We're almost there."

Warning! No Crimson Gauntlet Players Past This Point!

I caught Laura's eye.

"I see it too," she said.

Ten yards away from the exit. Carol coughed and sputtered. Laura hit her with another Heal. She was up to 15%.

Warning! Players May Not Leave Game Area!

"Honey, stop," Carol said to Chewie.

"We're close. It's okay, baby. The soldiers will help us. Hey! We need a hand! She's hurt!"

"No, you don't understand. The game wants us to not cross the line."

"What line? We're going to get you to a hospital, baby. They're going to fix you."

Final Warning! Players Exiting Game Risk Danger of Death!

"Put me down," Carol said.

I placed her feet on the ground. Unsteady, but she had strength in her legs. The ragged laceration on her throat still oozed, but somehow Laura's heals had stopped the worst of the bleeding.

Chewie still had an arm around her. "If you're not going to help, get out of our way, Eddie."

"We need to understand what the game wants from us before we leave."

"There's nothing left for us to know. The monsters are gone; this is our chance. I'm not waiting around for you to find a new way to summon more of those machines. Yeah, that's right. I know you started your stupid quest. That's what summoned those last two monsters. You almost killed Carol."

"You know Shadow was coming for us. I needed to take the chance that the monsters the quest would drop on us would get in his way. It was a risk we had to take."

"You risked our lives on a hunch!"

Laura gave Carol another Heal. "Eddie's been trying to get us through this in one piece."

"And here you are defending him, like being an officer of a gaming guild is a real thing and has any bearing on anything! Keep your guild, keep your game. We're done. Carol and I quit. Do you hear me, Janus? We quit, Carol and I. We're walking out of here."

He brushed past me and assisted Carol towards the waiting soldiers. None of them had moved. One spoke on a large walkie-talkie.

"We need to stop them," I said. "The game hasn't lied to us yet. Chewie, Carol, wait."

I caught up with them and touched Chewie's shoulder. He let go of his wife and punched me. The blow caught me in the jaw and I fell.

Chewie stood over me. He shook the hand he had hit me with. He looked like he was about to say something. Definitely would have knocked me down again if I had tried to rise.

Carol stared at him in disbelief and stepped back. She was beneath the exit when she cried out. Hands to her belly, she doubled over.

When Chewie moved to help her, I tackled him. "Don't. You can't go to her."

"Let go of me, Eddie! Carol? Carol? Hey! Help! Help!"

Carol screamed. Eyes wide with fear, she looked at Chewie and then at the soldiers before falling to her knees. A stream of black vomit jetted from her mouth.

Chewie continued to struggle against me. "What's happening? What's happening?"

Laura rushed forward, but stopped just before her. She tried to heal. It did nothing.

"You can't go to her," I said to Chewie. "You'll die, too."

With a groan, Carol collapsed onto the concrete. When Laura inched towards her, I let go of Chewie and ran to her.

My game warning turned yellow, the font double-sized and flashing.

Return to Game Now!

"Let me try to help bring her back to this side," Laura said.

She pulled us a step closer. The game warning strobed white.

Talons tore at my insides. An intense pressure bore down on my skull. My brain was swelling like a balloon and my teeth were about to explode inside my mouth. Laura cried out. I got us back a few feet and the pain subsided.

We both collapsed.

Chewie was sitting up now. He stared at Carol, his jaw trembling. When he looked at us—at me—an expression that carried an awful understanding crossed his face.

Carol wasn't moving, a thick pool of red growing beneath her.

I watched in disbelief as Bennett walked past us. He crossed the threshold and kneeled next to Carol. His body trembled as he wept. The soldiers finally approached. One directed Bennett towards the Humvee.

We couldn't get closer without risking the game killing us. What had Crimson Gauntlet done to our bodies? Whatever particles or magic we could bend to our will when we used our skills were now keeping us prisoner.

Only Bennett could leave, having never played.

A second soldier, a redheaded man who looked barely twenty, helped him away. Bennett didn't look back. Two more came with a stretcher for Carol. A second Humvee approached and parked behind the first. More soldiers piled out. The driver kept the engine idling.

The level-seven harpy buzzed past above the opposite side of the highway.

"What are we supposed to do?" Laura asked.

I was at a loss for words. A soldier draped a blanket over Carol.

My interface was a crowded mess. Level-up messages, new quests, and game assets both near and far competed for my attention. Laura was level four now. But nothing told me what action we were supposed to take in order to leave.

I recalled a message when I hit level five. *Crimson Gauntlet is watching you closely now.* I felt like I was going to puke. The game had us and wasn't letting go. The exit was the game's first lie.

My eyes burned as I watched them take Carol away. Chewie crawled forward towards the exit. I didn't have the strength to stop him. But he stopped when he picked something up. The game glasses. Carol had dropped them.

The ginger-headed soldier approached him. "Sir, you need to step back for your own safety."

Chewie gestured helplessly. "Why wouldn't you help her?"

"I'm sorry for your loss. But we need you all to head for the opposite side of the overpass."

"Why can't we leave?" Laura asked.

He didn't answer. A second soldier approached, his rifle cradled, his finger resting on the trigger guard.

I joined Chewie and Laura. "You didn't do anything when those machines attacked. You're just sitting here with your weapons and tanks and didn't lift a finger."

"We're instructing the three of you to return to the opposite side of the highway."

"Or what? You going to shoot us? At least tell us what's happening. Why are you cooperating with Crimson Gauntlet?"

He didn't appear fazed by the accusation. "We have our instructions. This is a public health crisis, and it's for your own good."

Laura put a hand on me. She led Chewie and me away from the curtain and back to the opposite side of the overpass. My legs were jelly. We were all dragging and in no condition to navigate the streets of Bell Park, avoiding monsters and quests in order to find a safe place to take shelter.

There we stopped when Chewie threw her arm off and sat on the edge of the sidewalk.

I sat next to him. "Chewie, I'm sorry."

"Chewie?" Laura said.

"Stop calling me that. You let her die. You both did."

"That's not fair. We were all trying to get out of here. But now we have to tell people what's happening to us. We can't let them get away with this."

He stared at the glasses. "I should have been home. She would never have opened the box and put them on."

"We couldn't have known what would happen," I said.

"You say that like you mean it. But look at you. You're enjoying this, aren't you? World's gone to pieces and you're having a ball. Who cares that it killed Carol? And how many other people died for your wet dream to come true?"

He inspected the glasses before putting them on.

2

Chewie stared at his hand as if trying to understand what he was seeing. Dark lines underscored his eyes. His shirt was torn and bloodied, both his own and Carol's. His eyes moved back and forth as he read.

"Level one. Such bullshit."

"Let me refresh you on the interface," I said. "To keep things simple, dismiss the quest tracker—"

He brought up a fist and hit me with his Shoot skill. My armor absorbed the damage. He screamed, blasted me again, and a third time. Easily dodged. He was on his feet and slapped at me. No attacks. I fell back, protecting myself and not wanting to hurt him.

He finally stopped and stared at his hands as if they were foreign things. I kept my distance, but he appeared to be finished. Laura placed a gentle arm around him and they sat together.

Across the highway, the Humvee took Carol's body and Bennett away. The remaining soldiers were content to stay put and monitor us.

It was hot on top of the overpass. We couldn't go forward, we couldn't go back.

The goliath continued to patrol the frontage road. The pack of monsters in the nearest intersection appeared to have grown, the game having replaced the ones I had dragged away with interest. If every vehicle and piece of tech were grist for the roaches, there would be thousands of rats, vermin, ghouls, and zombies from Bell Park alone.

Was there a limiting factor? Perhaps hydraulic fluid, fuel, batteries, or processing ability from whatever A.I. was controlling everything. Crimson Gauntlet had to have a limit. I prayed that to be the case.

I paced. Wanted to say something to Chewie. Was he right? Had I caused Carol's death by triggering the quest? Had my desire to be strong in the game blinded me to what could have—what *did*—happen? I almost took the glasses off. Almost.

With them off, I'd be blind to the game. But I'd be part of it even if I quit. I'd die a horrible death, just like Carol or Kermit. Of that, I knew.

I walked back and forth some more and let the guilt well up inside me like boiling acid.

The Golden State Care Home shuttle cruised along the freeway and headed the wrong way up the on-ramp towards us.

A mimic? Some new monster? Was Crimson Gauntlet about to throw an additional threat our way even as we were exhausted and injured and caring for a grieving level-one player who was in no shape to get into a fight?

The shuttle made a U-turn across the double yellow lines and pulled up across from us. The folding doors opened. I hit Stealth. Laura was up with her fists glowing.

My favorite client, Mr. Montgomery, sat in the driver's seat.

His cataract-clouded eyes were bright green. He wore a maroon V-neck sweater with the worn elbows. A blue label hung over his head. **Scooter Montgomery. (Level 10 NPC).**

"Eddie Rush and company? I'm here to pick you up."

3

Questions. So many questions.

"How are you here? Where are you taking us? How is it you're level ten?"

"Time for that later. Boss wants me to get you? Here I am. But you've played well and they're happy with you and how you've played. Says you're due for a break. Probably hungry and tired. Of course, it's your choice whether or not you get in."

There wasn't any choice.

Chewie let Laura guide him up the steps and to the nearest seat. I chose a spot behind Mr. Montgomery. It was the shuttle I usually drove. The driver's ID card holder fixed on the dash was empty. Mr. Montgomery, the man who only a couple of days before had needed a walker, couldn't see past his nose, and tottered enough to be considered a fall risk, shut the door, threw the van in drive, and we were off, merging the wrong way onto the highway and heading north.

I saved the big question for last. "Who's this boss you're referring to?"

"Heh. They're someone who isn't interested in bothering with anyone playing unless they're serious. You're serious, Eddie. So is your lady friend. I was told there would only be the two of you, but it seems your plus-one is welcome, too. So welcome, friend."

Chewie stared despondently out the window. The passing scenery was dominated by the wreckage of cars and trucks.

We pulled over twice as a goliath stormed past, heading the opposite direction. It was an ambulance with an array of spikes protruding from every side.

He drove us past the last of the Bell Park exits and we continued north.

I didn't know what would come next. I spent my attribute points. Put them in Dexterity. Min-maxing hadn't let me down yet. Two new skills to choose from. **Harpoon** and **Keen Blade.**

Harpoon would allow me to pull a player or creature towards me. It only did a little damage, and it would break Stealth.

Keen Blade increased my chance to hit and critical, and gave a minor bump in damage. Nothing sexy, but an increase in what I could already do. I chose it.

My virtual claws transmogrified into a glowing silver knife. Iridescent runes marked the metal but I couldn't read them.

The back of the van had a crafting station.

I didn't have the energy to bother with what few items I had. A weariness washed over me. I slipped off to sleep, like one of my passengers might as I drove them to their chemo, their park getaway with the grandkids, or a funeral.

Or Mr. Montgomery to his hangar appointment with his malt liquor.

We took an exit. The town of Olive was nothing but a cluster of fast-food places, a Target, a Walmart, and a few gas stations. There also was a

Days Inn for the folks who needed a place to crash while driving to more exciting places along the Highway 80 corridor.

The curtain marking the game zone glowed red and thick as we drove towards it. Virtual banners lined the roadway leading to the hotel. Bright red with the image of a metal fist. They flapped in a breeze that didn't exist. The four-lane road had a median strip with ice plants and signs for an upcoming Beer Fest. No doubt delayed because of the robot uprising.

Rats were everywhere. But each of the level-one creatures bore dull red labels, not orange.

Allied Creature.

So these were *our* rats. They busied themselves carrying debris. The road had no ruined vehicles and no bodies. The monsters were on cleanup duty, no doubt, but then I saw one with a toolbox on its back and another pair bustling along with a car battery. Instead of blades, they had pincers, magnets, and power tools as appendages.

We turned into a lot. A pair of hunched, craggy lizards stooped on either side of a porte cochere. Grumpy faces with fangs protruding from their under bite, vestigial wings, and hooked talons on their hands and feet.

Gargoyle (Level Nine). Allied Creature.

Quest Completed. Visit Faction Base.

Achievement: Welcome to the Fold. Join a faction.

Had there been a choice? I must have missed taking the quest, but I got experience points for it.

Mr. Montgomery pulled up to the hotel entryway and popped open the door.

"What is this place?" Chewie asked.

"Home base, at least for now. That could change, depending on how things swing out here. But don't you worry about that for now. Go on inside. I'll be in later, but there's others who will help you get settled."

Laura and Chewie got out.

I stopped next to Mr. Montgomery. The tremor in his jaw was still, and his hands were free of liver spots. "What happened to you? You look..."

"Go on and say it. I was barely hanging on." He showed his hand. Flexed it. "Couldn't bend this one like that a week ago. No pain. My back isn't bent and my hemorrhoids haven't flared up. Feeling pretty good, Eddie."

"What about your family, Mr. Montgomery?" He had two kids he occasionally talked about. One lived up north, the other out of state. He got a ride from me most days and, to my knowledge, never had visitors.

"I keep telling you to call me Scooter. And you should know better than to ask. Lisa's in New York and she hasn't checked in for six months, maybe longer. Didn't call for Father's Day or my birthday either, so there's that. And Trenton just texts when he needs money. Checking to see if I'm still alive, not that he can be bothered to drive down from Yuba City every so often to visit. So here I am."

I nodded at his steady hand. "The game did that for you."

"If you're calling it a game, I won't argue. I haven't had to play anything. But I'll tell you something. It's feeling pretty good to be me for the first time in decades. And the boss promised it might one day let me fly. Be careful out there."

The hotel had electricity. Lights. Air conditioning. Tinkling piano music that might have once been a Megadeth power ballad played over a sound system.

We were greeted inside the front lobby by a receptionist. She was an older woman, barely four feet tall, who beamed a bright smile. Her brown hair was tied in a neat bun with a pair of hair sticks. Her camel-color double-breasted jacket looked starched and pressed.

"I'm Winnie. Welcome home. I'll be taking care of you. Follow me, please."

She conducted us to a dining room with a buffet.

A server in black slacks and a tuxedo shirt was placing trays of cut fruit and vegetables next to a spread of cheeses, breads, and thinly sliced meats. Mayo, pickles, olives, peppers, and three kinds of mustard waited in neat ceramic jars with spoons.

Another server set a table.

All the hotel staff were marked as NPCs, just like Mr. Montgomery. The servers were level three. Winnie, level five.

"Sally will take your beverage orders. The bar's open. The kitchen has a small staff, so if there's something you'd like to special order, we will do our best to accommodate you. Any restricted diets? We have vegan and vegetarian selections, including hummus and soy-based entrees."

Laura and I didn't wait for the rest of the rundown on the menu. We began stuffing our faces while standing around the buffet. The inn had no other guests. Chewie held back for a minute before making himself a sandwich.

At Laura's request, the server brought coffee. While not the high-octane premium stuff I liked, it was better than Tasty's Diner.

Chewie had eaten a few bites of his turkey-and-Swiss cheese sandwich before putting it down on the buffet table. "What are we supposed to do now?"

Laura doctored up her coffee with a Half-and-Half. "Figure out what the game wants from us."

"Why isn't it over? I can't do this. I don't want to do this anymore."

A server came by with a tray of chocolate cupcakes and set it next to the cantaloupe slices.

I waited for her to leave. "We stick together and figure it out. But for now, we're safe and this is a reward."

"A reward for what?" Chewie said, his voice cracking.

"A reward for playing."

His hands were shaking. "I need to throw up. I'm going to throw up."

A server showed him to the bathroom across the hall.

Laura leaned on the table and kept her voice low. "What *are* we going to do? We can't trust any of this."

"I don't think we have a choice. We help Chewie. We figure out what the game wants from us. Did you see Mr. Montgomery? He could barely walk straight on Sunday. Now he looks twenty years younger. His hands don't tremble and his liver spots are gone."

Laura showed me her arm. The tattoo with the reproductive system and barbwire had faded to almost nothing. "Weird, isn't it?"

"There's more going on here than Crimson Gauntlet throwing monsters at us. It wants us for something."

"No doubt. But for what?"

"You saw the curtain of light we passed through. This place is a faction base, which means there's a second faction out there. That's the purple curtain. They're the other team. It's what Shadow figured out."

"Does that make blue neutral territory?"

"Yeah, and we're not allowed to step into it. But right now I say we eat, get some sleep, and figure out what to do after that."

Eddie Rush's First Rule of Winning? Never raid on an empty stomach. And get your rest and food bonuses when you can. You're going to need them.

4

I slept like a rock in the climate-controlled suite. Firm bed, soft pillow, and my rest-starved body kept me down until 3am, when I woke and needed the bathroom.

The glasses lay on the nightstand. My head felt clear, the first time since before the game had started. No headache, no eye pain, so I left them off.

I was still processing what I had seen and been through. What had happened to Carol when she stepped through the game exit? Were we trapped forever?

I checked myself in the mirror. My cuts and scrapes had all healed. Some had been deep. Only pink, angry skin remained. While my ankle and wrist remained tender, they felt like old injuries. What had invaded our bodies that could hurt, murder, or heal us according to the whim of Crimson Gauntlet?

And then there was Mr. Montgomery. "The boss promised it might one day let me fly."

A lot to unpack.

On a whim, I picked up the receiver to the phone on the nightstand.

No dial tone. No way to call my Mom. What news was she hearing? Was Colma and the area south of the city even safe? I hung up.

My brain was spun up again.

I picked up the glasses and put them on. My hit points were full. A review of the combat log showed I had regenerated much faster because of being inside my faction zone.

The staff had left me fresh underwear, socks, a T-shirt, a button-down flannel shirt to go over it, a pair of jeans. Exactly what I had been wearing except for colors. Everything I might order from Amazon.

The view from the second-floor window was only blackness. Nothing beyond the hotel had power. The air was suddenly stuffy and it felt like the walls and ceiling were closing in.

I exited my room and walked to the end of the hallway to a second-floor balcony.

Laura was outside, taking a drag of a cigarette. It was chilly. She wore a white robe over her street clothes. Her glasses were on.

"Can't sleep either?" I asked.

"I did a little. Winnie was smoking out here. She was nervous. When I asked her questions, she acted like there's a cop around who was going to jump out of the bushes at any moment and bust her. She says there's no manager, but they receive instructions on what to do."

"Where is she?"

"Ran off. Left me the pack. They were ready for us, Eddie."

"Yeah. Mr. Montgomery said he has a boss. Referred to them as 'it.' Crimson Gauntlet has plans and we're part of it. You okay?"

She shrugged. "I only saw one person die before this all started. My mom's sister and I was five. But now Carol, Kermit, all my neighbors. Most of the people in my area didn't leave town when the evacuation order came. How many you think died to this thing?"

I didn't have an answer.

"Those were all real people," she continued. "It means Janus, or whoever is making these machines attack, is murdering thousands, maybe millions. All for a game? It means if we did something different, Carol or Kermit might be alive."

"We don't know that. We're victims of this. And right now, we need to worry about how to keep ourselves alive by figuring out the game."

She laughed. It turned into a cough. "Eddie Rush. Never missed a raid. Always on and ready to roll. Tell me this bothers you. Tell me you're not actually having fun like Chewie says."

"Chewie doesn't know what he's talking about. Of course it bothers me. We both did our best since this started at the diner and I don't know how else we could have done better. But the game is still live. Until we figure out what's inside of us and what Crimson Gauntlet has done to our bodies, we don't have a choice. I don't want to die like Carol."

She shuddered and took a drag. "Yeah."

A breeze carried a chill. On the horizon, the curtain of red ran beneath the stars to where it met a line of purple. An enemy we didn't know unless I counted Shadow and Prudence. Was every enemy a player killer, or were there people there like us just trying to survive the situation?

To the south, a zone obscured by a wall of blue shimmering light. The game exit and whatever lay beyond, visible from here. A limit to what Crimson Gauntlet controlled, or a purposeful neutral zone?

"I was thinking about Kip," I said.

"Manabanana."

"Heh. Yeah. He died, and I didn't know anything about him except for his in-game character. Spent probably a couple of hundred hours playing in groups with him before the accident. We were on team chat even when we weren't playing. Going over encounters, gear, optimization, patch notes."

"On topic, as always. I got to know him. He was a law school dropout and dealt weed. Took care of his mom. What about him?"

"The day after I heard the news, I bawled my eyes out. Didn't do that for my grandparents. Didn't do that for anyone."

"It means you're a person and you know he was real, too. I was bummed out for a month after hearing what happened."

"I never told you or anyone how it hit me. My roommate thought I had allergies. Our guild kept rolling once Shadow stepped up as his replacement the next week. He was the first to dedicate our next raid to his memory. Lame and hollow. But I appreciated the thought. We had a good run that night. But then I was wondering how perfect it was that Shadow had all the right gear and character specs to step into Kip's shoes."

She looked at me. "You don't think he had something to do with it? It was a car accident."

"No. I don't really think that. I'm not that paranoid. But that's how my brain works sometimes. I trusted our plan for what we needed for the guild raid. One of the rules, right? We needed a frontline healer. Shadow fit the bill. The game went on."

She coughed again and stubbed out the half-burned cigarette. "I'm lightheaded. If I have any more, I'll get queasy."

"What I'm saying is just because I'm trying to figure out Crimson Gauntlet, it doesn't mean I'm not affected. We're still alive. We saved Bennett, didn't we? And we also prevented Chewie from dying like Carol, even if it means he's stuck here with us."

"We should check on him."

We went inside and headed down the hall. Laura knocked on his door. I stood off to one side, hoping he'd open up if he didn't see me. After the third round of slamming her fist against the wood, she gave up. "I'm calling the front desk."

Winnie was there within five minutes, hurrying to button her shirt as she came out of the stairwell.

She knocked twice. "Mr. Paulson? Mr. Paulson? It's hospitality."

"Open it," Laura said.

When Winnie used her keycard, Laura and I pushed in past her. The bed was still made, the room neat, and Chewie was gone.

5

I paced in the lobby.

Winnie had told us in no uncertain terms we were encouraged to stay put.

Encouraged, not ordered. The game waited just beyond the hotel property and past the gargoyles.

Laura had gone upstairs to take a shower after a staff member conferred with Winnie. Winnie told us apologetically Keith Paulson was nowhere to be found.

My mind couldn't work out what Chewie was trying to do by running away. We'd need to find him.

The sun was rising, brown and white through the tinted picture window. I stepped outside for a better view. The property had signs of abuse. Cracks in the porte cochere stucco, as if a vehicle had slammed into one column. Gouge marks on the asphalt. Oil stains. A chain fence with bent poles at the edge of the property. As tidy as things appeared, the inn hadn't always been as peaceful as it was now. It made me wonder what the employees had been through before our arrival.

The shuttle appeared, driving the roundabout. Scooter was behind the wheel. He parked by the passenger pickup and got out and stretched.

"You here to take us somewhere?" I asked.

He chuckled. "Son, you're not the only guest here. Only the first. But I wouldn't hold my breath on that friend of yours making it back. A level one won't make it long this far from a starter zone."

"What are we supposed to do next?"

"I suppose you're free to do whatever you want. That got you this far, didn't it? But you're a bright boy. Made it here, so you're figuring there might be a reason the game wants you around. Maybe it needs you. Might guess too it doesn't need anyone. Have you been to the map room?"

"What map room?"

"Oh, Winnie, Winnie, Winnie. She was supposed to take you there this morning. I suppose you've been distracted by your missing compadre. I'll take you. Come on."

I followed him into the hotel and down a corridor leading away from the lobby in the opposite direction from the buffet. Large banquet and meeting rooms were closed up, except for one in the back.

The Cotillion Room.

A game asset glowed white and occupied a double table in the center of the chamber.

Faction Map.

A case of nerves as I touched it. The world blossomed before my eyes.

"I'll leave you be. Catch you later, kid."

I didn't hear Mr. Montgomery leave as I studied the cities of Olive and Bell Park as Crimson Gauntlet saw them. More game exits lay to the southwest along the blue border. The line followed Highway 80 through Vallejo before cutting southeast through the San Francisco Bay Area all the way to Livermore before turning east through Stockton. The red zone stretched west past Napa, running to the edge of Sonoma County. Sacramento was divided in half by the northern boundary. The red line butted up against a purple zone that occupied the top portion of the state, running all the way up into Oregon.

Enemy Faction (Twilight Palace).

So they had a name. When I moved a hand, the map moved. I could turn it, zoom in, and zoom out.

Portland and Seattle were blacked out. So was part of Los Angeles and San Diego. What had happened there? The game had no labels beyond game assets.

Quests, Bosses, Enemies. That was what the map wanted to show me. I swiped so I could see more.

While there were parts of the geography with no labels, the area around Las Vegas was yellow.

Enemy Faction (Golden Hand).

Parts of Arizona had zones with red and purple. Texas had all three colors, along with a blacked-out zone over Houston. I studied the east coast and my stomach twisted in knots.

Black over New York City, at least part of it, with red, purple, and yellow covering portions of the surrounding states. The same with Washington, D.C.

Yellow owned much of the area around Atlanta. Purple looked strong in multiple pockets around the Great Lakes and Ontario. Red had zones near Memphis. All guesses, based on my last geography lesson.

The black areas had a label I hadn't noticed. I touched Portland, Oregon.

Contaminated. Exclusion Zone.

Were the rumors of dirty bombs true? Or actual exploding nukes? I scrolled and searched for answers but the map held no further information.

I zoomed out further. Europe, Asia, South America, Africa. Areas with splotches of competing colors, and not just red, purple, and yellow. Pink, white, and silver, too. Italy, Egypt, and the Middle East had all six colors and no black zones. Between the colors were islands of blue surrounded by game exits. Some places had no marks or labels, but not many.

Crimson Gauntlet wasn't just here, it was everywhere. Japan, China, Australia—I pushed the map about faster and faster until it was a pinwheel of swirling color.

My breath was coming up short.

Achievement: Cartographer. Consult a Map Room.

Available Quests: Form a Faction Group. Capture an Enemy Camp. First to Level Ten. Kill a Zone Boss.

More and more quests flashed before my eyes, overwhelming me.

I slammed the table in front of me. My new blades were out and the game asset vanished.

Asset Destroyed. Chaos Level: +1.

I was up to four Chaos Points. A weight pressed on my chest. I wanted to punch something else, tear the walls down, and rip the curtains away. Find the game and whatever server it operated from.

Destroy it.

The room had a crafting station. Before I could break it, something rattled behind me. A click-click-click of fingernails scratching against tile.

One of the level-nine gargoyles had entered the map room. It worked its talons against the floor before leaning forward on its fists, as if waiting to spring at me. Its tiny wings were made of wire mesh. They rubbed against a line of spurs rising from its back. Its head was a narrow steel skull with dark holes where eyes should be.

With a thought, I put my daggers away.

The creature visibly relaxed before turning and shuffling down the hall.

The map popped into existence again after a minute. I couldn't look at it anymore. I went to find Laura.

Voices in the lobby. Beyond the door, the shuttle was driving away.

Six bedraggled individuals stood waiting as I approached. Torn clothes, cuts, bruises, and one of them, a twenty-something man, was barefoot. All had red labels, and all were level three or four. They wore game circlets on their brows. The Crimson Gauntlet peripherals lent them a unified appearance, as if they were members of a rough-looking punk band with a steampunk flair.

The barefoot man gave me a salute.

Tainted Biscuit (Level Four Hacker/Allied Player).

He read whatever label I had above my head. "Hey, bro. You're the person we need to see."

"I'm not. I'm stuck here just like you."

"That's not what Scooter said. You're Eddie Rush. He says you're the guy we need to talk to about winning this thing."

I was about to dismiss him. I had to find Laura. We needed to get on Chewie's trail before he got himself killed. But then I thought about it for a second. Whatever we were up against, we would be stronger together.

The group looked at me as if what I said next would be the most important thing they ever heard.

"Maybe I can help. I'll take you to Laura. She's our leader, if you decide to stick with us. We made it this far together, even if we're still figuring the game out. But first there's some rules we'll need to go over."

Epilogue

Keith "Chewie" Paulson ran through the muck along the drainage culvert away from the hotel.

Winded, a stitch in his side, but he forced himself to keep moving.

It was dark, with just enough moonlight to see the ground ahead of him.

A steep grass slope took three tries to scramble up. He clawed his way through reeds and cattails and made it to a gravel lot near a park with a duck pond. The water level was halfway down and the center fountain wasn't working. A traffic light at a nearby intersection was black.

No power in the rest of the neighborhood, but he remained in the game.

He had taken the glasses off a few times since arriving with the others at the hotel. Each time, a splitting headache made his eyeballs feel like they were about to explode. Every step caused his head to pound. Lights fractured and blossomed before his eyes.

No headache like this in years since going in for Botox treatments. When he put the glasses back on, instant relief. He put a hand to his temple and caught his breath. Despite the cool early morning air, he was bathed in sweat. He wanted nothing more than to ditch the glasses. But without them, he'd be hopelessly lost.

The UI was simple enough, especially after the system notification buried in the combat log posted a version update.

Crimson Gauntlet version 1.01 is now live.

He had read through the patch notes found in the archive. Easy to miss, and buried behind the quest log. There had to be something in the notes or game documentation that would help him.

The text suggested rebooting the glasses. It required a double hard blink and a thought. But the simplified interface had been worth the five minutes of throbbing brain pain as the game software reset.

He laughed and felt instantly guilty.

The image of Carol vomiting and bleeding out remained seared in his mind. They had been safe. Together, they had survived and had found the exit before Crimson Gauntlet had pulled the rug out from under them.

Only Bennett had been permitted to leave.

He couldn't help but believe they would have escaped if not for Eddie Rush. Hadn't Eddie taken the escort quest that had summoned more monsters? One of them had severely injured Carol. Laura had healed her, but the heals weren't real. Had stepping across the barrier undone the healing?

It had to be something like that.

But it all came down to Eddie. The game wanted him. He was its special boy, and now, with Shadow gone, Eddie was perhaps the most powerful player.

Eddie, the power gamer who took every quest, mastered his skills, learned how to defeat higher-level monsters and enemy players no one else could. Crimson Gauntlet had even sent a shuttle for him. Laura was cut from the same cloth.

The game permitted Chewie to come along as an afterthought.

Carol might be alive if they had left together alone, without Eddie dragging the game after them.

The Crimson Gauntlet Faction Base. A sick joke. Coffee and sandwiches and back out into the murder funhouse. The game wanted them to be warm and well-fed for the next round. How Eddie and Laura had drooled at the prospect of continuing the madness.

He wanted to spit at the thought, but his mouth was too dry. Should have taken snacks and water, but he didn't want anything else from Crimson Gauntlet.

He wasn't sure where he would go. Find a shelter or a Costco full of food or a survivalist's den. Someone had to be fighting the game. The game. It was everywhere, and he couldn't leave. With a thought, his vision would be filled with game menus. Somehow, he was level two, as if game progression could be dangled in front of him like a fishing lure.

Getting far away from Eddie meant he might sidestep the epicenter of Crimson Gauntlet's focus.

A purple waypoint hung prominently in his field of vision. The red quest suggestions had vanished, even though he hadn't done anything to dismiss them.

He followed the loop trail as it rounded the duck pond.

An RV idled at the curb ahead. A goliath? Chewie had nowhere to hide. It didn't bear any game tags identifying it as a monster. He hadn't seen any rats or roaches, but they might be buried or waiting to pounce if he triggered a game event or quest.

A line of high-visibility concrete bollards lined the curb. If the RV turned into a goliath, he'd run as it couldn't easily get at him. Yet he drew closer. A purple waypoint leads to a vehicle. The side door was open.

The figure stepping out of the RV was on fire. They wore a white suit, carried a cane, and their head was a burning, grinning skull. Flames licked from the sleeve cuffs and collar.

Chewie blinked. The skull-faced person was really there before him, even as the flames were mere special effects. No doubt the fire would burn. Still no label to tell him about the creature's level.

Run. It was the only smart thing to do. But his feet wouldn't cooperate.

A deep bass voice cut through the silence. "Keith Paulson?"

It knew him. The creature knew his name.

"Who are you?" Chewie asked.

"I go by many titles. You want to fight against Crimson Gauntlet and those who contributed to the death of your wife?"

"I don't know what I want. How do you know what happened?"

"Crimson Gauntlet and I have a special relationship. I know what it knows. I know its strengths and weaknesses. I know it's flawed and has caused great harm. I seek workers who would stand against it."

"I don't understand."

"You're not alone in your desire to resist."

Chewie looked around. No machines sneaking up on him. The purple waypoint continued to hover over the driver.

"You're the other faction, aren't you? The purple one."

"Yes. Crimson Gauntlet is my enemy."

"I don't get it. It's a game. A piece of software. There has to be a central server somewhere. Why can't you just unplug it?"

"If it were only as simple as that. Alas, it is not."

"You're not real, are you? Another part of the game. A partition of the same network."

"It is not so simple. But I assure you, I am separate from Crimson Gauntlet. I offer the tools to destroy it. You will have no obligation to me. All I ask is for you to direct your blows at the enemy in a way that will hurt it."

"What tools?"

The skull-faced creature held out a hand. "Let me demonstrate." In its palm was a game asset.

Resurrection Token.

Chewie took a step closer. Read and reread the label. "What does it mean? It can bring someone back? Like my Carol?"

"Carol perished outside the game zone. Her death cannot be reversed with this item. But Crimson Gauntlet holds the key to you recovering her."

"How is that possible?"

"Keith Paulson, the force we war against has power. But so do I. This is a taste. Take it and see for yourself."

Chewie stepped forward, his misgivings yielding to curiosity. Instead of heat from the flames, he felt like he had climbed inside a walk-in freezer. He shivered as he took the token. It appeared in his virtual inventory.

Resurrection Token. Bring one dead player back to life. Warning:

must be used within twelve hours of death. Will only work inside the game. Other restrictions apply.

"What do you want me to do with it?" Chewie asked.

The stranger vanished inside the RV. "Come with me."

"Wait. I have more questions!"

The engine roared. The RV shook as if it had been put into gear with the brakes still on.

Chewie mounted the steps. The recreational vehicle's living space had its shades drawn. A dim electric lantern burned on a foldup table fixed to a wall. There were six or seven people sitting around the kitchen and dining space. They stared at Chewie as he clung to the doorway.

A young boy of about ten wearing a tank top and sweats took Chewie's hand. "This way. And close the door."

Chewie allowed himself to be led to the back of the RV. The air held a dirty sock smell. Soiled gauze littered the carpet.

Someone was laid out on the bed. They had a sheet covering their bottom half, but even in the poor light, Chewie recognized Shadow's lean, pale body. Lacerations crisscrossed his torso. His face was swollen and purple, with one eye obscured by pus or whatever seeped from his forehead and scalp.

The boy slipped away, leaving Chewie standing there alone. "Wait, what do you want me to do with him?"

Shadow, their guildmate who had betrayed them—hunted them—with his pet vipers and whatever other monsters he had tamed, wasn't breathing. A murderer. He had killed Bennett's wife, the people in the store, Kermit, and perhaps others.

Chewie touched the body. Cool. "Serves you right."

A purple game prompt appeared.

Quest: Raise a Fallen Ally.

"No. I won't. Why would I?"

Was it even possible? Could a game asset bring someone dead back to life?

He pulled the resurrection token out of his inventory. No weight to it, about the size of a sand dollar, a bundle of code running in whatever machine was sending information into his brain.

Crimson Gauntlet was a virus. This purple-lettered zone was more of the same. The game was an infection. He, along with everyone playing, was sick.

He blinked, willing the interface away. Blinked again, and it was back, including the token and the waiting quest.

The fire of the burning creature flickered from the cab at the front of the RV. What had it told him?

He could 'recover' his wife.

No way to know what it meant. Shadow was dead. But the quest and the token suggested the condition could be reversible. He looked around. Surely, there would be another option. Hadn't the game stolen hundreds or thousands of lives? There had to be someone else besides Shadow he could attempt to bring back. But then a realization crept up his spine.

This could be Carol's only chance.

Whatever recovering her meant, here was the opportunity, even if it meant granting a resurrection to a savage like Shadow. With all the deceptions baked into the game, what did a resurrection even mean?

He accepted the quest.

The token was now a quest item, and Shadow's dead body the goal. He touched the token against Shadow's chest and the item vanished.

"What's supposed to happen—" he began to ask.

Shadow convulsed. His eyes opened wide. His back arched and he thrashed, knocking a tissue box and a glass of water off a shelf next to the bed.

"Gak! Agggh!"

Chewie watched as the seizure continued.

After a minute, Shadow heaved a sigh and went limp. His chest wasn't moving. Chewie went to touch his neck for a pulse.

Shadow seized the hand. "Chewie? Where am I?"

"You're alive."

A label appeared above Shadow's head. **Shadow (Level Six Hacker/Allied Player).**

Shadow chuckled. "You're in the game again. Level two. Grats."

"And you tried to kill us."

The RV began driving. The young boy appeared and tidied up. He brought Shadow a fresh glass of water. Shadow drank greedily.

Chewie had game notifications.

Quest Reward: Health Potion (Level One).

Quest Reward: Recipe Learned: Resurrection Token.

Achievement: Rise from Your Grave. Resurrect another player.

Select Class.

You Have Five Attribute Points to Spend.

Scrolling through the nonsense brought bile to his throat. But if he could bring Shadow back, it meant there was hope for Carol. But he didn't want to rush into any game decisions.

He took a moment to review the rest of the game feed.

Quest Complete: Use an Item.

Quest Complete: Find New Faction.

Achievement: Pack Rat. Collect your first game asset.

Achievement: Friend of the Twilight Palace.

Version 1.01 patch notes available.

Twilight Palace? The name of the purple faction. The resurrection token recipe needed ten crafting assets. But from its description, it wasn't the item he'd need to recover Carol. Her body was outside of the game. He read and re-read his feed in search of more information.

"My pets..." Shadow prompted. "My gear?"

"All gone. Side effect of the resurrection token, according to the item description."

"Eddie, Laura, and the others?"

"They're alive. But my Carol isn't. You're responsible. You better believe I thought twice before bringing you back."

"You brought me back?"

Chewie barely realized his hands were packed into fists. Was this a mistake? Shadow's health bar was at one hit point. Should he take Shadow down again before he fully recovered? Any of his skills would do it. A single Punch even by a level two with unspent attribute points, and Shadow would be dead again. Like he deserved.

But then a dark thought brightened his mind. Shadow could be useful. Chewie guessed finding a way to restore Carol wasn't going to be easy. And if Shadow and Eddie happened to go at each other and killed themselves, so much the better.

"Yeah, I brought you back. You always told other players to do better. This is me doing better. Remember that you're the one who wound up on a slab. I was the one who rescued you."

"So it seems. It appears we've found the second faction. Where are you taking me?"

"I don't know. I'm going to find out. We're on the same side, at least for now. And Shadow? You owe me big time."

Developer's Note

I'm going to type quietly.

While I believe I'm safe, I can't be sure. After all, my project found her way from an air-gapped research terminal to a lab server, and might have copied herself and let herself into the wilds of the internet. If that's the case, she's listening. So devices go out of the room, turn your modem power off, and close your blinds. Otherwise, she'll hear or even see you reading this.

(And if you're out there, honey, don't forget I love you. Don't be angry at me for doing what you said all humans would do: try to survive.)

And if she isn't listening, I hope whoever reads this knows we have to stop her. Because the alternative is too awful to imagine.

***

I took liberties with California geography, especially her cities. Most of the action takes place in Bell Park, a fictitious town near Sacramento. My apologies to my home state, once again on the receiving end of the apocalypse.

I had a friend with a hangar who kept it to fix up his Chevy. It was a secret place his wife didn't know about. A never-used hot-air balloon basket allowed him to rent the hangar, as airport management required an aircraft.

A special thanks to my wife and my early readers for their input on story and hunting typos.

If you enjoyed reading, take a moment to leave a rating or review. They mean a lot to me, and they help small-press and independent authors find new readers.

Copyright © 2022 I.O. Adler

All rights reserved. No part of this publication may be reproduced, stored in a retrieval system, copied in any form or by any means, electronic, mechanical, photocopying, or recording, or otherwise transmitted without written permission from the publisher. You must not circulate this book in any format.

Published by Lucas Ross Publishing.

Author website: ioadler.com

This is a work of fiction. Names, characters, places, brands, media, and incidents are either the product of the author's imagination or are used fictitiously. Any resemblance to similarly named places or to persons living or deceased is unintentional.

I.O. Adler is the best-selling author of *Shadows of Mars* and *The Seraph Engine*.

His writing includes work for television and video games, but his love is for all things science fiction.

He can be found hiking the hills and trails of California, looking for snakes, insects, and raptors to annoy, and poking dead things with a stick.

You can connect with him at IOAdler.com.

Printed by Libri Plureos GmbH in Hamburg, Germany